RED DANUBE

A novel by David Gluck

For Dad.
Never forget.

1

———

The sight of produce piled high and on display carried Zoltan Gluck, Zoli to those closest to him, into a past full of color: a romanticized youth, before the pain.

By the mid-'80s, the stone fruits of his childhood were accompanied by all manner of out-of-season and wildly imported products. Light zigzagged though corridors of steel and concrete, fell onto the thin sliver of Fairway's storefront, the morning's calm shaking to the rattle of the cardboard-boxed bounty that slid from truck to subterranean storage over a metal conveyer. Like no other market on the Upper West Side, tucked between Gristedes and a Love's Discount Pharmacy, it presented the smells and colors of Zoli's childhood in Eastern Europe in their new and forever anachronistic setting.

Zoli carried plastic bags across the concrete plateau of New York City; a smile creased lines in his cheeks, exposed teeth yellowed by adolescent malnutrition and chipped through military service. His bright blue eyes were wide and present. Salt and pepper hair caught the cross-breeze of miles traveled as histories remained fastened to the soles of his feet, and in each free moment.

He moved on, mind ever-adrift to a time when families gathered to harvest the rewards of their labor. He could still see them. The fragrances were fresh in his nostrils, sharp on his tongue.

Townsfolk congregated to sell plums, peaches, and apricots; to barter and buy goods and services; farm-animal-produced milk, meat and cheeses; garlic and bunches of whole dried paprika on display; the harvest filled the air with the sweet smell of country living, available for the right price. He was there, saw the handful that hauled their bounty out of town on horseback and by the carriage-full, caravans of abundance.

He drowned in the expanse, waves of grassland that united the distant hills of his childhood, verdant terrain disturbed only by the orchards and farms that defined the region. He saw the rows of trees planted in antiquity that reached out over the horizon. Fruit that hung heavy off innumerable branches painted the hillside in a wash of color that marked the seasons. The villages that pocked the great field did much the same; born in service of the land, they were equally susceptible to the shifting conditions of the world around them.

"They annexed Austria." He still heard the whispers that travelled across borders so long ago, details of the Nuremberg Laws and the many nights of broken glass that followed. "We're next," was the collective conclusion of Jews and gypsies on the ever-redefined borders of Eastern Europe. Common ground, as logic dictated. "Who will save us? The Soviets? They're just as savage. We're damned either way," they'd spit in wretched agreement.

Zoli shook recollection. He knew times had changed, but the effects of his youth remained: Deadbolts locked against invasion clanked open from the outside. Zoli let himself into his spacious riverside apartment and locked the door behind him.

Elevated above the tree line of the adjacent park, sunlight danced in off the Hudson. Lost illuminants reached out across the living room and long gallery hall. Zoli hung his black overcoat on a hook, began unpacking groceries in the soft reflective light. Calloused hands, rough palms, torn up fingers squeezed stone fruit, and prompted sense-memory.

Viscid resin, concentrated juice, tacky to the touch and released by the slightest move, enveloped young hands and arms; ripe globules thick with pulp and sucrose sailed through the air, sloshed into baskets left by the foot of a mature plum tree picked clean. Fallen leaves sprinkled the landscape with deep purples and marked each of nine-year-old Zoli's steps with a satisfying crackle. He searched through dirt, blue eyes darting between branches and mulch to find every last imperfect plum. He was happy with the ones that had long lost their peels, oozing beneath topsoil, attracting bugs and rodents.

"GET THE ONES NO ONE WANTS," was yelled from afar and rippled through decades to live firmly in Zoli's recollections.

Remembrances interrupted, he turned toward footsteps, peered past a library of rarely opened books, across a collection of Hungarian paintings and porcelain that made their way across the Atlantic. He cracked a smile at the sight of his only son approaching. "Danny-kem," he whispered in an accent weathered by experience. "I told you, you didn't have to come with me."

"I know." Danny, short and husky, was in Bugle Boy cargo pants and a striped polo shirt, face broken out, red and irritated; a body built for the fields primped and styled to popular standards, hair gelled to perfection against the force of his natural curls in a dance of perpetual pubescent imbalance. "I just wanted to make sure you make it, Pops."

"Danny, come on. Vhy vouldn't I?" Zoli answered. They spoke in a hush through the morning light. His wife Julika and mother-in-law, Danny's live-in-grandmother, remained asleep while he sliced fruit for their cereal. He had rolled the sleeves of his sharp Pierre Cardin dress shirt in order to get banana into his son's bowl.

"You get all... you know..." The thought of his dad scared or uncomfortable snatched his ability to finish his sentence. The weight of his father's past, the family history, bunched up in Danny's shoulders, tightened his posture. He just sat quietly, eyes bloodshot as he considered the cumulative horror of his legacy, collecting the anxiety that had always been married to it.

Zoli got it. "Business is business."

Danny chewed and swallowed, was slow to continue. "He knew you and your brother..." His long corrected Hungarian accent resurfaced as he went on, "Your brother, János? Right?" He made it a point to get the name right, repeated himself, over accentuated the strong *ya* and Slavic *sh* sounds that bookended his late uncle's name: "János."

"Yes... Jenő." Zoli used the name most colloquial, the one he used as a child.

"Think this guy knows what happened to him?" Danny asked.

Zoli dared not answer; thinking about it contorted his face, agitated his jovial features. They sat silently, waited for answers within the ever-present aeioum of the city; the traffic, on land and above buildings, pedestrians at street level, distant sirens, the chaos and commotion all melded into a lulling constant.

"I don't even know if he vill remembers me, even though ve have ze same Hebrew name, Itzchak," Zoli said as ancient feelings crept up through his spine, locked in his gaze.

"I still can't believe he's represented by Perry Art Gallery, what are the odds?"

Zoli started clearing the table; light bounced off the river, cut shadows into the ceiling, across his face.

"OK, let's go," Zoli broke the static. "I vant to get there before they hang ze show."

They stepped out and away from a large brick building that grew out of an entire city block, joining the light morning motion of Manhattan: joggers and nannies, a spattering of kids running to Saturday morning sports in the nearby park.

"I don't tink Itzchak vill be there today," Zoli said, almost relieved.

"We'll havĕ to find him..." Danny interjected. "What if he knows something?"

Zoli stammered on a thought: "Vhat if it is someting I don't vant to hear?"

"You know I got your back."

"I know, Danny, I know," Zoli's affect flowed, connecting his son to different places and times. "You are so much like my fadher. Did you know Dani..." He emphasized the short-rounded-/ɒ/-sound that growled with an appropriate earthiness, a wash of the old country wrapped up in a long *ee* in his father's name.

"Yes, dad," Danny asserted. "I know all about your life on the farm. I feel like I lived there, for crying out loud."

"Who ever thought a little farm boy vould end up here?" Zoli thought out loud. "All ze tragedies..."

"All those things had to happen to get you here, Pops," Danny interrupted.

"Not quite, no vone vanted to drive around with Mr. Stern and sell his paintings, listen to him talk for days and days. I vas young. I vas a trained carpenter. I vanted to see America, and traveling is in our blood," Zoli laughed with his kid. "My fadher travelled to get ze best price at city markets, he'd travel days, sometimes veeks." He planted Danny in the middle of his far-reaching legacy. "Like me vith Mr. Stern, and you vill vith me. It vill be great to have you, kiddo, just this vonce time, till ze doctor says my old heart is strong again." He stopped to read disappointment on his young son's face; they both knew Danny's involvement would be permanent. "I promise you vill have your school vacation back."

Danny's mind wandered over elevated expectations of the idle time he'd miss with his friends over spring break and of the girls he wouldn't get to know better because he was off working with his dad. Zoli noticed.

"I vas much younger than you vhen I joined the family

business, I remember like yesterday... ve all vorked, but Jenő vas the toughest. He vas something else. I vould vatch him use his strength to load ze family vagon."

His words moved Danny, bent time, and coagulated space: Bushel upon bushel of fruits and vegetables were organized and placed by habit, Jenő's wide back and broad shoulders on display beneath his work-worn shirt, biceps flexed, weight-bearing thighs pushed to the task at hand.

Some of the younger girls in town would come to watch him work, giggling at caught glances, obvious affections offending a group of local boys that watched from a distance, side-eyed and malcontent.

Jenő felt their glare, turned to lock onto to the scowls of kids he grew up with, only to catch them spit in his direction. Disrespect met its mark. Jenő stepped to confront them, fists first, when his father stopped midstride.

"You have work to do, Jenő. Play with your friends later," Dani told him in their native tongue.

Jenő eased up, caught his kid brother Zoli with a playful shove. They watched their mother holding their baby-sister Magda in her arms while she dragged a couple of bushel baskets into their humble family market, wiping her hands clean on an already soiled apron. She turned to set out homemade jams and cakes, filled bins with animal feed, and rearranged hard-to-find farming essentials that Dani picked up along his travels.

"Come on, we're leaving," yelled Dani.

Irén moved to her husband's side. Antique brown hair caught an heirloom breeze, streaked grey. Dani's most mercurial impulses eased in her presence, tension evaporated from his shoulders as they held each other close, eyes half-closed, in a short-lived reprieve.

"Hurry back," a whisper turned stern, "in one piece."

They parted with a kiss. Dani joined long-time family friend Lukács György on the front bench of his wagon. The large gypsy had hair on his entire body thick enough to pierce the canvas clothes on his back. Both he and Dani hunched in their station, tasked to navigate the unsteady road ahead.

"Dose vere who my fadher vas friends vith, Jews and gypsies," Zoli stated. "Outsiders. Ve had to stick together."

"Wish I got to meet him." These shared moments bore down on Danny, had his entire life. "All of them. The whole family. The gypsies and everyone."

"Me too, kiddo." Zoli looked at his son; Jenő's eyes stared back at him, set his mind awhirl. "I can remember like it vas yesterday." He fell into a deep stare. "I vas just a little boy... and while my fadher vas away..."

He saw Jenő nod, and could feel his presence as they stood together to watch their father set out on dirt paths that had crumbled in the wake of one fallen empire after another.

"Your Uncle Laci," pronounced Lŭt-sī and short for Laszlo, "recruited me, had me till our fadher returned."

Laci displayed his inherited strength in the form of broad shoulders and a stick-straight posture, his intellect pronounced by his wide forehead and retreating hairline. He balanced a half-full basket of fruit in one arm and a shotgun in the other. The numbers danced through his mind; his pupils darted in addition and subtraction.

"Let's go, kis-Zoli," Laci said on the move.

Kis-Zoli stood still for a moment to consider the empty path his father rode off on, the feeling of his return lodged in his broken heart as he tried to imagine what lay over those hills, beyond the countryside. He dreamt of the markets his father would visit in cities that rose three stories, lights born of electricity, and fitted with indoor plumbing. His daydream was cut short by responsibilities. His already calloused hands dripped nectar, collected grime and trapped pests; a riot of bottom-feeders made easy work of the meal, larvae deposited, pulp left bruised and macerated. His young nails and fingers were destroyed in a testament of work accomplished, an exhaustion well-earned. He hoofed it past bare branches to catch up to Laci, who was prepared to negotiate terms with his littlest brother: "Pull the cart and I'll give you a raise. Five percent... total."

Joy swept in as kis-Zoli grabbed hold; he muscled their take into the thick of the forest that lined orchards planted before either of them were born. His young muscles strained to their limit as they blazed new trails through historical woodlands.

"You know, Felsővadász means beyond the woods, vhere ze trees vonce stood," Zoli tested his son.

"Yes, dad," Danny said, "I speak Hungarian, remember?"

"Of course I remember. Now can I finish?" Zoli took a dramatic pause before he continued. "My fadher built something from nothing for ze people up in the woods ven no vone else vould..."

"And that's why we sell paintings door-to-door?" Danny asked sarcastically, "I don't get it..."

"Yes, it's vhat ve know, ve gather vhat ve can and hit ze road," Zoli explained. "I'll give you five percent like your Uncle Laci gave to me...."

"To start."

"Ok," Zoli smiled as he cinched his overcoat by the lapels, over his loose tie, and examined the alleyway behind the grand old Ansonia. The iconic building had hosted icons Ziegfeld, Toscanini, Stravinsky, Babe Ruth, Jack Dempsey, and Isaac Bashevis Singer—a storied past that was lost on the immigrant.

Zoli took the time to inspect the hidden nooks and corners of the old Beaux-Art residential hotel. He scanned gothic shadows that fell behind the imposing structure, looked for the perfect place to hide from the endless storm that lurked behind every corner of his youth, prepared for its return.

"Ze woods of my youth vere thick, tangled branches made vay for a clearing..." Zoli colored his speech with photorealism; his accent added texture like brush strokes to his telling. "I vas just a little guy, squatting in a tree vith a shotgun. I tink I vas nine-year-old and ready to shoot while your uncle vorked on his large copper pot." He chuckled as he continued. "He vould always break screws, yell 'BULLSHIT!' for each piece he lost. I vould just vatch. He'd dump basket after basket of that rotting fruit into ze large vat, stirred it all in. I remember the smell, it vas so strong, I had to take my hand off ze gun to cover my nose." Zoli commented as muscle memory matched the actions of his youth. "It took him years to come up vith a vay to cool the vapors." He drew plans in the air with a raised finger; Danny stared into the empty space as it filled with family history. "His design moved steam through pipes right into ze forest. They ran through dirt, several feet underground, and after all that, ve aged ze booze in barrels he made from ze same Magyar Zemplén oak that grew all around us back then. He had this funny little glass that he vould always use." Zoli pantomimed his way back to when young Laci retrieved the out-of-place stemware from his inside pocket. Complete with manufacturer's stamp, it was a relic found in the dusty corner of some long forgotten barn.

Laci promptly filled this glass with liquor and enjoyed its contents with a pinkie raised.

Kis-Zoli watched his oldest brother swirl his concoction, note the rate at which the viscous liquid streamed down the inside of his glass, appreciating the depths of its aroma, its hue. He took a sip, immediately comforted by the warmth it offered.

"Can I taste?" Kis-Zoli's innocent blue eyes sparkled. Laci happily shared, laughing when the kid gagged on the pálinka's bite.

They got back to work. Jugs overflowed, replaced empty ones, corked full containers loaded on the back of his wagon, ready for market.

"It's not like that anymore, Dad."

"It is just like that, Danny-kem, vhether you sell cars, coats, paintings or booze, you make ze opportunity." They circumvented pedestrian traffic, Broadway bustling in the organized chaos of the city; the 1,2,3, or 9 train station jutted out of the Avenue. Zoli opened the heavy city-worn doors that exposed them to the urban undertow as he continued. "No vone can tell you how to do it..." Danny watched his dad's mind charge through six decades of experience, intimate moments boiling over and lingering as unintended parables. "We got ze wagon back to Felső-vadász without spilling a drop. Your Uncle Laci placed his shotgun in ze wagon before ve turned kegs to the customers. Those casks vere all ze advertising ve needed. Everyone in town knew about it, knew vhen each batch vas going to be done. People crossed borders to get a taste, all happy to vait for their turn at your Uncle Laci's kegs."

The young entrepreneur collected payment; the size of his billfold grew. He got top krona, pengő, or whatever other currency was available, doing business in whatever language he needed to speak. He made time to barter for screws, new piping, and other necessities from friends and neighbors, with a chorus of drunk Hungarians in the background: "Laci, you make the best stuff! You're a genius, I love you!" It was a drunken celebration of the brew doled out by Kis-Zoli.

But, not everyone welcomed this increasingly habitual event. Above the celebration, unknowingly to the amassed, a rock hung on the wind, curved to gravity, and hit its mark with the animus intended. Kis-Zoli watched it crack his older brother's head; blood spilled furiously, pooled at his feet. Laci watched it turn black in concentrate, his knees buckled, dead weight brought him crashing into the unpaved road, rendered motionless.

The townsfolk who had gathered to drink stood stunned, quieted by the act, turned towards the young men responsible. Longtime Felsővadász neighbors, a few child-hood school friends, had shattered the festivities.

"You people buy this swill from a Jew?" They came prepared; some carried bats, others had knives. "We know these people, been their neighbors for generations. They steal our kids, take our jobs. They get rich while we stay poor…"

"My family has roots in this land…" Laci protested as soon as he gained consciousness, struggling to his feet as his head continued to bleed.

His argument was met with a fist, then more. The pack pounced, punched Laci till he dropped, kicking him while he was down, before he could utter another word.

Friends and neighbors were hushed, none stepped in to stop the beating.

"Someone do something!" Kis-Zoli yelled. No one moved. He continued to howl. "They're killing him!"

"The little Jew thinks he can save his brother," a hooligan snarled as he approached. The crowd turned, began to add to the clamor. "Is this little son of a whore joking?"

Kis-Zoli caught sight of the shotgun, jumped to get his hands on it, but didn't get far. The mob surrounded him. The intensity in Zoli's eyes gave way to fear. He was outnumbered, cornered. They snatched the gun right out of his hands, turned it back on him with a finger on the trigger.

The sound of a charging horse roaring to a gallop rendered the rabble thunderstruck. The entire gathering grew tight with anticipation.

"LACI!" It was a yell that shook birds off trees, traveling the length of long dirt roads; born in an oak thick core, urgency laced the battle-cry. "ZOLI!"

Jenő arrived in a fury, his farmer's build held tight to his galloping steed; a full head of brown curls straightened in the force of his advance.

Attila was Jenő's first and favorite horse. The two were well-practiced in charging to the rescue. He leapt off midstride, knocked a brute out with a single blow, and swiped the shotgun back from another in one fluid move.

"Jenő grabbed me," Zoli told his son; he tried to act it out. His hands pumped with excitement as he continued. "Svept me up onto his horse..."

Brothers sped above harm's way, shared a look; Zoli knew Jenő would keep him safe. He always had.

Jenő beat their way towards Laci; each of his defensive blows riled the prejudiced mob. Laci stirred conscious, opened his eyes, and struggled to his feet in time for his rescue. Jenő swung him up over Attila's back. Laci tilted back to see his drunken customers, their friends and neighbors, help themselves to what he had worked so hard for.

"Those vere tough times, but..." Zoli shined proud, straightened himself out in layers of business attire, tightening his tie as he stepped down to the subway platform. "Jenő single-handedly took them on. He took care of everything back then. He vas someting else..."

"You looked up to him," Danny noted.

"Of course," Zoli said. "Vhat a question."

Generations of long-gone relatives whispered in Danny's ear, filled his mind. "Maybe you'll find out what happened to him." They allowed themselves to get caught up in the thought. "Someday."

"If only, at least, I knew vhere he vas buried, how he died," Zoli announced with eyes tear-shot. "I could say a

Kaddish for him like I could for ze rest of my family..." He gasped at the thought. "Now, that vould be someting..."

The roar of the oncoming 9 train shook the station, grew ever-present, slowed to a halt in front of them.

"They vere all tough guys..." Zoli drifted in thought; they boarded. "Did I ever tell you vhen my fadher charged to stop my modder from marrying another guy?" He shook his head, stuck in memories as thick as hot asphalt. "A goy..."

Danny had, a thousand times, but listened as they stood by for the closing doors. The train disappeared into its prescribed trip through the darkness.

"Tough times," Zoli echoed from the abyss. "Tough guys."

2
___

After a youth spent in the company of transients, throwing punches and training horses, Zoli's father, Glück Dani, found meaning in his family, was grounded by the work his land required; his wife Irén was elbow deep and by his side from the beginning. They saw those who drank themselves into the landscape become indistinguishable from it; to them their success came off like pure luck in the tide of European uncertainty. The Glück surname didn't even exist until the 12th century. Before then, it was purely ornamental, given to those who exhibited good fortune. Dani wasn't one of those types; he didn't believe in luck. He knew about being at the right place with the right attitude; his sleeves were permanently rolled above the elbows. The fragility of family fueled his every effort.

He took over the family farm when his hometown was more of an encampment than a village. Migrants had always pitched tents and parked wagons parallel to the Great Hungarian Plain in time for the harvest; these extra hands helped clear swaths of the expansive forest, worked the topsoil, and primed larger fields for more crops for as long as any of them could remember. Dani and his wife took what he had and made it into something else. He was in the fields and she did the numbers, built the grocery. Before they knew it, their market was feeding a community that grew out of the countryside, a center of commerce sprouted in the middle of nowhere. Their doors were open to everyone.

Lukács György called no land home and happily planted his family on Glück land annually. He made camp beside communal groves as a young man, worked the fields for Dani for as long as either of them could remember, met his wife and had a family of his own under rows of trees they planted, and weathered short seasons as best they could. It was where he found acceptance, a reprieve from unwavering discrimination. György wondered if he would ever be considered anything but a gypsy. Dani often thought the same about his Judaism. A foreseeable precipice drew them together, kept them close. They trudged to city markets not out of greed but for maintenance. The goal of working hard and making more for their children set them on paths less traveled, strengthened the core of the family tree. They were there for each other, a practice that grew to be more than habitual; it became familial. Aware of the difficulties they faced, both held witness to more than a few youthful transgressions, aggressions that lingered in the sinew of their relationship.

The difficult courtship of Tepper Irén stood out, always made them laugh. Back when her parents made decisions for her, and after years of Dani's intense pursuit, Irén found herself attached to someone else's star. Her parents had decided they wanted more than a life on a farm by the Great Hungarian Plain for their only daughter, felt the need to shield her from her own Judaism, and made arrangements accordingly; marrying into a well-to-do Christian family would keep her from more than just a few hardships.

Dani had other plans.

György would never forget the day he chased his young love-drawn friend through the countryside. Dani tore through a trip that usually took two days by carriage in two hours on horseback. György remembered watching him bank over inclines and dart between trees until the forest made way for towns that grew in size the further he rode. All burgs eclipsed Felsővadász in every possible way, homes were larger, buildings taller, streets paved, filled with pedestrian traffic, cramped spaces. Dani rode undeterred by urban obstacles. *Magyar* grandeur refined by age and history flew by in a blur that painted his travel in streaks of red, white, and green.

A rich Rococo interior, left worse for wear by wars and occupations, hosted a celebration; the tears in once fine upholstery were carefully tucked from sight, looted paintings unavoidably left their darkened prints on long unexposed swaths of sun-lightened wallpaper, the craftsmanship of their hand-carved frames outlined within the discoloration. The fray left behind by the Great War, and especially the Treaty of Trianon that diminished the great Hungarian empire, left countrymen minorities behind newly minted borders.

A lone violinist played Bartok, then a *chárdásh*. The

inebriated swirled in the spirit of *pálinka*, the brandy made of local fruits, and wine as red as bull's blood; booze flowed freely, passed in jugs, drunk with abandon. All imbibed, attempting to drown out the misery. The stringed instrument was met by the percussion of fists against the tabletops, the banging of worn soles on the chafed wooden floor by fervent dance, an entire party grown out of the frustrations left on the other side of the ornate hand-carved door. They danced and drank and reveled in unabashed defiance of their lost identity.

A blade pierced skin, sliced fat, *szalonna* slid right off a whole smoked hog that hung in the butcher's stall at the local open-air market. It was carried out of the square and down the streets by the mother-of-the-groom herself. At home, she cut pork belly into one-and-a-half inch cubes, roasted them in the oven with onions, garlic, and home-dried, fresh-ground paprika until the bacon crackled and the onions dissolved into the pools of fat and gristle that collected on the bottom of the pan, burnt to its sides. Geese were grabbed, their necks snapped, feathers pulled. She chopped their heads off with a single drop of a heavy-headed cleaver, every part of their carcasses used; whole bodies were turned over an outdoor spit, pan-cooked innards and gizzards whipped into a pâté with cream, peppercorns, paprika, and a most precious splash of Cognac. Their engorged livers were set aside, cooked whole then sliced into accommodating pieces, coarse salt, jam, and bread served in accompaniment. A cauldron of goulash was brought to a boil, carrots and cabbage stirred into a mélange of lamb and beef, taken off the direct flame to simmer. Hot *rakott krumpli* moved to make way; the stacks of sliced potatoes, onions, sausage, and hardboiled eggs bubbled over in loads of sour cream, cooked till golden brown. Farmer's cheese, butter, mustard, anchovies, sliced green onions, paprika, and paprika paste were mixed together, bowled, and set amongst deviled eggs, pickled and smoked fish, dried and fresh fruits from the plain, preserves and compotes straight off local trees. A lavish feast was presented in the family's finest porcelain.

Tepper Irén wore white, a wedding dress that had been passed down through the ages, her grandmother and her mother and her mother had all hand stitched the lace, leaving their legacy in its seams. She danced to old songs with her new husband, Nagy Peter, whom had won her hand with a substantial offer, a gesture that fell short of dowries of the past but was more than fair for the time. Her mother wanted more for her daughter, but this marriage would take Irén away from the menial labor of country life her family had known, save her the discriminations their religion carried, bring her into the larger world growing around them, of the twentieth century.

The newlyweds twirled to toasts bellowed in their honor, and Peter led his young bride across the dance floor.

Tepper Marika, the mother of the bride, stood conflicted. She was relieved to see the day but her eyes welled with an uncertainty veined through decades. She prayed for stability, hoped she did right by her only daughter. Irén returned her mother's gaze, recognizing that both their faces were lined with resignation. A historical stoicism drew them together. They had both given in to the currents of expectations long ago. Few in this area had ever known their own decision, made their own way.

Things were done with larger considerations in mind. Tepper Marika married off her daughter for the family and for her future, not love.

The party continued, the gathered pinged off walls, ate fattening food with fresh bread and wine. They danced to the torrents of folk music that were allowed in mixed company. An accordion joined the whirl. Stomping, clapping, wails of joy shielded the revelers from the sound of the front door rattling. Everyone just kept dancing; drunkenly, joyously unaware as the banging continued.

With one swift thrust, all of György's bodyweight proved enough to rip hinges from frame; the heavy wooden door slammed to the floor, brought instant silence to the room.

Musicians stopped, drinks were tabled, old ladies turned in their seats, waiting in silence for the dust to settle.

Dani slipped in past György. Groomsmen lost their jackets, rolled sleeves, took heavy steps towards their uninvited guests.

From across the room, Dani and Irén shared a full moment in each other's eyes; the second lingered, slowed time, replaced words, but never lasted. Dani was forced to leap onto the reception table to avoid Peter and his friends.

The roaming musicians continued playing to the sounds of shattered glass, breaking plates setting the tempo, the yells of women maintaining the harried tone.

Dani used whatever he could get his hands on to ward off the onslaught; mothers cried for each dish destroyed. He dodged furniture and profanities, knocked food and beverage from the stretch of table. Unsheathed knives usually used for slaughter were drawn in his direction. At the far edge of the table with his back up against the wall, he defended himself from the blades, catching sharp edges across his arms and torso.

György tore through the crowd, disrupting the onslaught. His size alone was enough to move people out of the way, to extricate his friend unscathed. Making their getaway, Dani reached out for Irén. They lit up on contact, the wind taken from their lungs. The surrounding bedlam faded into the ether as Dani wrapped her up in his farm-built arms.

György barreled them outside. Dani took care to keep Irén low until they got to his horse. Their eyes locked, time slowed within the chaos as Dani whirled his stolen bride up onto a waiting saddle, besmirching the fine lace of her dress with his calloused, bloodied hands. Smiles were exchanged. Irén tilted in gratitude, reached out to the large gypsy.

A groomsman was the first to catch up to them. György grunted confidently, urging Dani up onto the horse before turning to grab the guest by the lapel of his suit with one hand, knocking him out with the other. The well-dressed man writhed on the ground between the gypsy and the rest of the wedding party. György hung back, stood guard, gave the couple his blessing.

The gathering turned to watch Dani and Irén ride off on horseback. György looked up in time to catch them disappearing into the next village.

. . .

"Your grandfadher vasn't afraid to chase, to gamble," Zoli reflected. "Didn't worry about vhat it took, he vent head first."

The rattle of subterranean progress shifted a spattering of Saturday morning straphangers in all directions. A few riders, long familiar with the dips and shifts of MTA rail service, weathered the imbalance, surfed the train; tourists were lifted from their feet, sliding about in their seats, interrupting Zoli's story.

"Vat is zis? Rocks and rolls?" He smirked, looked over to his kid. "I didn't ask for no music."

"It's running express, dad."

"Like a horse bouncing around, except you don't have to stop to feed it." He continued, struck by a thought, "Or ven it has to pee."

They smiled, and laughed, and sat close to one another even though the train was practically empty. The bright fluorescent light turned everything blue, and everyone green.

"We can transfer to the local on 14th."

"Ve go vhere ve have to go, do vhat ve have to do, kiddo." He leaned in. "It is in our blood, remember..."

The gypsy György accompanied Zoli's father on trips to regional markets. One day, they were on their way back to the same town that hosted the aforementioned wedding. The burg Dani saved Irén from.

Szikszó was the largest town in a string of hamlets that hugged the southern side of the Great Hungarian Plain. Farmers and craftsmen rode from miles to hock their goods at its market, meet and do business with merchants and retailers. Some, like Dani, traveled for days to be there. The abundance fueled this bazaar's growth and popularity. Dani knew he could make more here than he ever could at his store back home—more than he could make anywhere, for that matter.

Their wagon wound through the streets of Szikszó. The town had grown over the year, proved to be the perfect midpoint for the city and country. The duo was quick to breach the borders of its marketplace, found their usual stall. They unloaded their wagon. Flats of stone fruit, plums and apricots, the last of this season's apples and pears filled their space. As György continued unloading, Dani unsheathed a blade, began cutting samples.

He assured anyone who'd listen that his fruit was not only the best but also the cheapest, truths that bothered his competition. One of Peter's groomsman, now aged and disgruntled by his lot in life, recognized Dani from long ago.

He scanned the duo with disdain, pointed them out to friends and neighbors, eager recipients of his belligerent perspective.

György and Dani were too busy selling their goods to notice.

"FILTHY JEW."

"TAKE YOUR GYPSY DOG BACK TO THE POUND YOU FOUND HIM IN."

"THEY'RE TAKING OVER OUR MARKET!"

György swung toward the insult, his hand moving to the hilt of his blade. He scoped their surroundings, unable to identify the person who yelled from within the bustle. The few became the many. Hate flew from all angles.

"GO HOME, JEW!"

"STRING UP THE GYPSY!"

"HIM AND THE GODDAMN JEW!"

György drew his blade, its razor sharp edge catching the sun as he prepared to take matters into his own hands. His first step toward the growing prejudice was met by Dani's restraint; he held his friend back with both hands.

"We're not kids anymore." He fought György's primal march, his own frustrations, and reminded his large friend, reminded them both: "We have families to take care of."

György eased in his friend's hands, took a deep breath.

They locked eyes. Shared history had led them both to this most respectable place. Neither of them wanted to ruin what they had worked so hard for. The realization worked to calm György. Dani watched his friend put the knife back in its scabbard.

Their restraint had little influence. The crowd continued to grow unruly, a mob well-formed; chants rose from the mass, epithets turned ugly.

"GO BACK TO THE DESERT, YOU CHRIST-KILLING, SHYLOCK!"

"HOOKNOSE!"

"MONEY-GRUBBER!"

The verbal insults turned physical. Merchants and their customers added to the confrontation. A wave of prejudice washed over Dani's stand, fruit laid waste, stomped and smashed by a herd mentality.

Dani pulled György toward their wagon as the crowd drew close, applied pressure. They packed what they could before the mass enveloped them, shook their ride as they made their escape.

"DON'T COME BACK!"

"WE DON'T WANT YOU HERE!"

"ANIMALS, THE BOTH OF YOU."

Dani and György shared few words on their long drive home, the silence embraced them through the stark Hungarian landscape. Their newly damaged carriage was repaired with what little was available. Only two of Dani's crates returned home with them. Both men showed signs of their struggled departure: ripped clothes, swelled faces, coagulated blood gathered in fresh wounds drawn over old scars.

"And zat is just how my fadher told it to me," Zoli wrapped it up with a shrug. "Zat vas ze vay tings vere, and he vanted to make sure I knew."

"And now, I know," Danny added.

The shriek off the third rail accompanied the flicker of interior lighting. Cracked electricity turned fragments of darkness blue, threw howling shadows inside and out of the speeding train.

"Vell," Zoli digressed, "experience is ze best teacher, kiddo, but experience isn't alvays good."

They fell quiet under the rattle of subterranean travel; transmutable considerations rippled away from them and into the folds of time.

3
———

Danny charged up and out of the Canal Street station, immediately engulfed in a current of pedestrian madness, avoiding elbows and making way. People worked the sidewalks of this wide throughway from all angles, invaded space, and gave little room for the unprepared.

"Gucci, Louis Louis. Gucci, Marc Jacobs, Louis Louis," barked an older Chinese woman with a slapped on smile and three-week old perm. "You want han-bag? Wallet? Sunglass? Good price."

Zoli emerged, collected within the mayhem. Together, they walked east, took a left on West Broadway, and continued north, away from where a wall once kept indigenous people at bay and allowed for a great expansion. The neighborhood just south of Houston had changed a lot over the years. Subjected to a rollercoaster ride of urban economics, the once gilded streets of the 1800s had been reduced to an industrial area filled with semi-legit import/export houses, trucking companies that could take advantage of the Canal Street corridor that connected all of lower Manhattan to the outer boroughs—and garbage, lots of garbage.

The dirty '70s helped turn the magnificent old buildings retrofitted with elaborate cast iron facades that lined narrow cobblestoned streets into makeshift warehouses available for the rag trade. Wholesale textile firms and inexpensive clothing outlets that employed mainly low-income and undocumented minority workers set the tone and kept things grimy, graffiti-littered, pollution-stained.

This rundown plot of the Rotten Apple was long considered the wasteland of the city, and the low rents that came with the moniker attracted a new breed of resident. From the '50s on, artists had quietly made the area south of Houston home. By the '80s, thanks largely to a boom in the downtown art scene and Reagan's go-go economy, broader interest returned. At this point in time, there was something for everyone.

"This way," Danny called out, excited to be downtown and in the mix, but eager to get to their destination, to unravel history, the mystery.

"Ve have a little time." Zoli veered off course, not as prepared to face his past; nerves boiled up through his spine, jerked his posture, welled his eyes with thoughts of things he wasn't prepared to hear. He turned a corner. Danny remained close behind him as they entered a parking lot filled with the ordered chaos of commerce.

"Are you serious?" Danny questioned. "We're like a block away. Aren't you dying to get over there?"

"Yes, of course," cracked through Zoli's reluctance, "but, I love to look..." He had the perfect distractions laid out before him, and he stepped to bury his anxiety in it.

The whole area was a marketplace. Huge spray painted murals a mess with random graffiti tags covered real estate cheap enough to accommodate all types of businesses; street vendors hawked handmade wares, artists painted or pieced together works on the spot; peddlers pitched piles of reclaimed trash, old typewriters, and bootleg audiotapes: *Thriller* and *Like a Virgin*, The Talking Heads and The Police available for a dollar a pop, maybe three for two if you played it cool.

Transvestite hustlers worked the crowd from the shadows, alternated with salesmen well-supplied with the latest and greatest commodities of vice. Stock brokers and businesspeople comingled. Crackheads helped the refined score some refined, were paid in powder alone; they passed joints and girlfriends and boyfriends and needles and Chinese takeout containers to one another in fare trade. All manner of commerce fueled the energy that attracted so many.

Zoli wore a grey suit that complemented the streaks of white in his hair, remained youthful amid wrinkles well-worn. His overall appearance, freshly-shined dress shoes, combed back hair, and a military formed gait cleared a path through the radiant crowd as they whispered warnings of approaching: "5-0. 5-0."

"Yo, chief-chief." One local crossed Zoli's path, dark eyes floated deep in their sockets. "You cop, cop?"

"No," Zoli turned to him, cool in his reaction, straightened his lapel, and smiled as he continued on his way. "I am Hungarian."

The duo took their time moving from stall to stall, appreciated the wealth of goods being offered. Danny poked through piles of city refuse turned to treasure by time, discarded trinkets brought into New York long ago; old coins from distant lands, subway tokens from decades past, Native American artifacts excavated from construction sites that dated back to before The City existed. He stalled on used books. Well-read New Yorkers left literature in their wake; it piled up on street corners and in garbage rooms before it hit the market and fueled an entire subculture. The booksellers of New York City could teach literature at any major American university.

"Hey, yo, read dis one..." the bookseller announced as his sales pitch, held a book of poetry out for Danny to grab. "I think it's what you need in yo' life."

Danny looked at the cover, flipped open its pages, skimmed some lines: *brimming cup, stormy sea, a new door, waited for us...*

He paid the man. It was the first book of poetry he'd ever owned.

His dad, on the other hand, was there on business. Zoli had found an artist, had already started setting paintings aside. He made it a habit to listen to stories, histories, learn of their places of origin. He bathed in the melting pot that was New York.

The artist was a painter from Nigeria, thin and narrow, with long fingers that made every one of his motions, no matter how remedial, seem elegant; the dark purple that reflected off his skin added to his incongruous regality within the noise and clutter of the city. He bent Zoli's ear with trials that rang familiar; the feelings he shared were palatable, running from one to the other. It bound the two refugees.

Zoli appreciated the connection, encouraged it. "I cannot tell you how similar my life vas…"

Their accents mingled in a parade of authenticity, augmented English blessed with smiles and camaraderie. They faced the wrath of merciless leaders out to extinguish a particular people from a region, destroyed the beauty and culture of the land with goals of total domination, environmental and spiritual devastation.

"Too familiar, Bernard. Too familiar." Zoli placed his hand on the artist's shoulder. They locked eyes, shook hands. "To some people it doesn't matter vat side of ze border you come from, they just hate you for how you vere born."

"So true. After two years of civil war I finally made it to the Ivory Coast. I had to leave everyone behind. I had to go alone. I lost my mother." His crisp accent was formed before he was born, shaped by decades of British colonization.

"Our mothers…" Zoli joined his new friend in a long hard moment, then another.

Bernard continued to connect. "But there has been no peace since. You cannot live there in peace." He shook his head. "They always find something to fight over, religion, tribes, oil, is the same. How many have to die in the name of their greed?"

"Terrible," Zoli shook his head. "Vhen vill ve learn?" he asked, taken in by the artist's undying efforts in the face of adversity; introspection was interrupted by the matter at hand, the artwork Zoli had already set aside. "How much do you vant for all these?"

He shared a smile with the fellow immigrant and went on to buy the entire bundle on the spot; paintings alive with African subject matter and vibrant colors, red, black, and green jumped from the canvases in a swirl of abundance, depictions of daily life in Africa that were easy on the eyes.

Zoli knew he could turn them around no problem, and promised, "I will return for more once I sell these."

Danny took the lead as they continued off side streets, away from the market and far from the starving artists who defined that area. They continued toward a row of galleries that had opened throughout the neighborhood to find and enter Perry Art Gallery, Broome Street.

"Mr. Gluck." A warm welcome turned them toward Israel Perry, a slight man with broad shoulders and unnaturally dark hair. He came to them with his hand held out in greeting. "The two Mr. Glucks."

Israel Perry's path to New York may have been different than Zoli's, but the obstacles were most similar; discrimination followed the Jews no matter where they went or came from, breeding a camaraderie that was near impossible to extinguish. A united distrust propelled Semites into business with one another, turned relationships sacred; Yiddish was the language that kept them connected.

"*Abi gezunt!*" Zoli announced as a greeting Mr. Perry appreciated; Yiddish, Yiddish, and more Yiddish, handshakes and an invitation out of the polished gallery space and into a backroom followed.

"Shaineh raaineh keporah." All was good.

Danny was accustomed to gallery life. His earliest memories were from his crib in the main room of his dad's gallery in Provincetown; the depth and colors of works his father had collected over decades swirled in his subconscious. Each sale, every purchase, the good years and the stress of the slim ones fought for their place within the kid's amygdala, and held steady around his throat. However, he had learned to pay attention, consciously pick up on the minutia.

Zoli smiled and laughed with an ease that accompanied every transaction; the adrenaline that pumped through his body was addictive. Perry fell into its cadence. "How long has it been?"

Danny shifted in his seat as they reminisced; living in Israel at the time they were there seemed so foreign, so romantic. They described Kibbutz ideals; both Zoli and Perry were transported back to the holiest of starscapes. "Milky dew off pre-morning grass lifted between our toes, dates that dripped honey were always within reach." A long sigh of relief blanketed them both. They were finally home.

"I stayed in Israel far longer than your father," Perry explained. His sharp Israeli accent bit the head off his every utterance. "You will see the artists I represent reflect my time there."

Canvases that hung on clean white walls worked like windows, sent viewers into sprawling landscapes thick with the textures of life. Zoli readily drifted through the fields of his youth, his hands permanently soiled by the earth of his childhood.

Art as it had come up around them in New York in the

'70s and '80s did not connect with Zoli. It wasn't what he enjoyed. Never educated in the arts, not even graduating from elementary school, he learned solely from experience, approaching his trade the only way he knew how. He took a personal path, sought bridges to his past, continued in the niche of his life lived. He couldn't sell anything as foreign as soup cans or fine art graffiti. He didn't connect to the avant-garde or overtly intellectual, new wave, rock and punk music, drug-fueled loft parties, and pretentious gallery openings. It was all a distraction compared to how he connected to the works he represented. His inner soliloquy churned at the thought of changing his tastes; he knew giving into the consensus of a singularly-minded crowd was dangerous.

Zoli was drawn to artists whose lives ran parallel to his own. His Provincetown gallery exhibited the depth of those experiences, from European Landscapes and Hungarian primitives to American impressions of the sea and sand off Cape Cod. He had perfectly curated a collection of chapters lived. This genuine connection to the art he sold endeared him to both artists and collectors, added depth to the relationships he held with both, and would lead to nights in studios and living rooms entertaining deals made through friendship.

Aware of his talents, marveling at his unconventional business model, artists, dealers, and private collectors all consigned artwork to Zoli. They were all confident he could turn the deal.

Clients were willing participants in Zoli's explorations, drawn into the experiences he set out before them. Over the years, Zoli had compiled a large list of customers outside of the New York area that he would drive to see as often as he had art to show, and later, whenever Danny was off of school to help. Middle Americans who couldn't get enough of Zoli's charm wanted him over whenever he was in town; his accent was enough of an excuse to throw parties where he could show off, "a collection of ze finest original artworks," each piece presented with a sales pitch wrapped in a reflection.

Hosts made sure to show off their New York City art dealer to envious friends and neighbors. Housewives around the Great Lakes and throughout the South, all the way down to Florida and out to Texas, hung on Zoli's every word; a trip through Europe dangled on each dip and twirl of his inflection. They encouraged his return by making sizable purchases a habit.

Mr. Perry led father and son down narrow steps. The gallery's shiny facade made way for remnants of old New York; exposed brick, concrete floors, and unabated asbestos completed the reality behind the curtains of Soho luxury.

Yet-to-be-stretched canvases still curled from shipping were stacked on a worktable as old as the building itself. A gallery assistant jointed long pieces of wood together to form large rectangles and squares that were stapled together in an afterthought of repetition. He went on to carefully unravel a piece from the top of the pile, slowly revealing a wealth of color, a striking beauty, bold lines that were hidden from sight.

"This is the artist I wanted to show you, Zoli," Perry said.

"Ze one you mentioned on ze phone?" Zoli questioned, amazed. "This is his work?"

"First things first." Mr. Perry invited them in for a closer look with arm gently raised.

It was a large 40 x 46-inch acrylic portrait of a young lady seated beside a bowl of fruit on an unnaturally flat table top, her head gently tilted. Blue eye-shadow painted across her half closed lids pronounced the ethereal calm of this modern woman.

They watched as the gallery assistant continued to unpack, each piece expertly mounted, affixed to simple frames with a nail on each side, then propped against the exposed brick as he turned to the next in line.

Zoli stepped to flip through the accumulation, falling enchanted in the process. Artwork screamed out with fauvist exuberances. Broad swaths of color jumped off canvases with a bravado reminiscent of early modernism. A reintroduction of Matisse colors, Degas grace, depictions of Lautrecian leisure drew Zoli off his feet. He floated through the whimsy, found the light behind every corner, and took his turn at the cafes and balconies depicted.

"I don'ts believes it," Zoli exclaimed. "*Itzchak Tarkai* painted these?"

"Yes," Perry stated. He had first met the artist at a retrospective of notable alumni of the Avni Art institute in Tel Aviv. Mr. Perry's initial attraction to the paintings were amplified by the artist's history, and convinced the artist to let him represent his works in the United States.

"The same boy from the camps?" Zoli asserted, repeated; saying it out loud made it real. "The same kid I knew at *Mauthausen?*"

A long pause allowed the fact to float across the room, land on Danny's shoulders. "That's where you were with *Jenő*, right dad?"

"Yes..." Zoli stepped away from the artwork, lifted his head, eyes glazed in memories that rushed through him like white river rapids; the chill in his bones wiped the color from his face, wrung his bypassed coronary arteries tight. "I vas..." Words cracked with pain. "Ve vere..."

"Maybe he'd know what happened to your brother?" Danny blurted out, too young to respect the heaviness in the room.

Zoli's heart skipped, pangs of pressure traveled up his sternum, pounded pounds. He took a second glance at the signature unfolded before him; one canvas after another, like an old time nickelodeon, sped to animation, and flickered into the past.

"They are using his images to launch the inaugural ArtEXPO for the new convention center. You know, Jacob Javits opens later this year, down by the old train yards." Mr. Perry went on, "I'm sure he will be there..."

"He could know something," Danny repeated. "We have to go."

Zoli stood silently in front of Tarkai's work, a backdrop of smooth lines and vibrant colors contrasted emotions that welled within. The thought of a reunion, of revisiting what they had gone through as children charged through Zoli's veins like ice water. Memories rushed into the now, recollections Zoli had long wished to forget remained as raw as wounds left to fester.

"It's been so long."

4

———

Farmhands raked in a steady haul of fruits and vegetables, picked through the bounty, pruned branches, and loaded baskets; wagons perpetually rolled out of sight while others came back for more, an efficient and ongoing effort maintained by a seemingly endless supply of tireless workers. Stalks of wheat and barley required a gentler touch when cultivated manually. Small fingers made easy work of releasing the grain from its chaff; children shuffled through the rows of grain that sprouted at their feet. They checked each stalk for sustenance produced, tedious work done under the afternoon sun.

Highly regimented, a finely tuned machine, all parts worked as one; crops were retrieved and transferred as soon as they were available. Field hands were pressed to keep an unseen schedule; teams of boys, none older than sixteen, were stressed, compartmentalized, and kept on task.

Fourteen-year-old Zoli was slender with a full head of

dark brown hair that waved left in its natural oils. His sky blue eyes opened to the horizon, homed clouds, and held the future. It was all a mirage.

He wiped sweat from his brow, took a moment to catch his breath, familiarize himself with the land.

"Back to work!" German commands encouraged job performance. Canvas sleeves unrolled in Zoli's frantic effort revealed stripes that ran the length of his long unwashed uniform, a pattern interrupted solely by a yellow Star of David that had been sewn on its chest.

Zoli stood frail, limbs bone thin. The cut of his cheeks accentuated his neck, exposed veins. Work in Nazi fields, its forced and unrewarded repetition, left an apparition in the young boy's place; Zoli hung his head low in servitude, focused on survival. He moved to instruct another boy, Chaim Kemény, ten years old at the time, on how to tend to each plant grown in the field. Hungarian was the language that kept them close throughout internment. "Some fruit is cut at the stem," Zoli illustrated with the blunt instrument issued. "Ideally sharper."

Chaim was careful, copied Zoli's every move, stayed close. They shivered through peak harvest season. Fear fueled their trial by fire; Chaim clung to Zoli like a shadow. They filled wagons and waited on new ones to arrive, changed crops and retrieval methods along the way. "These require a gentler touch," Zoli instructed.

Kids worked to no end, turned insignificant within the huge Nazi field, hours, days, and lives diminished by design.

Carrots were pulled from dirt, land moved to loosen sugar beets from their roots, mounds of cabbage set aside.

Zoli and Chaim moved together, dug through their take. They set rotting and insect-infested crops aside, shared a grimace. The feigned revulsion protected them from the hunger, their frail frames forced to handle food that they could not eat. A lack of strength hung their arms, hunched backs; lifeless through the effort, their eyes were hollowed by starvation and fixed in a lifeless stare.

They wheel-barreled imperfect produce over to a nearby barn. Animals that were kept for their milk and meat ate better than they had in months. They watched bovine and fowl tear into their meal, ripping food from their hands with a force that threw food every which way, cabbage gobbled by whatever animal stood closest, carrots swallowed whole, a frenzy amplified in the want of the two boys.

Outside, from behind gates and fences, barbed wire and armed guard, stood a farmhouse silhouetted by distance. Zoli stared at the trees that arced to the sun and the movements of a child picking fruit from them as her mother called her home. The glimmer was just that, gone as quickly as it came.

The entire labor force, from the farm that provided life for the march of fascism to the prisoners that worked the quarries, toiled in devastated silence. An egress was weaponized and referred to as the stairs of death, prisoners were made to carry granite and quartz blocks up and down its 186 steps in brutal 12-hour shifts. The exhausted crumbled under the weight of the Sisyphean task. They fell over, caused an avalanche of the infirmed; the stones they carried broke limbs and lives. Their agony repressed by force, remained near silent.

The SS called Mauthausen *knochenmühle*, bone grinder. There were no distractions, just labor and death. A Nazi flag caught the winds of a brewing storm around them, cracking ominously against the eerie calm.

Within the sanctuary of a barn, Zoli stepped to feed a colony of rabbits crammed into tiny chicken-wired pens. Mammals bunched up and indistinguishable, one large mass of bunny-fur caked in the grime of necessity, uncontrolled and overpopulated, underfed and fecal stained.

Hunger pains persisted through young Zoli as he tore heads of cabbage into manageable pieces. Rabbits trampled each other to get their share. Zoli dropped food onto the mayhem; docile animals turned ferocious out of need.

Zoli lifted his head, checked his surroundings, tilted to Chaim in a moment dragged long by quickened heart beats, pure fear, before sneaking a single cabbage leaf into his mouth. He kept a hand in front of his face to shield his chewing from sight, eyes darting with heightened anxiety as he frantically digested food meant for livestock. His vacant innards churned in the nearly forgotten sensation.

Chaim swung to follow Zoli to their next task. They threw the last of the produce in, gathered hay before stepping towards the dairy cattle.

The vacancy in Zoli's eyes made way for opportunity; he fell to his knees, an intentional accident that left him face first in the mud, laid out in order to steal sips of milk spilt beneath the cows he was ordered to feed.

Chaim couldn't contain himself, blatantly stuffing whatever he could into his mouth.

Zoli caught sight of the conspicuous act, stopped what he was doing, and got to his feet. He inched closer to

Chaim. The boy fought Zoli's efforts and continued to cram food into the void.

Zoli saved Chaim from certain death before; upon arriving to Mauthausen in 1944, Jews were examined by the Nazi Doctor Oskar Paul Dirlewanger. A proud German who had worked his way up the ranks of the Reich by committing the most heinous acts; mass murder, rape and rumored cannibalism were among his credits. He carried those experiences and that expertise through every task gathered. He was both feared and exalted for the malevolence of his work and the undying enthusiasm he had for the job.

Dirlewanger separated incoming Jews into manageable groups. Artists and intellectuals, Jewish doctors and lawyers were immediately put on latrine duty, kept alive in order to receive as much humiliation as he could give; the more accomplished the Jew, the lower the task. He was interested in athletic male subjects around the age of eighteen and was allowed to conduct experiments on fit young men, similar to those his peer Dr. Josef Mengele was doing at Dachau on twins. Dirlewanger enjoyed pushing the limits of cruelty. He operated on the lucid and boiled the heads of his victims clean for keepsakes. There was a cabinet of skulls in his office, a row of perfect smiles exposed and on display. He sent countless people to their deaths in the gas chambers and turned the quarries of Mauthausen into a mass grave. A litany of atrocities sanctioned by a Nazi party that needed men of his resolve, he was given free reign as reward.

Kapo August Adam was there to keep himself alive.

The career criminal—and half-Jew—took orders from the Nazis for extra food and cigarettes, charged to keep his kind in line. The camp encouraged his demons; all the anti-social behavior he exhibited on the outside was rectified, put to good use. He made Dirlewanger's needs his own, reveled in dehumanizing his own people, considered it payback for his prewar incarceration.

Families were destroyed in an instant; the old and infirmed, females of any age were filed in for showers that would be their last. Zoli watched his parents get hauled away. Uncompliant Jews were shot on the spot. Jenő stayed close to his little brother for as long as he could, kept Zoli from running out after their family. Neither imagined that this glimpse would be the last they would ever have of their mother.

There was no time to mourn for any of them, not their parents or grandparents, brothers or baby sisters. The remaining young were herded into a separate line where Dr. Oskar Paul Dirlewanger made his final selection. Toddlers and infants were reunited with their families to wait unknowingly for their imminent deaths; fit males were sent to work camps, sentenced to death on their feet in mines and manufacturing plants, while young boys were handpicked for more specific duties.

Jenő held Zoli tight, their clothes in rags, breath never recovered. Zoli noticed another little boy next to them lost in a daze, his little body clenched by shock, unable to cry. Zoli instinctively reached out to pull him in.

Jenő pleaded with the Nazi doctor, humbled by the situation: "*Nein, nein...*" Propelled by familial pride, he hid his strength, avoided eye contact, and begged for the three boys with what little German he knew. *"Kleiner, kleiner."*

"What is the age?" Dirlewanger asked in German.

Neither Jenő nor Zoli understood a word. Kapo Adams was nearby and available to translate into Hungarian. Jenő insisted: "All three of us haven't been bar-mitzvahed," a lie that dangled on a moment of trepidation, their fate locked in the slow moving seconds of the doctor's consideration.

"Ya, but you're strong enough to work, maybe I'll give you an extra hard job," howled the Nazi, his language cold and harsh as the troops tore Jenő from his protectorate.

Zoli was separated from the last of his family. Jenő went easily; the fight inside him flickered in the depths of their loss.

Dr. Oskar Paul Dirlewanger yelled out, ordered the young and recently orphaned to work the fields that fueled their final solution. Handpicked pre-pubescents were given a reprieve of farm life, cruel healing from what they had all witnessed.

Being so close to death so often was too much for Chaim, the joy of feeding himself too much to contain. He broke out in hysterical laughter as handfuls of food traveled through his insides. Pure joy was interrupted when Zoli went silent, hurried back to work.

Chaim was struck still, his mouth left full of half-masticated food as a familiar heaviness bore down on every inch of his being. Commandant Ziereis stood above him, his full Nazi uniform kept crisp by the comforts of rank; the cattle prod held casually in his right hand was lifted, brought down in a series of sharp swings that landed with a snap of flesh.

Chaim wanted to cry, needed to cry, but had no more tears. The routine was familiar, had turned habitual, the abuse was expected. The pain gave him an excuse to feel again. His knees buckled, gave way, dropped him in the waste that collected on the most unholy floor of the pig's pen. Swine closed in on the boy; snorts and snouts tempted appetites, teeth grinding with anticipation, dissuaded from their meal only when Commandant Ziereis swatted them out of the way.

"See. I saved you," said Ziereis. His crooked smile punctuated his meaning.

Zoli watched Ziereis's guards retrieve Chaim's lifeless body. He carried the little boy out of their eye-line and toward the gates of the nearby concentration camp.

Mauthausen jutted off of the banks of the Danube like a soar, built by the first held captive within its stone walls in 1938, with sub-camps that sprawled out over appropriated Austria like a virus, infecting the whole world around it. The majestic river, like the trains that came to the local station, was now used to transport the last of Europe's Jews from Hungary and the outlying countryside.

Months passed, the cyclone continued, the final solution moved ahead full steam; chimneys spewed swirls of smoke in testament to the success of their infernal efforts, Jews marched to their deaths to maximize casualties, beaten to save bullets. Prisoner quarters slowly emptied; the arrival of boats and trains carrying dehumanized cargo slowed.

Zoli grew up in an instant, maturity driven into his teenage frame by the sight of innumerable nightmares, countless murders. He focused on survival, muttering to himself, "Keep going," as he pushed through tasks designed to facilitate his demise.

Jews fought unconsciousness while pushing their bodies towards it, faked strength to avoid being shot for dead weight. They carried supplies, tended to the fields, dug mass graves, and mined for minerals. Battered bodies, bloodied and splintered, held infections and disease that fought for flesh appropriated, shells of human beings infested with nits and lice and vermin. They kept their hands busy in order to stay alive.

Nazis unloaded cattle cars of human cargo, a spattering of undesirables from the Hungarian-Yugoslav border. The interned and indoctrinated were immediate ordered to fill the trains with food and munitions redirected to resupply the front lines.

One new arrival, a boy no more than nine years old, tore Zoli's attention. The fear in his eyes rang familiar.

"Come over here. Jew, this way, this way, stupid dog..." The turn of momentum, advancing allied armies, and lost nation-states brought pangs of desperation to the orders barked by their captors. Still, Kapo Adam was ever keen to humiliate in his native tongue: "I will put you where the Jew-lovers will never find you."

The newly imprisoned were lined up; Nazis compartmentalized them into the useful and the useless. Young children were immediately filed in for the labor force, left to watch their few remaining loved ones herded to extermination.

Zoli and his group were taken off task, immediately pushed into the next. New underage boys joined the walk back to the farm; dangerously low food supplies fueled

Nazi desperation, the stress of war available around every corner. Nazi soldiers, barely older than the Jews were on the farm, prepared themselves for the front. The young and fit boarded passenger cars with seats and windows; they acted their age, laughed and ate, enjoyed the freedoms that their captive audience had stripped. Food and drink spilled as they shuffled towards their ride; one soldier turned to notice the kids in the adjacent field.

He laughed and joked with his friends, then hurled a pieces of bread out toward them like pigeons in the park, for his amusement, before boarding the waiting train.

Food landed in mud. Zoli stood nearby, numb to the temptation, natural impulses beaten out of him. He watched new recruits hurry as fast as their bodies would carry them. They fought for what little was offered, turned ferocious out of necessity.

The child Zoli saw at the train station stood nearby, stripped of family, of a regular life. Zoli watched him take struggled steps towards sustenance, dragging one foot out in front of the other.

Scabs perforated his slight frame, wounds gnawed at by all manner of insect. Creatures flew, crawled, and squirmed to infect gashes, sharp pierces, open wounds; coagulated blood hosted thousands of their eggs. Maladies worked in concert to make waste of ravaged youth. Only the child's bones kept him upright, there was no muscle, no baby fat. He dropped to his knees, pulled himself towards the bread that sat at arm's length, fingers extended, at the ready, glands prepared, stomach growling, about to feed.

Zoli kicked the food out of his reach, twisted in the inhumanity of his effort.

The child looked up with a dry and devastated smack of his lips; Zoli would never forget his face as they watched the food disappear into the brush.

Zoli turned to immediately tend to the crop-lines, got the kid to his feet, put his rake in his hands. "Get back to work," he urged. "They will kill you."

Traumatized, their tearless eyes watched others eating. The starving tore through the crust of recently baked goods, chewed, swallowed, spit crumbs with unadulterated vigor that transported them out of their lives, and went on long enough to attract unwanted attention.

Commandant Franz Ziereis had risen in rank, earned full Commandant status the year he took over the farm and train depot at Mauthausen. His productivity had become a thing of legend. His particular brand of motivation, and employment of techniques recommended by Dr. Dirlewanger, were equally lauded by peers and superiors alike. Many thought that he had mastered the art of training Jews, breaking them down to the subservient subspecies they were. Many fantastic rumors had formed but the facts spoke for themselves. Ziereis was able to maintain steady food production and distribution during his time at Mauthausen, and expectations remained high as the Nazi war effort was beginning to stretch itself thin. For the first time, the Commandant felt pressure meeting the demands made by the SS command. He charged into the field, shot the children who were still feeding themselves on the spot. Mass graves opened to all manner of maggot and unholy disruption were filled by those who dared take food out of the mouths of the Aryan race.

Survivors remained, moved fruits and vegetables as

directed, and never again considered eating any of it. Tension draped their dwindling numbers, infected every action within it; even the sunset was perverted by the malevolence. Rays of light pierced clouds of human ash, tinted the entire world in a deathly red haze.

Zoli dared to break the despondency as they began their march back to the barracks, whispering in Hungarian, "What's your name?"

The kid sparked to the sound of his native language. It acted as a reminder, momentarily connected the child to where he was from and who he was.

Zoli introduced himself, helped the kid walk.

The boy tilted up, looked to Zoli. The six-year age difference was magnified in a moment; Zoli was a man molded by circumstance, bar mitzvahed by the horrors of war, their collective loss. He led the young boy through gruesome circumstances. All the sadness, fear, and anxiety welled the child's eyes, affected the way he walked, his gait pressed down by the force of this new life.

"Itzchak..." the young boy replied in a cough, under the weight of complete and utter loss. Every inch of his diminutive prepubescent frame soiled by miles of dehumanization, dirt residing in every orifice of his long uncared for body; he cleared his throat, tried again: "Itzchak... Tarkai."

"Itzchak is my Hebrew name..." Zoli shared. They locked onto one another. "Now, I will never forget yours."

5

Hungarians displaced and left homeless after either World War, on the run from any of the many revolutions, communist and otherwise, were all looking for a better life in the United States of America. They congregated in New York, Cleveland, and Miami, seasonally in the Catskills or wherever else they could find work; a preexisting Hungarian community was often the main draw. They were waiters and counter girls, dressed display windows and bussed tables, all the while immersed in their European heritage.

A neighborhood grew out of that need, Second Avenue on the Upper East Side of Manhattan was long known colloquially as Goulash Alley; chess grand masters, future Hollywood icons and Governors were raised on the paprika that flowed through its streets. Hungarians had filled an area that stretched twenty square-blocks with carts and vendors that would evolve into butcher shops and bakeries, every imaginable Hungarian delicacy eaten at the outdoor cafés that lined the streets. Evenings were paired with *pálinka* and wine as music filled the air, a *chárdásh* in every restaurant, *paprikás csirke* on every plate.

The *Magyar* language bellowed through corridors of steel and concrete, crescendoed in all manner of communication; love, hate, respect, and disdain manifested in a holler.

Men congregated behind a tobacco shop off Second Avenue and 79th street, and what started out as a scheme to sell more cigarettes turned into a place to talk politics or literature, do business, drink, and play cards. Pocketknives divvied up cheeses and salami brought to the games by the grocer himself. Every war, every occupation, every threat to *Magyarorszag* brought refugees to the city. The amassed quickly grew out of their informal meeting space.

Churches and social halls grew to accommodate the boisterous camaraderie. By 1889, The First Hungarian Literary Society was born. It moved around for decades, from farmhouses to the newly erected buildings that pocked the vanishing open spaces of upper Manhattan. Hungarians flush from the economic boom of the Jazz Age co-operatively bought land at what would be 323 East 79th street; their four-story row house was ready for them on October 11, 1925. On the southern border of the very German Yorkville neighborhood, The Club, as its members would come to call it, remained the only owner/resident of that property until selling out in 2017.

Membership grew, especially after women were allowed to join as Jewish refugees found sanctuary in New York City following the Holocaust. Affected by the horrors witnessed, these men and women sought stability, family, whatever routine that could reestablish normalcy. They went forth and retained that long lost sense of community with lots of food and drink. A new zest for life filled large card rooms, staffed kitchens with refugees, sustained by grandchildren turned waitstaff.

But time went by, the turn-of-the-century crowd began to thin out and The Club's dynamic began to better represent the needs of its craftiest members. Not every Hungarian came to work their fingers to the bone; some came with dreams of making something of their own, of seeing the new world, of living the American dream as best they understood it. They worked their way up to respectable stations in life in the hospitality industry, utilizing crafts brought from the old country, working with family in the Diamond District, or jumping into the fledgling film business. By the mid-twentieth century, Hungarians were making a name for themselves in America.

Another wave of Hungarian refugees was encouraged by the nationalist revolt of '56 that did little to change the Soviet's hold on Eastern Europe. But, the brief uprising did displace the Red Army long enough to give Hungarians the slightest opportunity to escape the uncertainties that lurked in the shadow cast behind the Iron Curtain.

Different from the Jews who fled extermination at the hands of the fascists in the forties, the Hungarians who fled communism had something to prove. Not dehumanized in the same way as those who preceded them, the immigrants in the late '50s wanted their lives for themselves, not for the state, not for their neighbor, and they wanted it right now.

The *maîtres d'* at an upscale restaurant near The First Hungarian Literary Society stole booze from work, sold open bottles in The Club at a discount. Ruffians with questionable revenue streams and living situations with nicknames like *Banán* (Banana), *Kenyér-Evő* (Bread-Eater) and *Kis-Orosz* (Little Russian) were seldom judged by the ranks of established businessmen who kept their company. They were here to exploit the free-market system and came to The Club for the same reasons as everyone else: to have a meal, play cards, and feel at home. They bought and sold hard to find goods from across the Atlantic; others just "knew a guy in Queens."

Beyond the obvious and illicit interests, Hungarian art and culture flourished; theatres and cabarets came to life. The neighborhood, known as Little Budapest, drew visitors and elicited multiple New York Times articles. At a time when newspapers and tastemakers lauded Peggy Guggenheim's European art collection, endangered paintings from the "old country" were in high demand within a displaced community grasping for their roots.

Laszlo Stern, who went by Lester after immigrating to the States, was one of those Hungarians. His early life in Hungary left him soured and generally unimpressed with the world. He channeled the sentiment into his work as a film critic for the *Magyar Távirati Iroda*, the long-lasting Hungarian Telegraphic Office in the heart of Buda that would be bought up and restructured by Reuters decades later. His work kept him close to the cultural tides of the time. With access to filmmakers, artists, and all the museums and galleries, he was able to develop personal relationships with curators, to entrench himself in the cultural affairs of a nation trying to maintain its identity through post-WWII redistribution.

Hungarian artists and thinkers had long grown accustomed to the ever-changing political landscape and the repression it bred. They were prepared for it to happen again; rumblings of revolution floated through the squares and markets, filled the cafes with booming Hungarian chatter, people could no longer function under Soviet rule. Some charged towards the flames, others away from the fire, but all saw the conflagration in the distance.

Jewish as well as non-Jewish artists knew their works were perpetually in danger as they teetered on the sharp edge of acceptability under established communist doctrine; Mr. Stern jumped at the uncertainty, took paintings by François Gall, Antal Berkes, and Fried Pal right off the walls of different collections. Venerable Professor Béla Kontuly gave Mr. Stern as much work as he could carry, inspired others to do the same. Even prior to the Budapest uprising of '56, artists and patrons were anxious to protect as much Hungarian culture as possible. The short-lived fracture in communist rule gave them an opportunity to do so.

Mr. Stern left the country of his birth with rolls of paintings tucked under his arm. He followed writers, artists, and filmmakers to Vienna, then Paris, into the embrace of the salon lifestyle, the connections it offered. He befriended other repatriates, added to his collection; the promise of taking paintings to America was an attractive one to many of the young artists he reached out to. Mr. Stern's collection grew increasingly refined by the addition of French painters Antoine Blanchard, Edouard Cortès, and Lucien Delarue, among others.

In the United States, The First Hungarian Literary

Society was one of Mr. Stern's first stops. He showed works smuggled overseas and available for purchase, unknowingly competing with legitimate Hungarian art dealers Alexander Kahan and Herbert Arnot down the street. But, he didn't care; after his long journey, Mr. Stern stood content to display his collection in the main hall of the now long standing social club.

Without the overhead, Mr. Stern was able to offer his paintings at a fraction of the cost that the established galleries could; he also had a list of recently immigrated art collectors who were expecting to hear from him as soon as he got state-side. Unfortunately, due to his practical blindness, Mr. Stern wore glasses an inch thick that kept him from driving. Also, his unfamiliarity of America made tracking the diaspora nearly impossible; Hungarian enclaves spread across the nation, were separated by thousands of miles. Mr. Stern looked for help within The Club's ranks. He intended to take his collection out of New York and travel through the Catskills, Cleveland, and the suburbs of Detroit, Miami Beach, Los Angeles, Dallas, and maybe Vegas.

Fortunately for him, Zoltan Gluck, young and exhilarated by his newfound freedom, had recently immigrated to the United States from Israel and was looking for a way to see the country. With no experience in the arts but a carpenter by trade with an available car, Zoli approached the old film critic.

"Excuse me, Stern-*bacsi*," he addressed his elders formally as was expected when introducing oneself, especially to someone you hoped to be employed by. "I hear you are looking for a driver."

Zoli's blue eyes and strong back, easy features, and sincere smile made all the difference, was good for all involved. His charms and sense of humor had further developed; every day was now a gift to be relished and people couldn't get enough of his good will and insatiable appetite. He was hired on the spot.

The town of Fleischmanns, tucked into the valley of the Catskill Mountains, was to be their first stop, not just because of the Hungarian-Jews who called this community home but because Mr. Stern wanted to introduce Zoli to his other passion: the ponies. They stayed in a boarding house, rented rooms with shared baths, and spent days waiting for evening appointments at Monticello Raceway.

The park offered daily harness racing throughout the spring and summer seasons. Mr. Stern preferred this to the jockey on horseback variety, although he would go to whatever race was closest and open. There was just something about this type of race: jockeys pulled in wagons behind a stampede, like modern day gladiators charging through the dust of battle. Mr. Stern was in his element, teaching Zoli along the way. "Zoli, the two greatest thrills of the races," Mr. Stern insisted, "are winning AND losing."

Zoli found that many of their trips revolved around the schedule of a specific close-by track. It was what drew Mr. Stern to retire to Miami-Dade County; the lure of multiple tracks within bussing distance was too much for the old man to resist.

He studied racing forms intently but always bet the favorite. Zoli took advantage of his youth on the farm and went to the paddocks to see the animals up close and in the flesh before making any sort of wager. Unlike the methodical Mr. Stern, young Zoli preferred to gamble, had nothing to lose after losing it all; he chased the big bucks, bet trifecta boxes, included the field, always took a stab at the daily-double, a pick 6 if it were available, a combination of cross-back-bets racking up the cost of each trip to the betting-cage. Zoli knew he just needed to hit one of these bets to make his day whole. Mr. Stern would curse every available deity after realizing that a day of betting sure things didn't even cover gas and the price of admission.

From city to city, throughout their five-year partnership, the two spent their days at the track and nights setting out a collection of the finest works Mr. Stern had to offer.

Over the years, their territory grew; friends told friends of the Hungarian gentlemen from New York City who would come to your home and put up a private art show of works straight from Paris, Budapest, parts unknown. Zoli drove from coast to coast, down through Texas, and into Florida, carried portfolios in and out of clients' homes, made conversation, stretched canvases, built frames, hung paintings on bare walls while charming his way into the next deal. His involvement fueled their business, ran their supplies short.

"We have enough paintings for two more shows, that's it," Mr. Stern announced back in their guest room as he counted profits and noted inventory.

Zoli faced the reality, a decision, another fork in the road. He considered his life on the road, the American landscape flying by open windows on open highways, but never thought about returning to Europe. That reality rolled over him like a tsunami, toppling him through a twirl of memories, distant and recent, some more available than others, but all set aside for the sake of business. He knew his customers and what they were buying, and reacted accordingly. "Then ve need to go to vhere ze paintings are."

In Europe, Mr. Stern introduced his protégé to the artists they represented and the dealers he knew. Those who didn't speak Hungarian spoke Hebrew, with Yiddish well-represented and spoken close to the chest among dealers and artisans locked in the Eastern Bloc. Some couldn't communicate at all, so their dealings had to be translated from French and Italian, were inevitably pantomimed by the time they reached the smoldering cafes of Montmartre, too drunk to care.

Zoli attempted to speak the native tongue no matter the country. At this point, he had been immersed in life on four different continents; fluency in Hungarian, German, Yiddish, Hebrew, and English were gifts of those trials.

Through their buying trip, Zoli felt at home dealing with other expatriates, no matter what country they lived in or came from. They ate and drank and laughed at their good fortune; a life of poverty painted romantic by the fruits of their collective labor and a long fought freedom, in paintings that displayed their feelings, pronounced their pain. Long sad brushstrokes draped melancholy in an autumn landscape, subtleties in the eyes of subject matter who gently tilt from the hardships of the past. Abstract carnival tableaus that lit up canvases with depictions of the good life, movement, depth, and excitement roared off compositions, changed the tune. Bearded men who smoked pipes and used pocketknives to cut through bread and cheese were bound by more than just commerce. Artist and Art Dealer were brethren, baptized in a hellfire that ignited a shared enthusiasm for living life.

Mr. Stern hooked Zoli into the current of his debt-based business model that obligated servitude. With a roll of paintings and no cash, Zoli had to go on the road with Mr. Stern or be left broke after each working vacation that lingered way past being professional in the dark cafés and biergartens that lined the old cobble stoned streets of Europe. Before long, the pattern was all they knew.

"It is fine to travel and meet such lovely people," Zoli's accent would glide by housewives and female houseguests. Women of all ages and in every city, town, and township hung on his utterance. His sapphire eyes encouraged their smiles into giggles when they were caught staring. "God bless America," he thought.

Days free and pockets full of money propelled Mr. Stern to the races; Zoli followed breadcrumbs instead, a trail left by the ladies. Women he met in local businesses and in passing, from their art shows and their customers, fell victim to his charms; hotel doors swung open, family homes beckoned, clothes and inhibitions were left in the wind. His rendezvous took place under paintings sold, and occasionally involved escaping from husbands home early.

Other afternoons were spent in local bakeries with relocated friends, young and blue collar family men, uninterested in art, looking, for any excuse to speak Yiddish and talk of the old country, for hours. Tales made the rounds. Zoli's natural talents shined.

"Beautiful people, strong with freedom. Can you feel

it?" He crossed eyes with a corner table full of survivors. "Dis country is ze land of opportunity, a land of dreams." His silky accent gathered steam with an experience-fueled swagger, enveloped all within earshot, made Zoli an attractive novelty for the non-Hungarian clients that began to hear of the traveling art dealers.

Their territory expanded, parts of the South they usually drove past were becoming new markets. Zoli, ignorant of the local customs, stood in front of a urinal in a "colored only" bathroom, sat at the colored section at the diner, both he and Mr. Stern unaware of why they were calling so much attention to themselves.

"Hello," Zoli politely acknowledged their neighbor at the counter.

"You sure you want to sit here, sir?" the young black man seated next to them asked. His eyes extended concern and he wore a crooked smile that quivered with unease. His calloused hands hovered over the counter so as not to assert too much pressure on the hard linoleum surface.

"Vhy not?" Zoli asked with a smile, naive to the dissonance he was providing. "I'm hungry. Vhat is good in zis place?" Zoli craned to get a better look at his neighbor's plate; the sight and smells slapped his salivary glands, waffles smothered with gravy, grilled onions, cheese, and an egg on top, evoking all the near-burnt goodness he had learned to love since being dunked into the abundance of this great country and its regional cuisines and compartmentalized cultures. "Looks good. Vhat is that?"

His curiosity was interrupted by a gathering of the unseen southern status quo. "We keep things clean down here," someone growled.

"Hey, Benjy," the kid at the counter interjected, spinning around to a white man whose sunburnt face was beginning to flush even redder with agitation. "These two don't know any better, just let them be."

"You talking to me, boy?" the man named Benjy led out, privilege hitting its mark with the twang of southern discomfort. "I'll deal with you later, Versh."

Zoli's fellow diner sat still for a moment, seething over his remaining breakfast.

Confused by the exchange, Mr. Stern adjusted his glasses on the tip of his nose in order to better see what was going on around them. Both he and Zoli simultaneously wondered how the diverse land that they idealized, this great melting pot, could allow this to happen. *We haven't traveled so far after all,* they both thought in unison, with not so many words.

"Everyting is fine, gentlemens," Zoli insisted, his charm cracking under the pressure. "Ve just want to eat in peace. Right, Versh?" He shot his counter-mate a playful glance that was immediately interrupted by a chorus of dissenters.

"That ain't how we do things around here."

"Where you from?"

"They ain't American, tell you what."

Someone grabbed Zoli by the back of the collar, lifted him out of his seat. Any resistance was met by resolve. A mob mentality swept in, a wave that carried the immigrants out of their seats and into the streets.

"Vhat is happening?" was all that Mr. Stern could muster as he watched Zoli hit the ground with a thud. Three men stood above his protégé.

Black children playing in the streets, barefoot and

malnourished, were shooed away from the spectacle like vermin, an all too familiar muscle memory; those kids already knew their place in the world. The parallels were apparent, and it took the shine out of Zoli's eyes, resuscitating his own fear-driven reflexes. He wanted nothing more than to follow the children into the dark shadows of this unfamiliar American landscape.

The growing crowd of spectators rumbled, mumbled in concert.

"You hear that accent?"

"Bet they're Jews."

"Or commies. No good city-slickin' reds."

Benjy closed in, reached out, about to lay hands on Zoli when he was promptly shoved aside.

Versh stood in his place, turned to the crowd. "What is wrong with you people? Get on your business," he yelled. "These fellas just passing through, don't need no problems."

"What the fuck you doing, Versh?" Benjy demanded answers. "Fuckin' dare put hands on me, boy?"

"Don't make me tell Mr. Jason what you up to, Benjy." Versh's retort landed as intended. Benjy was struck reluctant to continue.

Versh extended his hand, helped Zoli to his feet. They locked eyes as they met shoulder to shoulder; a sensation, like a lost memory, one repressed and unfamiliar, urged its way to the surface, remained undecipherable.

"Mr. Jason been eyein' on bankin' in on that new highway that cuts town, you know. He been real protective of dere reputation," Versh stated before turning to Zoli. "Now, you and the old man best get going."

"Are you going to be ok?" Zoli interjected.

A simple question met with complicated history, a prejudice that ran through the veins of time, existed in DNA.

"Don't worry 'bout me. I've known these peckerwoods since we was all shittin' ourselves," Versh insisted. "My momma work for their daddy and his daddy before him, like her mamma was for the one before them. She bring order to all their squakin' and madness, they'd be lost without her." Zoli thought he caught a hint of a smile in Versh's expression. "Ain't nothing too bad gonna happen to me."

No sense could penetrate the static indifference of Jim Crow's status quo; Zoli tightened up as he was transported back to a time when similar ideologies prevailed, but was brought back to the present by Mr. Stern's sweaty palms grabbing him by the forearm and urging him toward their car.

"Let's not bring this up with our customers," Mr. Stern said as they walked quickly away from the fracas. Zoli agreed, unable to bring himself to look back.

They kept to themselves for the remainder of their trip, waited in their hotel room until their showing, and agreed to never return to the region.

After Mr. Stern retired, Zoli happily continued the business on his own, hosted art shows in private homes across the nation and at The Club in NYC where in '65 he dropped a painting on his soon-to-be second-wife, Julika. By then, he had seen America but remained happiest within the embrace of the Hungarian-American community of New York; marrying Julika cemented that relationship as she ran in the same circles. She would join him in the art trade the way she joined her two previous husbands in their work. She sat behind the register at a Hungarian restaurant on the Upper West Side for the last one and, as a seventeen-year-old waif after WWII, came out of hiding to follow her first husband the violinist across the concert halls of Europe, and she would follow Zoli on his buying trips.

Working vacations took them from the Danube to the Seine, slurping clams and sharing cigarettes with artists in bistros tucked away on the cobblestone streets of Montmartre or backstage at the Moulin Rouge that was long run by a Hungarian expatriate they knew. Lautrec's legacy was thick in the air as glasses were hoisted into smoke overhead. Zoli's French grew proficient enough to get a laugh. He made a toast, made his way through the room, slowing for conversations and craning to flirt with scantily clad showgirls.

Paris was attractive for a number of reasons to the artists who had fled Hungary; some were drawn to the familiar architecture and the reputable art scene, others had sought to have their more irrational needs fulfilled.

Aside from the obvious, and lascivious, one Hungarian painter, Tibor David, famous for his clown portraits and carnival scenes that belonged in many well-respected collections worldwide (as Mr. Stern's sales pitch went) thought he could only work with brushes found at a particular Parisian art supply store. That was enough of a reason for him to call the Left Bank home. Zoli had all this stored away for later use. He took it all in, filing useful details away for the right occasion, sharing it all as often as he could.

They continued the tradition of traveling to the customers that grew out of Mr. Stern's original list. Clients throughout the United States waited on Zoli's return. Young children grew up accustomed to his annual visit; the paintings, his stories, the funny accent all readjusted their Middle-American routine.

In 1972, their son Danny was born, and in 1973 they moved Julika's mom out of a one-bedroom at 135 West 79th street and into a three-bedroom that they couldn't afford six blocks south. She was to pay rent and watch Danny, but only did the latter, laying Hungarian in as his first language —but it was worth it: With a live-in grandmother on hand to watch their kid, Zoli and Julika were free to expand the business, travel in excess to support it.

They went from state to state, country to country, collecting experiences and expenses, eating and drinking, laughing and selling, making do with what they had even when they didn't have much. But they kept at it, unde-terred. Zoli loved the hustle, Julika did the books. Every penny was accounted for. They saved enough to open The Zoltan Gluck Art Gallery in Provincetown, Massachusetts, moved it from its original location at 424 Commercial Street to 398 Commercial Street in 1972.

After a mortgage was added to the expense of their life-style, Zoli and Julika quickly realized that they weren't going to make ends meet by selling the Eurocentric artworks that moved so freely in New York and beyond. They decided to offer inexpensive mass-produced seascapes to the hordes that came into town for whale watches, dune tours, and foot long hot dogs. Through the ArtEXPO and other conventions attended, Zoli had connected with *Dae Ryung*, a Korean family owned framing company that operated out of Jersey. They employed a room full of art students who churned out landscape after seascape, street scenes and still lives painted in a window-less warehouse right off the highway at a strip mall in Hackensack off Route 46, a ballet of brush strokes that left innumerable fictitious beach scenes ready for sale at a variety of resort towns across the country. Zoli would bring rolls and rolls of them up to Cape Cod, stretched loose canvases and stacked them upright and in rows that tourists could flip through. He devised a system where he could hang the painting on the wall in order to help a customer choose a frame, a very hands-on approach that carried over from his fine arts experiences. He tried to make everyone feel as if they were a real collector.

The decision was a simple matter of mathematics, they set themselves a quota on the number of paintings in the 10 to 100-dollar range they needed to sell per season to break even. Any more than that and they would be able to quit waiting tables, dressing windows, and doing whatever else they had to keep themselves afloat. The plan worked, selling what Zoli's friend and artist Romanos Rizk called, "inexpensive 'schlock' seascapes to day-trippers unaware of Provincetown's cultural significance," paid the bills. They were able to make the rest of the year available for the road and beyond, leaving their kid in New York City in his grandmother's care.

They would take every available weekend of the off season prior to their cross-country selling trip to prepare.

The tradition of all things Mr. Stern continued, stories shared, work ethic engrained. Julika watched. Zoli had it all planned out and dove in headfirst. He sized out cardboard reclaimed from the streets of New York City for paintings on the move, closed works into their protective embrace with cords slipped tight. Art from New York and Europe, Cape Cod and Israel converged in the main room of 398 Commercial Street, brought by Fed Ex or the artists themselves. Local painters Samuel Edmund Oppenheim, Romanos Rizk, John Dowd, Jonathan Blum and Raphael Soyer arrived on foot or by bicycle; all happy to consign them their work—the good stuff.

They would stay and chat, try to keep warm in the uninsulated space that was once a Captain's house; the winds swept over the harbor, grazed salt off the water, added to the thickness in the cold air that penetrated the gallery's walls.

Their last day of prep revolved around packing the Dodge van, a large-scale jigsaw puzzle, fine art slipped upright where backseats once were.

After years on the road, Julika's presence was welcomed. She kept Zoli company over countless miles, talked to hosts while he went on to unload and carry works in and out of their appointments. Julika would then light a cigarette and watch Zoli work magic with one eye; the other remained on housewives and other female fans who couldn't get enough of their young Hungarian art dealer.

Zoli's power of persuasion was on full display, no matter where they were, was well-practiced in the presentation. He unveiled one piece at a time, checking the artist's name as it was written on each box before starting his pitch, guiding clients in a seamless explanation and an available anecdote that connected them directly to the painting in hand.

"Ah, Emil Lindenfeld... had a two man show in New York City vith Frank Lloyd Wright in 1967..." Zoli said, then paused to collect his thoughts; his broken English saved to captivate his audience. "He left Hungary before ze var, vas treated like a maestro in ze Italian mountains, children vould bring him gifts, families gave him food..."

Their collection grew beyond the Hungarian works that appealed to those draped in a cultural birthright; the pieces now better reflected a broader journey, referenced Zoli's experiences. He had curated a traveling art show that transformed living rooms, corporate offices, and party halls into windows onto his past. Every piece came with a story, a recollection; true or not, Zoli made his musings a part of the artwork.

Faded turn-of-the-century oils of The Great Hungarian Plain by artists passed down from Mr. Stern joined the newly acquired, allowed for an intimate glimpse of Zoli's path. New York painters fresh from shows in world-renowned galleries, Cape Cod artists who apprenticed under the fathers of American Impressionism, reflected miles traveled.

Zoli stood shoulder to shoulder with doctors, lawyers, CEOs. They hung on his every word as he referred to whichever painting was held in their eye-line. Julika was ever-present in order to place one piece down to retrieve another by the same artist, while coordinating with the running monologue: "The vorkers in ze field take me back to Hungary. Lindenfeld alvays painted these hard working people, ze movement in ze painting, ze colors, take me back to simpler time..."

A sprinkle of nostalgia was usually enough to loosen the purse strings. Checkbooks and hard cash came out at the end of most evenings.

"Yes, very much in ze style of Wyeth." Armed with reference points, Zoli continued, "but, Adolf Sehring is ze only American to be commissioned by ze Vatican to make portrait of ze Pope..." He went on, directed the client to paintings Julika leaned against the walls; the softly lit hyper-realistic oils drew them in to conversation. "Vith ze help of a Father Milewski. Do you know Father Milewski?" Some did, others did not; he continued either way, body language, and hand gestures surreptitiously stimulated enthusiasm. "Yes, right here at St. Mary's on Orchard Lake... Vell, ve made big show of ze painting before I packed it up and Father Milewski got on a plane and took it to ze Vatican himself."

On cue, Julika handed him an accordion file folder full of bios and letters of authenticity. Zoli riffled through it and, after much anticipation, proudly displayed a thank-you letter from the Vatican.

Unpacking, showing, selling, and hanging were all part of the plan, Zoli got to work as soon as they pulled into any driveway. He prepared his sales pitch, went down the line of paintings he thought were right for his customers. Living rooms across the country were full of artworks, leaned atop one another, against walls and counters, moved to view and hang.

His tour through the collection continued. He stacked paintings on top of one another until they were almost out;

rooms ran short of space towards the end of his presentation.

He set large acrylics on canvas and a few watercolors out for reception. The paintings projected the simple elegance of ladies who lunch, serenity awash in bold colors that did not distract from its intended tranquility. They surrounded their audience, transported them to Paris, to the edge of the Danube, the Mediterranean, or the Plaza Hotel, circa 1920.

The pieces on display were enhanced with emotional relevance: "I have known dis artist my entire life," Zoli said, confidence taken over by sentiment. "As children, ve vere in a concentration camp togeder," he trailed off ever-quiet, and into a memory. "Ve saw a lot togeder."

6

The current of the second largest river in Europe careened off its bank, ran through forests in full bloom, crowded with leaves, fruit, and flowers that cast long shadows. It redefined its borders with ripples that traveled the length of the waterway; a stillness fractured by the cracking of explosives dropped from the sky. A barrage of munitions collided with the landscape, clouds of flak hovered in darkness, plumes of gunpowder hung in place, masked the world in a dreary rain.

Marches designed to wear Jews to their deaths slowed; an entire railway system was brought to a complete halt in a hail of liberation that fell from above.

Nazi guards had no one to fight, panicked. They shot into the air at planes long out of range; the American B-17 bomber and its 2,000-pound payload, bullets and bombs produced to combat the Axis powers, had free reign within the clouds; thinned out defenses gave them the right of way, a path to destruction.

With other planes in its class, the war craft sped through the skies of occupied Europe in box formation, carnage brought to every mile. The mess of reorganization. Gunners sat at 12.7 mm machine guns set in the plane's nose, wings, and tail. A .50 caliber machine gun rested atop this "flying fortress," establishing air dominance with booms that rattled sound waves and shook the earth. The bombardier, at a swivel seat domed in state-of-the-art Plexiglas, kept an eye on the enemy, was designated to fend off any air-to-air threat. He leaned into the effort, simultaneously jarred and steadied by the force of his defensive fire, hanging onto his just mission as enemy bullets cracked the 360-degree view, He panted, fighting to focus as the percussion of war thumped beneath his trigger-finger.

Smoke ejected, force released, projectiles spat through Nazi steel and flesh; blood splattered out of exit wounds, stained clouds, and left Nazi pilots slumped over their flight controls. Planes fell from the sky, smoldering tailspins that ended in pieces on subjugated land.

The crew of the American B-17 was given the moment they needed to hand munitions off to gravity, men working together for a singular cause, passing bombs off, a fireman's brigade of explosives placed and deployed, a cycle continued as their efforts were drawn to the Earth below, on mark and in a rapid eruptive freefall.

The sound and fury of the attack bathed Jews crammed into the slightest spaces with hope. Their lives were now secondary to the reparations that fell from above like the frogs and locusts that plagued Egypt, a god-sent wrath designed to smite the persecutor of the Jews. A pious hum of prayer, long kept hushed, rang out to the sounds of liberation; men joined together, believed again.

Nazi guards were in a panic, some dropped their guns and ran for cover; others tried to cover their heinous acts, freed prisoners from locked cattle cars, released them from bunk houses that packed ten to a bed and had no plumbing whatsoever. They rid themselves of any evidence of the atrocities they had committed, pushed the starving mass in the right direction, and encouraged their escape before charging off on their own.

Jews clawed for fresh air, a sigh of relief eviscerated in the continued bombardment. They scrambled in a disorganized stampede, the mayhem of warfare. Under cover, undernourished and emaciated, their knees buckled under the crush of limited freedom. The countryside was overrun by the release of the neglected. The tortured. The dehumanized. Left to their own devices, they found nowhere to go. They huddled together or wandered aimlessly to desperately search for friends, family, and food.

Names yelled out in agony for mothers, fathers, brothers, and sisters were accompanied by the blistering pangs of destruction; Nazi infrastructure toppled as their calls for reconciliation echoed across the forever fractured globe.

Men in their late twenties, maybe the oldest remaining survivors, gathered within the mayhem, donned improvised yarmulkes, found contentment in prayer as bombs went off around them.

Still a young man, nineteen years old when Zoli found him, Jenő's body had turned inward. His face and eyes were yellowed with jaundice. Fever adjusted his complexion, turned him green. His bones pressed against skin from the inside. Failing organs distended his abdominal cavities.

Zoli ran over as quickly as he could, dropped to his brother's side, stayed close as the war raged on around them. They tightened their grip on each other, continued hand in hand.

"Zoli, get out of here," Jenő whimpered Hungarian in near death, grasping at his atrophied strength and spirit. Zoli wasn't going anywhere. He stayed close, looking through the amassed and tried to make out faces within the crowd.

"ITZCHAK!" Zoli yelled. The young man attempted to get his brother off the ground, forced to burrow himself under Jenő in order to get him upright. He bore his weight, carried them into their escape, and continued to yell for his friends. "CHAIM!"

His weary lungs taxed in the act, despondency added to the sound of innumerable survivors calling out for friends and family, and help in general. Jews struggled to stay alive long enough to reconnect.

"ITZCHAK!" Zoli continued until he saw his other friend. "CHAIM? CHAIM?"

Zoli watched the young boy get swallowed up in the commotion. The haze of war blew through, then cleared; a group of Nazis gathered where Chaim just stood.

"CHAIM!"

Jenő tugged at his distraught brother, used what little strength he had left to pull him away from the Nazis who just released him from a forced march.

Jews continued to flood into the fields by the train-full. In an instant, the quiet countryside was inundated with the recently imprisoned, louse infested and burning with disease.

Ten-year-old Itzchak Tarkai bounced through the blind escape; people scattered away from explosions, vacated anything that could be considered a target from above. Trains, buildings, and bridges were all destroyed in an instant that lingered in smoldering remnants, uncontrolled fires.

Children nurtured in concentration camps looked for food scraps in trashcans; adults were right behind them. They ate whatever they could find, fought for what little there was left. The starved lingered close to the hazards of war, the dead at their feet. Brethren were torn to pieces, flesh removed from bone, turned to dust, skeletons left in pieces right before young Itzchak Tarkai's eyes.

From out of nowhere, Zoli grabbed Itzchak before the next bomb landed; Jenő pulled the trio through the fractured Bavarian countryside, struggled to keep them close. Urgency propelled each footstep, kept them moving, kept Jenő upright.

"Come on," Zoli urged Itzchak with as much enthusiasm as he could muster, only an inkling of hope allowed to reveal itself within the madness. "We can make it. I know a place..."

The more they moved, the weaker Jenő got. Both Zoli and Itzchak bore the weight of his efforts, one under each arm, moving steadily out of harm's way.

"We're almost there. Just over that hill."

Frau Baumann was left her farmhouse after Nazi appropriation; her husband was one of its first victims. He was killed before the farm that had been in his family for generations was turned into one that would be run for the sole purpose of feeding those the Nazis deemed deserving. Frau Baumann's family would never again be able to work and live off the land, a fate shared by all of the farm owners in the region. Slave labor, child labor, provided by and for the Reich took over, all benefits were to the state. Frau Baumann and her daughter, Anja, had been prisoners in their own home since.

Their farmhouse was isolated within its rural setting. It stood alone against the large fields they had tended to, the majority of the land developed for the Reich, the comforts of country living decimated by the occupying government. An entire nation subjugated by their manufactured consent were left to pay for the consequences in full. Those who never spoke out about the atrocities perpetrated on their front door were now burdened by the weight of that decision; the streets were emptied by their shame.

Little Anja huddled in the sitting room, flinched uncontrollably to the sounds of distant detonations. She watched her mom stand stoic by the front door with an anticipation that churned deep inside and out. The slightest sound caught her attention; Frau Baumann yanked the front door open, found three boys on her front porch. She hurried them all inside before anyone could see.

"I'm so glad you thought to come here." The emaciated boys only understood half of her German. She tucked all three in a corner away from windows and doors. "Let's all stay out of sight. Yes?"

The boys huddled around Jenő, watched dysentery rot him from the inside out. Drained of all his fluid, his orifices seeped the viscous remains of his long eroded innards. Dirt and waste, human and animal, soiled every inch of their bodies, their mouths, their souls forever compromised.

Anja brought in a pitcher of milk, a loaf of bread, a pot of preserves. The well-trained boys sat in shivers, waited on Frau Baumann, too scared to make any sudden moves.

"Please, it is for you, eat..." She urged them towards the meal, pushed the plates closer. "Don't be frightened."

German words were met with skepticism. The boys were unsure of its kind inflection. They turned to Jenő. Zoli's big brother could barely keep his eyes open, as death set in, was given approval.

Itzchak dug in: milk spilt in his haste, dropped bread eaten off the floor, as jam shoveled in by the handful. Zoli reached out, retrieved food for two, fed Jenő first.

"It has been so hard to watch what you all have gone through and not be able to do anything about it." Mother and child watched with tears in their eyes; callous indifference washed away in the display. "I am so sorry for what you have gone through. All of you... How could this have happened?"

Cold sweats, eyes crusted shut, limbs limp as infection branched out into Jenő's every last vein. He refused food. He refused water. On the floor of Frau Baumann's kitchen, he was given peaceful moments he didn't have to fight for.

The allied effort grew distant, the sound of their assault reduced to timbre indistinguishable from the ambient ring of all things destroyed. The immediate area drowned under a veil of devastation, shocked quiet, roads emptied.

Zoli looked at his brother. The glance held, unraveled their repressed humanity, spoke silently. Zoli brought a glass of milk to his lips. The first sip being the hardest, Zoli helped Jenő force the calories down.

"Not so fast..." Jenő warned the youngsters, struggled on. "You'll hurt yourself, stomach isn't strong enough."

Itzchak locked eyes with Jenő as he struggled to slow down. Their angst was relieved in deliberate chewing, as bread made its way around. Each bite, every breath, everything swallowed replenished their humanity. Jenő drifted in the sanctuary, allowed himself an easy smile as he faded from consciousness.

Anja sat by the kitchen door, on her usual perch by the window. It was from here, carefully and from behind the curtains, she kept watch, unable to blink, tension stretched her young lids wide.

Buildings reduced to dust clouds lingered over the remnants of Deutschland infrastructure. Black-shirts and SS soldiers lay waste, bodies charred, a bone and flesh mess of pierced skin and scattered intestines. Swastikas ripped from uniforms and knocked off flagpoles burned in the cinder left by Americans. Surviving Nazis took off their uniforms, threw down their arms. They ran to hide from the fall of the Third Reich, the destruction of the Wehrmacht, and the inevitable arrival of Allied ground forces.

Frau Baumann grabbed an old dishrag, dunked it in a barrel of well water, took Zoli's place beside Jenő, catching him before he tipped over. She placed the cold compress on his head, leaned in to force bread through his cracked lips, helped him chew. She reached for a hand-knit afghan, wrapped it around Jenő's protrusion; bones, his spine, each joint jutted from the slope of his hardships.

The kettle whistled atop a wood-burning stove.

Zoli tilted from the sight of his weakened brother, locked on to the kind stranger as she got up to make tea, noticing the large cross on the kitchen wall behind her. He stared at it for a long moment, examined the details of the religious accessory, and sighed.

Frau Baumann poured them some more milk, washed the dirt off their faces to reveal the children buried beneath. Her eyes welled, heart skipped, pained her core. "God bless you."

Outside, the sun refracted through fumes of battle, diffused and redirected. Only the orders of high-ranking Nazis could be heard through the aftermath; their indignant hollers echoing across a collective recoil.

"*DIES IST NICHT ÜBER!*"

"*HEIL HITLER!*"

Nazi SS, uniformed and loyal, yelled at service men, spitting mad inches from their faces. They forced the rank and file to regroup.

The Allied bombing grew distant; like remnants of a dream, only an occasional reverberation traveled kilometers to shake the still occupied land.

Commandant Franz Ziereis stood firm, watched his men fan out into the fractured countryside. They rounded up Jews, murdered the ones too weak to march to their deaths.

"Find my boys." Dr. Oskar Paul Dirlewanger was present, had the commandant's ear; a twisted sincerity fluffed his order. The doctor thought the boys couldn't survive without him. His eyes narrowed, pushed a foul mucus from the corners of his scowl as he scanned the countryside for his collection.

Sitting on Frau Baumann's kitchen floor, Jenő sat over hot tea, steam lifted to bathe his face. He closed his eyes to dream about it burning away what ailed him, the years of ruin. He cracked his eyes to find Zoli and Itzchak seated at his feet, all three hushed by the weight of the day: April 27th 1945.

Their long deserved calm was annihilated the instant Anja reeled from the window.

The boys froze, too petrified to speak, to move, to live; Frau Baumann took her daughter's place, carefully looked outside, and instantaneously swung toward the boys. By this point in their lives, frantic German was under-standable.

"You must go. You must go, now," urged Frau Baumann. She gathered food, assembled provisions. "What are you doing? Help me." She called in a panic; Anja gathered what she could, what little they had in the cupboards, sealed it all in a kerchief tied at the corners. She handed the package off to her mother before returning to the window.

Frau Baumann helped get the boys up off the floor, panicked empathy saturating her every pore. The poor widow was overrun by emotion. Memories of what her home used to be rushed in. The place where her daughter was once allowed to act her age was now filled with grief, regret, and fear. Young Anja could not help but cry along with her mother as they did what they could to help their Jewish guests out of their home for their own sake. They banged their way through the living room, barely-there accoutrement knocked to the floor in the urgency, apologies left unsaid as they rushed to exit.

Winds temporarily cleared visibility before ushering in another reminder of the day's dire significance; smoke black with lives lost, Jew and German, death and destruction. A blood red overcast hung heavy, perverted the depths of terrestrial disarray, turned the landscape inhuman, unrecognizable.

Dogs barked through the confusion, grew ever-present.

Blades of light pierced the aftermath, sporadically illuminated fields with the imbalanced glow. It gave the three boys the moment they needed to shuffle out of the farmhouse's back door.

Mother and child watched their escape before a forceful knock at the front door brought end to their reprieve.

Anja watched her mother make her way to the front door; long, slow, careful steps, Frau Baumann's hand shook as she reached out, but it was too late. The entrance was kicked in from the outside. Anja watched on in horror as Nazis barged into their home, infected the space, beat her mother where she fell.

"*WO SIND DIE JUDEN?*" they yelled through the thrashing, Frau Baumann given no time answer. "*WO SIND DIE JUDEN JUGEND?*"

A distorted grief rose up from Anja's insides. Tears were permanently branded onto her psyche; a youth twisted by all she had witnessed culminated in a state sanctioned home invasion.

Through the haze, struggling to remain on their feet, the three boys dragged themselves through the brush. The sound of Nazis regrouping chirped through the unnatural calm they found in overgrown evergreens that surrounded the lot.

"We have to keep moving," Jenő decided for them. "They'll find us here." He coughed up blood, spit Hungarian through his fever.

They looked back, crouched low, tore through fields, lurched out of the cabbage patch, and found cover in the tall stalks of wheat that ran towards the town of Mauthausen. The Nazi train station that stood there this morning had been replaced by a twist of steel and toppled stone, salvation from above that had yet to return.

"They will kill us." Jenő's eyes welled with the collective struggle of all Jewry, all the prejudice, all the hatred, from the times of Pharaoh on to the present institutionalized disdain. He eyed the minors and gathered his strength, led them towards an imagined sanctuary where the ash in the air was cleansed in the breeze that floated off the nearby river, the Danube.

The boys slowed, lingered, meters from toppled businesses, remnants of residential and commercial buildings; everything was quiet, too quiet.

"JUDE! HIER RECHTS. JUDE!"

The distant call prompted them to move. Barking dogs were audible once more.

"*ANHALTEN!*"

Zoli pulled Itzchak by the arm. Jenő huddled over them both. They were almost safely behind the rubble, out of sight.

"*ANHALTEN, JUDE!*"

One bullet shattered their effort; defeated without

reaction, there were no tears left. Zoli held Itzchak close. They watched Jenő fall to the ground in front of them.

"JENŐ!" Zoli's emotional outburst accompanied him to his brother's side, turned unwanted attention their way.

Itzchak's face contorted to spots of lights that led predators their way.

"RUN!" A command yelled as prayer, but Zoli couldn't. He stuck to his brother, stayed glued to him.

Itzchak couldn't contain himself, sprung to escape, but gained little ground. A German Shepherd leapt on his back, another caught him by the calf, a third snapped close, rendered everything dark again.

7

Rubber touched tarmac with a bounce, prompted a screech abrupt enough to jar Zoli from his slumber. Lufthansa flight number 2305 touched down at the Ferenc Liszt International Airport in Budapest. He fell back into his seat, tilted to watch Julika put her cigarette out in the armrest's built-in ashtray. The last of the smoke lifted out of the confined fire-proof box, dissipated into the muted light of cabin haze.

Her plan had come to fruition. By now, Danny had been left with his unassimilated grandmother through his formative years, started high school under her oblivious watch, so that his parents could go on one of any and many working vacations.

"Let's eat at Jancsi Neni's," she said excitedly; taste buds and salivary glands danced to the memory of great meals enjoyed amid numerous celebrations on the restaurant's outdoor patio.

"Don't ve alvays," Zoli replied with a smile.

Their comfortable rapport was born in the common interests of eating, drinking, gambling, and travel. They turned from the thought of food to stare out onto the country of their births, mixed emotions veined in their arrival. The unremarkable airport caught the weight of their return in its coarse concrete facade.

The cab ride from the airport was accompanied by the familiar Hungarian landscape. No matter the frequency and fervor of their return, the depths of their collective past remained ever-present in the hills that surrounded Budapest.

The driver picked up on an American accent in Zoli's Hungarian.

"We have lived in New York for close to thirty years," Zoli answered, making sure to accentuate his native tongue, never fully realizing how his life in the United States had changed his affect. He remained too distracted by the view to fully explore how and where the change had occurred, was lost in the sight of the approaching city, and the familiar elevation that sloped up from it.

Julika grew up in Hűvösvölgy, located in the hills of Buda. She couldn't help but think of her father Sandor as they drove by the location of what was once his very successful lumberyard in the city. He, like so many, came in from the countryside to provide for his family, to import his expertise along with goods from the hill. Years of labor and growth, flesh left in gears, blood soaked in its foundation, all taken away by the Nazis and ultimately kept by the Communists. Their home was divided to accommodate: a policewoman and her sister moved into the top floor, their childhood housekeeper would reside in what was once a bathroomless back storage room for the rest of her life.

Zoli and Julika always stayed at the grand Gellért Hotel when in Budapest. Built in 1918, half the building had to be pieced back together after the war, and required another major renovation of its interior in the seventies. But through it all, and even within these dying years of communism, the structure and its rooms retained much of their original charm. The thermal baths it was built upon were as therapeutic as ever, now complete with modern amenities built by the people for the people; the locker rooms, saunas, and swimming pools were accessible to all while only its façade of exclusivity remained.

The pair got out of the cab, turned to notice a hard cold-concrete viewing plaza built since their last visit. They left their bags with the porter, crossed the boulevard, and took the few steps needed to admire the venerable river. The platform built at a particular angle invited all to take in the scope of the city around them; the historical hotel, Parliament, the depths of the urban landscape sliced wide by the Danube; the twist and turns of the artery held Pest apart from the rolling countryside of Buda, its current rolled in from the past, kept time by watching empires come and rot, reborn all over again, then again.

A breeze from deep within the Hungarian hillside fell over them, baptized them in a thick *Magyar* air that moved on to travel the length of the Danube, dissipating off into the horizon.

Horvat Gabor had worked at the Gellért for decades, the head of customer relations since being placed there by the government. He walked amid the synthesis of old

architectural characteristics and the roots of national identity; Rococo grandeur mixed with folk culture, bohemian
charm; waitresses dressed like gypsies served *pálinka*, ice
cold in hand-blown stemware. Gabor made sure the deca-
dent ornamentation was preserved in every room and
swept across the large curves that opened up to the expansive lobby where he stood in wait.

"*Jó napot kivánol*," rolled off his tongue without a
thought, an instinctive welcome for all his guests, but
familiarity instantaneously broke Gabor's formality.
History drew him toward a particular entrance. He immediately jumped to embrace Zoli and Julika in an attempt to
drain them of freedoms enjoyed state-side. He pulled away
with a smile, producing a gift for his friends who had
gotten away.

"Welcome home."

"Thanks, Gabi." Zoli smiled.

"Open it."

Zoli untied Eastern-bloc twine, unraveled the plain
brown paper wrapper and revealed a bottle of local homemade *pálinka*.

"Just like you used to make."

They shook hands, a real connection made between
two palms.

Gabor was Julika's childhood neighbor, who, thanks to
his family's religious and political inclinations, had avoided
much of what her family had gone through. They had kept
in touch between and during current political occupations.
The Gellért's location gave Gabor a prime view of the ever
changing occupants of the Parliament on the opposite side
of the river. He liked to be in the know and made sure the

Glucks were treated like family whenever they visited. Thanks in part to Gabor's connections, and a fabulous exchange rate, great meals, nights out at the newly reopened Hungarian State Opera House and in the very exclusive state run casino were always an integral part of their business trips.

Deep down inside Zoli wanted to reclaim his national identity, to be himself in Hungary, again. He relished the opportunity to reconnect with the artists and local dealers that he had now been working with for decades. Zoli met them on their own turf, in their own studios, neighborhood cafes, and drinking holes.

Their once-easy conversations had slowly, over the years, turned to recollections, comforting moments of shared history that worked to solidify relationships in memories.

Artists were excited to provide Zoli with their work; primitive towns painted in the primal colors of traditional Hungarian accouterments, little villages with tiny fields, the country's lost innocence confined in each piece Zoli purchased; portfolios of charcoals, stacks of watercolors, oils rolled and slid into tubes, changed hands. The power of the American Dollar dictated each transaction.

Nights went long into the morning; Zoli and Julika endured, stayed awake for that fifth meal only Hungarians know about. Cold cuts and hot peppers were served with wine and cigarettes in the wee hours of the morning; men staved off the monotony of the coming day by dancing together under the illumination of a single light bulb in some ancient wine cellar buried deep beneath Pest.

The veil of night lifted on hung over mornings. Zoli

pulled the drapes aside to wash himself in the new day, to wake Julika. The two happily trudged to the complimentary breakfast set out in one of the larger ballrooms. An assortment of fresh juices and pastries famous throughout the region, jams and country butter, ham and eggs were set out on tables in the middle of a cavernous hall. Sixteen-foot ceilings and gold-leafed interiors were accessible only to the registered guests of the hotel; Communism's open door policy had no place at the buffet line.

Along with the required elbow rubbing, soiree attending, and art buying, the duo always made it a point to take in the sights. They went to their usual spots, places Julika remembered from childhood, restaurants run by old friends, as well as some obvious tourist destinations. The famous indoor market across the bridge from their hotel in a building the size of an airplane hangar was usually their first stop.

Aromatic herbs and spices, mostly paprika and garlic, wafted through the wide aisles, confections and cold cuts sold by the kilo in stalls where *Téliszalámi* hung from the ceiling, as it always had.

Julika bought goose liver, foie gras, religiously at the altar of familiarity. Known locally as *libamáj*, Hungary was the world's second largest producer of the delicacy; France was obviously the first. She filled her shopping bags with cans of various sizes, all the while romanticizing about how things were with vendors who remembered it well. "My mother used to force feed geese during her childhood on the farm. She'd watched her dad butcher the birds. We'd have a great feast."

They imagined her father cutting the engorged livers

out of slaughtered birds, carcasses roasted with onions and potatoes, salt, pepper, and paprika, till golden brown, with skin turned crispy, crackling in the cool air, fat rendered in a pool meant to be mopped up with fresh crusty bread; all served with a cucumber salad made with produce fresh from their garden, sliced thin, tossed in vinegar and a teaspoon of sugar.

"You're making me hungry," Zoli half-joked.

Nostalgia took the couple through the streets of Budapest, accompanied their every meal, led them through winding streets and public squares. Architecture influenced by the countless occupiers throughout antiquity was left unchanged for hundreds, even thousands of years; the backdrop of the past ever-present, as if time had failed to proceed.

Every corner was familiar from either Julika's childhood, their innumerable trips back, or of their darkest days. They charted the city with experiences, and with the good came the most horrid; reminders of what was grew increasingly apparent as streets narrowed in the part of town that was once the cramped Jewish ghetto.

The *Dohány Utcai Zsinagóg*, the largest synagogue in Europe and second largest in the world, anchored what was once a neighborhood of oppression with hope and remembrance. Completed in 1859, the building's two oval domes, perched upon its twin towers, stood watch over the tenements that defined the neighborhood.

An assemblage of architectural styles was employed to welcome all through its door; a Moorish revival exterior complemented by Byzantine, Romantic, and Gothic elements, details that were influenced by Islamic models that came from North Africa and Medieval Spain. (It was a deliberate confluence described by its Viennese architect, Ludwig Forster, as, "related to the Israelite people, and in particular the Arabs."

Zoli and Julika covered their heads and stepped away from the rose colored stained glass that sat above the temple's large entryway. They made careful progress into the main hall of the atypically ornate place of worship that still showed signs of past traumas.

It had been bombed by the anti-Semitic Arrow Cross Party on February 3, 1939 and then used as a stable when Hungary aligned with Nazi Germany soon after. The Soviet's land grab, the 1945 Siege of Budapest, only added to the damage. Restorations were kept to a minimum under communism; just enough was done to make it accessible to the people; it stood as a memento of the victory over fascism.

Cracks in its façade tore into its interior, displayed the ire of its legacy, reflected the struggles of the European Jews who continued to worship within these worse-for-wear walls.

The trademark frescoes and golden geometric shapes added by the Hungarian romantic architect, Frigyes Feszi, remained magnificent, adorned all corners of the interior, lit up the Torah ark. Under an inch of horrid history, the colors and scope of his workmanship shined through. Details and dimensions hosted visitors in its warmth, drew worshippers into the holiest part of the temple, past the male seating area, women meant to pray from the mezzanine, all the way up to the ark at the front of the building. The large embellished cabinet housed the remnants of all the Torah-scrolls from all the European synagogues that were burnt down throughout the Shoah.

Emotions ran deep, bittersweet for Julika. "My parents were married here," she'd mention to anyone willing to listen. The gold trim of the altar that had once sparkled brightly on the day of their union stood decades away from its glory.

They continued through the temple, stepped through a side door, and out into a complex that had grown in memoriam over the years.

In the final years of WWII, as part of the Eichmann plan, the Ghetto next to the shule was overrun by 70,000 transplanted Jews. They were kept there until the Soviets liberated them on January 18, 1945. But, thousands of men, women, and children were unable to make it through that harsh winter; faceless human beings were unceremoniously buried in a mass grave dug in the land behind the synagogue where they now stood.

The Heroes' Temple, originally built to commemorate the Jews who gave their lives during the First World War, took on dual meaning, grew to honor those who were slaughtered without a fight as well.

Julika grieved before two simple granite memorial walls erected on the far side of the courtyard. It bore the names of congregation members who didn't survive the ordeal, who may or may not have been buried in the mass grave underfoot.

"Can you find some stones for me?" she asked.

Zoli found rocks in the landscaping, joined Julika. He followed her tearful eye-line across the names engraved in the monument; hollowed out arches sat atop each name, accommodated stones left by the descendants of the unforgotten, a remembrance that unlike flowers would never die, and would always keep the dearly departed close to their progeny, and vice versa.

Julika placed a rock in the space allotted to her father; his name, Samuel Sole, and date of his death, January 18th, 1943, commemorated a life lost too soon. The date had been arbitrarily picked from a letter her family received from the Red Cross; they would never really know what happened to their father.

Samuel Sole was forced into the Hungarian Labor Force in 1941 and only saw his family one more time before the war came to Hungary; on March 19th 1944, Julika and her younger sister, Aniko, were playing in the family garden when the Nazi-supported Arrow Cross marched through Budapest. By April 6th, every Jew in the city had a yellow star stitched to their clothes. They were no longer allowed to handle money or own a business before they were rounded up and packed away in the worst parts of town.

Julika's Uncle Béla took it upon himself to acquire false papers for the entire family. He was her mother's oldest brother and heir apparent to the family manufacturing business that was built from nothing by their father, Nandor Neumann. He rented an apartment for the Soles on *Bánat Utca* on the other side of town, far from the ghettos; the entire family was spread across the city, barred from visiting one another in order to assure their anonymity.

Ilona, Julika's mother, snuck her kids through Buda under the cover of night. She burned their yellow stars in a pile of refuse on the way to their supposed sanctuary, new identities. However, their papers were so bad that they were all in constant fear of having to show them to anyone, including their new landlord who was blissfully unaware that she was renting her attic apartment out to a Jewish family. They lived on pins and needles. Little Aniko was kept from leaving the apartment; tenacious and proud, she refused to go by her new name, to live under their new identity. Her childhood fancy was all-encompassing. The family voluntarily stayed put for the remainder of the war, watched Soviets fight Nazis from their window.

Ripples through time reverberated, accompanied Julika and Zoli out of the hallowed hall, back into the streets of Budapest. Dizzied and emotional, they made their way through the city, silent. Both were long trained by the litany of tragedies to distance themselves from feeling too deeply.

The details of their thoughts, the pain of their loss, their solemn contemplation was interrupted by the vilest intrusion yelled from across the street.

"GO HOME FILTHY JEWS!" The words were spewed in Hungarian familiar.

European Jews had long been the scapegoats for a host of social problems, misdirection from above; ill intent packaged in propaganda had nations, continents, and empires loathe the Semitic people for no real reason. Rulers, parties, and philosophies rallied their practitioners with an unfortunately familiar and resilient war cry.

"We don't want you here!"

Young Hungarian bigots always had a reason to hate the Jews; they were long designated as unclean, subhuman, but somehow, at the same time, were blamed for a variety of political, socioeconomic, and ethical problems. They were both the rats and the rulers, neither worth embracing, forever labeled a danger to the very fabric of European life. Those who knew nothing of the Holocaust now thought communism was a byproduct of Jewish intellectualism. A significant number of Jews did play a part in the establishment of the short lived Hungarian Soviet Republic born in March 21st, 1919 but their efforts died shortly after, the rumor resurrected now for the sake of prejudice alone.

"Too bad Nazis didn't finish job," echoed off the Old World stones that surrounded Zoli and Julika's retreat. "I'm sure there was room in the ovens for you two."

Three young men in Iron Curtain available wares followed them, continued to yell. "Look at them, fanciest clothes, fanciest life."

In their escape, the couple stepped out from the confines of the cramped neighborhood, the old ghetto. They cleared a public square. Zoli swung back to notice the hooligans gaining speed, closing in.

"You leave us your Communism!" the tallest of the three spat in malice, razor sharp features cinched with anger.

"You make us Communists!"

"They keep us down." The three of them now talked in a mash of hate passed down like a precious heirloom fully developed in the present tense.

"See how we live, Jew? You get all the money." The posse was nearly on top of them.

They slipped through the crowd, past markets and

cafes, hoped to have lost the aggressors as they reached the river's edge.

Zoli stopped short. Julika turned to watch him look out onto the majestic body of water that flowed at eye-level. The current that was bound by history, the worst kind of connectivity, flowed in from the past; the delta along the ports of the Black Sea crossed the borders of Moldova and Romania, its progress took it to the cities of Bucharest, Belgrade, Budapest, and Vienna. Its banks witnessed the atrocities of every war, each conflict, uprising, and upheaval that the European continent had ever known.

His face contorted to the discomfort of long buried sense-memory. He had been here before.

8

A gunshot spewed hate; its bang bounced off the land-scape, birds were disturbed into flight away from the banks of the Danube. Lukács György's fall from existence was slow, his dehumanization immediate; his powerful frame was taken out from under him, left to bleed out in the waterway, brilliant red turned burgundy, pooled black. His corpse slid through mud, was swept up in a wretched procession of the recently murdered, people regarded as undesirable flushed away in the current of popular opinion.

"Dirty Roma," was the only eulogy he would ever receive. The river's once magnificent blue current turned red by the depths of the Nazi transgression. Families floated by. Vacant eyes left open stared out on those awaiting a similar fate. Mouths gaped wide in screams no one would ever hear.

"This is our country," vitriol spit by familiar faces.

Friend, families, children born and raised alongside the perpetually vilified were caught up in group detestations.

They learned what they were meant to think, felt the way they were told. A consensus of hatred that fed off mass miseducation, old prejudices churned under the guise of nationalistic pride. The division of the populations, those with and those without, the scapegoats and the self-appointed victims, grew in facts engineered to limit a variance of opinion.

"Hungary is for Hungarians, not Jews!"

Following German ratification of the Nuremberg Laws on September 15, 1935, the Hungarian government implemented prejudicial policies of their own. Institutionalized discrimination restricted Jews from full citizenship and negated their basic human rights. By 1938, Hungarian Jews were prohibited from owning businesses, handling money, or holding authority over any non-Jewish person. Aligning with the Axis powers in their fight against the Soviet Union not only guaranteed Hungary a pseudo-sovereignty but also won them back territories lost over time.

Lands annexed by long expired empires, the rewritten borders shared with Czechoslovakia and Sub-Carpathia, were adjusted to complete historical boundaries that favored the Magyars. It reconnected forests and farmlands, families divided by politics were reunited after decades apart, but the reconstruction came with a burden, and a most insidious expectation.

The newly acquired territories added to Hungary's Jewish population; this became an immediate concern for those drenched in national pride and those eager to please the Axis powers. The Hungarian people took it upon themselves to round up the Jews. In October of 1944, in an act of allegiance to the Third Reich, Hungary's right wing extremist party The Arrow Cross, led by countryman Ferenc Szálasi, murdered thousands of Jews on the banks of the Danube. The rest were shipped off to parts unknown; waterways, train cars, and military trucks were available for deportation. Friends and neighbors had come from the remotest corners of the nation to witness the forced exile. Vilification spread through the countryside; a cascade of evil left a trail of blood and tears in its wake. Well-taught hatred tightened its hold on the simple minds of the many.

Arrow Cross members were welcomed into small towns and big villages with open arms, often directed to the nearest Jewish family. Little kids would join their march towards instant redemption, some dressed like their fascist heroes. These children were brought to excitable laughter, grins shared with the gathered before doors were kicked off their hinges. A rush of revelry flooded homes, exposed the occupants inside. They tore through one home after another, collected those deemed lesser-than.

"Together we will purge the impurities that have long spoiled the progress of the Hungarian people."

Fascists forcibly removed families from their lifelong homes, killed the old and disabled on sight, dragged patriarchs through the failure of their provisions, reveling in each cruel moment.

Jenő, along with his older brother Miki, stood with their father, saddled up to defend the family home. They looked to one another, anticipated the worst, hope fractured by the stark reality that marched towards them.

Irén locked herself inside with her two youngest, held them both in her arms; love, fear, and instinct took over.

"It'll be alright, everything is alright. You know your father."

Little Zoli struggled to catch a glimpse of what was happening outside, was able to free himself from his mother's restraint to get a better look. She joined him. With his sister in her arms, they watched.

"Get off my land!" Dani yelled in mid-gallop, meeting the trespassers the moment they stepped on his land. His boys were by his side; Jenő jumped off Attila and met the threat with his bare hands. Punches were thrown, knuckles received; the three farm-bred men defended their home from the onslaught; knocked brown-shirts out with a well-practiced right hook. Dani turned his barebacked horse around, leaned in, dug into its ribs with his feet to draw it to buck. Always under his control, the animal tucked its head and began kicking its hind legs. Meeting their mark, fascists were knocked to the ground. Dani warded them off for as long as he could.

"FATHER!"

Outraged and eager, Jenő pounded his way through the field, muscled opponents to the ground. His heel pivoted on the jaws of the beaten, angled a new approach, fought the contemptuous as their numbers continued to grow.

Tides turned in the buildup; a tsunami of aggression washed over the family, flooded the farm.

"Get him. Show the filthy Jew what he's worth. Nothing." They yelled as they pulled Dani from his steed.

"Stop. Stop right there. I'll shoot you, you sonofawhore," Jenő fired. People bled. He reloaded, took aim. "I'll kill the next horse's cock I see." He couldn't get another shot off, drowned in the wave of animus, fought the entire way down.

György broke through the landscape, bringing a mob of his own. An all-out brawl bloomed in the great fields of Hungary. Fascists and farmhands were at each other's throats, but one was better supplied than the other. Aggression boiled over, built steam from the base of the village, gathered momentum and attracted participants. Soon, the entire Gluck property was overrun by the livid, - by nationalists. Townsfolk had come out to stand with the Arrow Cross.

"Who do these Jews think they are with the only store in town?"

"Burn it down. Burn the store down."

Dani was unable to keep the family market from destruction. Efforts to intervene were met with arrest. He was bound and forced to watch; windows were broken, the structure ablaze, their nearby home looted before catching the fire.

The last of the fight was torn from them, Dani was brought to his knees, forced to watch Miki lose his life. His second oldest son was born sick, bedridden and fevered for most his adolescence. This day was no different. The frail young man used stringy muscle mass developed on the farm to swing tools turned into weapons with no avail. He was quickly overpowered, caught underfoot; his dying gurgle muffled under the charge of destruction.

Gypsies and Jews fought shoulder to shoulder; Jenő faced infectious culture eye to eye, fought to his feet, fought through the pain, through the blood. A myopic precision forcibly broken, beaten to near death. They all stood against the consensus for as long as they could.

Confined and loaded, inventoried like cattle. Dani's family, along with others, were stacked on the back of wagons owned and driven by longtime friends and neighbors, no words spoken as they disappeared off the only road in town. The weight of long, unmoving fog hugged the countryside, obstructed the path ahead.

"Oh, my family. My family." Mothers howled in a chorus of pain felt deep inside, traveled through the ages, collected in an eruption; trans-generational mourning for the entirety of their ancestral line.

Irén cradled Magda, thought of her only daughter being pushed into an uncertain future, their shared fate. She looked at her two sons, worse for wear, bruised and beaten. She wondered about her oldest; László had been taken to the Hungarian Work Force early in the war, required to work in support of the Axis powers. She didn't know if he was alive or dead.

Dani was pushed into the mayhem; thousands upon thousands of citizen-prisoners were efficiently handed over for transport. Dani laid eyes on his nation's capital, Budapest, the curves of the Danube perverted by acts committed in plain sight. He turned from the unbelievable to reach out to Irén, but was struck by the butt of a rifle before he could make contact.

She watched her battered husband fall into the crowd, disappear as the conquered were herded onto waiting ferries.

Coarse German was yelled, moved the amassed, angered György. The surly gypsy swung elbows to make way, help his friend. A scuffle ensued, Hungarian Military, members of the Arrow Cross, and their Nazi mentors intervened, attempted to reign the nomad back in line. Hands on the man released a fury; the last of György 's fight ended by a single bullet, smoke lifting from the barrel of the gun used.

Dani watched his friend fall, murdered by doctrine, institutionalized hatred accepted en masse and without question.

"Dirty Roma."

Gunfire rang out to accentuate the urgency of an unseen schedule, humans that survived were reclassified as chattel in a parade of degradation.

Dani shielded his family from the sight of the innumerable corpses that floated past them. Irén buried her youngest into her nature, attempted to nurture them away from reality.

They all caught sight of the bodies that bobbed downstream, an inescapable fate; family and friends were among the dead, among the soon-to-be. The subjugated were pushed and prodded into line; victims turned to catch more than one familiar face snarling at them from within the singular entity that the crowd had become.

"You sons of bitches."

"Rot in hell, Jews."

"Go fuck your whore mother."

Pure disdain dealt in an avalanche of profanity fueled the judge, jury, and executioner. The assemblage lost all sense of individuality, could better recite the party line than their own hopes and dreams.

Customers from various markets, wholesalers, and

retailers who had known the Glucks for generations had traveled for days to see their deportation. Childhood friends and classmates made the journey with their parents. Neighbors relished in the fact that they would never have to set sight on another Jew again. A blind hysteria ran through the proletariat like a virus that fed off irrational fear, threatened immunity, and required the lives of the innocent to threat its symptoms.

Children were peeled off parents, torn from mothers' love; outstretched arms and shrieks rang out in a crescendo of suffering, emotions antagonized by gunfire.

Dani found himself close to Jenő, close enough to gauge his son's boiling rage. He reached out, put his hand on his shoulder. Jenő turned to reveal a fury long ossified in his eyes; indignation reaped for millennia, sowed under Pharaohs and cultivated ever since.

"You want to be face down in the river?" A cold whisper charged with the force of a final roar. Dani couldn't exert himself anymore. He pulled Jenő close, desperation fueled his words. "You take care of this family. You."

"Father..." Jenő locked on to his only mentor. Zoli peeked out from the folds of his mother's hem. They all watched the inevitable with unexpected clarity.

"LOAD THEM UP." The orders were yelled in Hungarian by Hungarians; Jews were stripped of the last of their national identity. "GET THIS GARBAGE OUT OF HERE."

Soldiers barely older than Dani's oldest tore families apart, followed orders; women and children were separated from the men, men separated by age, health, and strength.

The entire mass pushed and pulled, directed down the line, out of sight and out of mind.

Dani attempted to keep his family together within a collection of victims trying to do the same. Mothers called out for their daughters, husbands for their newlywed wives; infant children were left to be trampled to death by the vile procession.

"Jenő, listen to me. You are the strongest." Dani's brood was inconsolable by an assertion neither were prepared to hear. "You take care of this family," he struggled to continue. "No matter what."

Fourteen-year-old Zoli shut his eyes, wished the world away.

"You hear me, son?" His eyes pierced Jenő's. The fury waned, sorrow overwhelmed, flushed his cheeks. "You survive this!"

Screams of, "Not my child, not my child," were silenced with a bang, ended out of convenience; the elderly, invalids, and disabled were stomped silent at the boot-end of contempt. The jeers never ended, accentuated the violence.

"THIS IS OUR HOME."

"THIS IS OUR LAND!"

"GO BACK TO WHERE YOU CAME FROM!"

"I was born here!" Dani turned to address the gathered. "I was your neighbor. Your friend. Shame on you. Shame on all of you!"

Dani scrutinized his surrounding, a flash of familiarity destroyed by a malignant mentality. He saw so many faces from so many places, a rush of memories spoiled in this most heinous moment. Men barreled over in laughter, children threw tomatoes in an exercise so pleasing that even little old ladies partook. Dani was singed by their collective delight, it evacuated the air from his lungs in an instant. His hurt regurgitated up through his bowels and into his stomach, acids built and secreted, burnt lining stuck by needles and burrs. He had lived to see the prejudice he had always known become the status quo.

The vice grip of the scared and small minded closed in on the young family; Dani grabbed hold as the guards worked them apart.

"Leave us be. What do you think you'll get from treating people this way?" His pleas were redirected. Nazi guards doubled their efforts, grew increasingly violent, threw people around like objects.

"No, not the children, leave them with their mother. Keep us together."

Arrow Cross was available to do the dirty work for their Nazi allies, relished the opportunity to split families apart. Dani stood defiantly in harm's way, caught the brunt of their impatience across his face. He stared at Jenő as blood spilled. His eyes urged his son's restraint through punches served.

Jenő stood conflicted in purpose, impulses and expectation gnawed at each other. His temples throbbed with frustration, muscles clenched in indignation.

Irén held onto all she had left in the world, little Magda pressed close to her chest, under a blanket, shielded from wicked inertia. A mournful resolve was set, Irén laid eyes on her men for the last time.

Jews were filed into cattle cars, loaded onto riverboats, set off on foot over infrastructure that connected the evil empire; large metal doors sealed human cargo in with their own horrors. The stench of what was to come had already developed within the confines.

Jenő guided his father's steps through boarding, held Zoli close. The youngest boy of the clan scanned the world around him, a far cry from the happy childhood that was wiped from existence. Redefined.

Zoli reeled from the cruelty, was fevered by the vitriol, but all that hatred paled to a sight. His young heart twisted, skipped beats, aortas bound. He was thrown into a panic when he noticed neighbors within the assembled. One of Zoli's childhood play-mates stood in shock, confusion slowed in amber. The two boys connected in a moment that transcended time, halted the mayhem, drew them to one another. Zoli's young friend squirmed with discomfort, shame lodged in his nerve tissue, wrenched agony deep in his gut. He wiped tears from his eyes, watching Zoli getting pushed further into the abyss. The child's demeanor contrasted to the festivities around him, he was deeply ashamed.

It was his family that had told the Arrow Cross where the Glucks lived, information that led to the destruction of the store, the looting of their home. Longtime neighbors who were first to wish them the worst brought the family to watch the continued humiliation; their child stood tattered in the wake of his family's unreasoned animus.

"Why does Zoli have to go too?"

Bottomless distress defined their gaze, existed between two kids on opposite sides of the same coin. Zoli was adrift on the tragic side of the bewilderment; unable to understand why his neighbors felt the way they did about his family.

"What did we do?" little Zoli whispered to himself, waited for the nonexistent answer in the eternity.

His little friend's face was the last thing Zoli would ever see of his childhood, the road ahead drowned in uncertainty.

9

———

Highways Zoli had learned over twenty-five years of traveling to customers sped by, miles and miles of asphalt connecting the United States were laid out as an invitation. Lane dividers and mile markers slung past, sped through decades, a blur of all roads traveled.

"If ve leave at 9 o'clock ve can be there by 3." He could estimate times of arrival days in advance, from hundreds of miles out. He calculated alternate-side-of-the-street-parking regulations in New York City while in Ohio, could catch the last breakfast service in Jacksonville from Fort Lauderdale. He once had Danny drive 100 miles to an appointment two states away and back, never once falling off his unforgiving schedule.

By the late '80s, he exclusively brought Danny on the road with him; Julika stayed in New York to do all the bookkeeping and enjoyed the fruits of their labor with her mother; they spent nights at the opera or in the First Hungarian Literary Society on the East Side while being spared the travel required to earn a living. It was father and son on the road from there on out.

Zoli filled a hole from his past with his own two hands, remedied his childhood regret of never getting to go to market with his own dad. He looked to his son as they hurled towards the unreachable horizon. Even though his packed Dodge Ram left them little leg room, it made plenty of space for Zoli's exuberance.

The 6 off Cape Cod connected to the 95, a main artery that led them to their clients; they headed south down to Florida or connected with another interstate that took them to the Midwest, Texas or wherever they had a lead.

They visited professionals and retirees with disposable incomes, fixed and dividend yielding, as well as those who needed to sell old purchases to make ends meet.

"Mrs. Halpern, of course I give you more zan I sold it to you for..." Zoli enjoyed being able to help out, his accent ever generous. "Plus, I get to see you again, darling."

"Thank you, thank you. You have always been such a nice man." Old ladies were left overjoyed with profits when they needed them most.

Zoli always had a collector lined up to make the deal more than worth his while. Sometimes his prospects lived right down the street, other times it took days, years to find a piece a new home. Unsold art would inevitably find its way to hang on Zoli's living room wall, a constant rotation of paintings in stock and for sale.

They traveled around Danny's school vacations. By then he had taken on multiple responsibilities in the family business; framing, stretching, retouching, hanging, and sales in the gallery or on the road.

"On ze road again..." Zoli sang the chorus of a Willie Nelson song he may have never heard in full. They left from the gallery on Provincetown in a Dodge Caravan full of art to venture through the United States together.

In the beginning, Danny wasn't even old enough to have a learner's permit. He rode in the passenger's seat; mixed feelings whirled in his head as he considered alternate spring breaks, getting high with friends and chasing girls instead of bringing home the bacon.

They aimed for country club communities on golf courses with five-star amenities; six-bedroom homes built on lakes, accessible through private drives that wound through rural tree-lined paths with spectacular views. Mansions built in the suburbs of Cleveland, Detroit, and Chicago, beachfront estates along the coast of Florida and the panhandle left their doors open in anticipation of the traveling art show. They traversed topographical changes, flat lands and urban sprawl that led them to customers in the suburbs of Michigan and Illinois, sometimes getting on the I-80 to visit Youngstown, Ohio where the local Butler Museum featured works by Raphael Soyer and Reginald Marsh and other artists in their traveling collection, and visiting town like Akron that still basked in their former glory, the glow of the Firestone/Ford marriage that occurred within their county lines in '47 remained long after.

But, no matter how nice the home, and however dear the occupants, they always refused invitations to spend the night. Zoli preferred the privacy of the closest Hampton Inn, comforted by the clean familiarity it offered. He also needed a break from the nightly performance.

In any indistinguishable hotel room, Danny watched his dad work the phone. Zoli sat in his underwear, a tank top over-worn and overdue for recycling, swaddled in the banal beige interior of the lifestyle. The chain motel and its cup of complimentary lobby coffee always within reach was a constant comfort.

Zoli held the phone's receiver between his shoulder and chin. "Of course, ve would be very happy to see you then." He'd shoot Danny a thumbs up. His smile shined through sapphire eyes, pure joy transmitted. "Yes, yes, my son is with me. Great. Great. See you then."

He'd chart their course according to prospects uncovered.

Danny struggled with restlessness, vacant days in absent neighborhoods with little to nothing to do, books and muted TV were the reprieve du jour. Long hours, 600 hundred miles traveled per day, empty afternoons in motels also left time to share stories that always tied up with Zoli's hard-learned mantra: "Experience is ze best teacher."

He shared his dire history, their most personal family struggles, over chess games and in between syndicated television shows; they spent all day and all night together, talking, remembering, learning.

"To be ze only one, imagine vat I felt like vhen I learned your uncle Laci vas living in Queens." The burden of survival apparent in hindsight, the trials of subjugation needled Zoli's posture, each prick a lesson in the true nature of freedom. "You have to make your own way, Danny. There are all kinds of tings around us to look out for, make sure you don't get caught in one that vill end it all."

Danny listened to tales from his father's youth, biblical parables and drawn out parallels; Jacob's trials were much like Zoli's own, forced to be his own man after emerging from a tragic disposition. Their camaraderie transcended the usual parent-child relationship; every one of their trips together was a mission, a battle for the family's prosperity. The responsibility fell on them the way it always had, the way it was back in Felsővadász.

Danny writhed in the traditionalism. Ultimately unaware of the root of his angst, the teenager twisted between the subconscious forces of ancient expectations and the envy he felt not living the way he thought a normal American teenager would. It was all so European; it always had been.

Zoli's mother-in-law played matriarch over the household as Zoli worked every angle, juiced every dollar, earned every callous. Any resentment he felt over her expectations was tempered by the gratitude for the classic six they had to move into when she moved in to look after adolescent Danny. The large apartment made the situation almost bearable.

"Miserable creature," he would whisper under his breath at the end of a rant better left unsaid.

"I had no one, nowhere. I cannot tell you how that feels..." He made sure not to sugarcoat his experiences. The weight of a great exodus that took him through Europe to the life of an officer in the Israeli army, alone, bore down on his ascension. Fighting for the liberation of his historical homeland while still only a teenager molded him; he chipped his front left incisor on a grenade in the heat of battle, got his helmet shot off his head, and evaded death before being trained as a sniper. He even served alongside the fledgling nation-state's future Prime Minister Ariel Sharon.

"I don't want you to ever ever feel that way, Danny-kem. You do not need to know what it feels like to be grateful for food that has fallen in shit." He shook his head, tried to shake the memory. His accent blended recollections: "I can still remember how sveet that cabbage tasted that morning, how happy ve vere to steal vegetables from rabbits." No matter how difficult the memory, Zoli smiled through his recitation. "Ve vere so lucky to be able to steal milk from the puddles that formed in the shit beneath the cows, and through it all, I can't believe it..."

Danny's adolescent impatience overcompensated; he shifted between the unmade sheet on his temporary bed, watched Zoli reach across their economical accommodations with an open palm that led to a yawn.

"Look at us now!" Danny added.

Lost to the sarcasm, Zoli considered the now; he always did. A long silence consumed by the constant reminder of his collective experiences that existed in perpetuity, defied time and space, lived beyond tense and case. He was the little boy in the camps and the suave art dealer, the army sniper and the loving father, played on the great plains of Hungary as the sun set in a swirl of history relived, and replayed on the shores of Cape Cod.

"I cannot believe that after all that, we have Tarkai's work in our collection. He was just a little boy..."

"You think he'd remember you?" his clients always wondered; the facts and emotional details were never kept from the customers who treated each of Zoli's visits like a history lesson, with some notable exceptions.

Visits to the Klugman home in Flint, an hour's drive from their hotel off telegraph in suburban Detroit, were conducted by Mrs. Klugman herself. Front and center, no hands in your pockets, eyes were expected to be on her the entire time. Humoring her stories of strangers in the attic, anti-Semites poisoning her drinking water, was part of each visit to her home. She was convinced that the government followed her no matter where she went, and could go on for hours about all of it. But, listening to her was time well-spent; she filled her home twice over as they decided to replace their entire collection after their home mysteriously burnt to the ground.

Zoli added Romanos Rizk's three six-foot by three-foot Water Lilies, Provincetown's ponds fully analyzed, revitalized in a wash of an ethereal blue-green hue, a natural subtlety wrapped in each canvas, and John Dowd's crisp Cape Cod townscapes, depictions of two-hundred-year old cottage homes adrift in the mist that rolled off the harbor and into her collection.

Mrs. Klugman always inquired about Zoli's youth. She relished in the agony. Although not a survivor of genocide, she related to the torment, almost enjoyed it. Zoli paid close attention, played along, and recounted, "My vife and I vere in Europe, on a buying trip, visiting friends and family and..." His thick accent laid out the narrative sans seams; octogenarian Ben Klugman jarred from his nap as Zoli continued. "The same hatred is there. They vould have me back in a camp if they could." He kept busy entertaining his hosts with stories of his past, left the menial labor for his son.

Danny stood by the Dodge, rain or shine, in front of rows and rows of fine art; sometimes their hosts had kids his age who would keep him company, shared a drink or a smoke. Zoli was there to make sure Danny didn't have too much fun if customers' daughters showed any interest that could affect business.

"This sucks," Danny grumbled to himself, mostly left alone with his work. He slipped the collection into the space where back seats once were. One appointment after the other, he unpacked then repacked paintings between the custom wooden partitions that were screwed into place, cut to size, and designed by his dad. A case erected for the sole purpose of carrying a collection across the country; hundreds of thousands of dollars' worth of art boxed in reclaimed cardboard were marked with the artist's name and their price. Danny would place them upright, smaller pieces fit in any available corner of the vehicle that he could find once the larger unsold pieces were in place. Reloaded and repacked.

"Don't force anyting, sometimes backwards is the only direction you can take. Have to pull tings apart to get them to fit…" The art of packing art, packing goods, packing for the market was his rite of passage. Zoli insisted on hauling paintings they weren't able to sell for decades. "Just in case, you never know," he thought eternally.

Danny unloaded and unpacked, took his father's lead, and always left the same artist for last. He stepped over to boxes bound by a slip knots easily unfastened, pried framed works gently from their custom sized boxes, and exposed large acrylic paintings recently consigned from Perry Art in New York City. Ethereal ladies who lunch, tranquil teatime, and contemplative moments caught on canvas were revealed one at a time. Clients watched as the pieces were placed atop the already exposed collection; in doing so he turned the entire room into a one man show for Itzchak Tarkai.

The awe of attraction made way for the sentiment fixed in Zoli's heart. He happily shared some unlikely facts; customers stood aghast at the thought that he and the artist had spent time in a concentration camp together, most were held speechless, some were more willing to inquire. Zoli's whole story was wrapped tight in recollection, an entire struggle supported by the lines on his face and the chip in his front left incisor.

He went through memories of being alone in Europe, the random call to join the exodus to Palestine, a life in the bare Judean Desert. Customers showed compassion, connected to the pain; the Hippocratic Oath kicked into effect as Zoli continued by painting a silver lining over every dark cloud of his life.

"But, that is how it vas, and now, this is how it is. But, it vasn't all bad getting here."

Brushstrokes of kibbutz living, apprenticing for tailors and carpenters under unpolluted skies, colored his life before he learned that his oldest brother Laszlo had made it to America. Laci, as every Hungarian called him, lived in Queens with his family, had a young daughter named Irene after their mother. These were the feelings he focused on while keeping the pain of his past on the periphery.

"Ze good life just jumps off ze picture..." Zoli continued. "No matter vat ze artist vent through, the positivity in his surrounding, after childhood of hardship, he bathes in the tranquility of his work. Itzchak Tarkai is a survivor in the truest sense, he not just lived through the bad times, he shares his triumph vith each of his paintings..."

Danny disassembled smaller boxes that held water-colors by the same artist, representations of an ease unob-tainable to most, a sentiment perpetually accentuated by the master salesman.

"To come out of vhat ve vent through, the struggle, the starvation. We vere happy to eat ze food not fit for the livestock, ve shared vater with animals." He waited on reac-tions, continued with eye contact, heart strings in his palms. "Ve did, me and ze artist, it's true, and you know vhat?"

A long pause by design, for everyone's sake; Zoli didn't cry, never did, but he felt, and it showed. Their hosts held feelings behind disbelief, housewives hid behind cocktail napkins at the thought of what had happened and waited on Zoli to answer his own question.

"Ve vere happy about it. Ve had to be. It vas the only real food we had." He turned from his audience, took a long moment to look at the pieces he had to offer, each an exquisite example of the artist's style and perspective. "And, now Tarkai can have his peace, found peace, after all that... so much that he is able to share it in such a vay, vith all of us."

No matter the audience, no matter what the room, whomever heard Zoli's story had to fight off the urge to applaud; they would show their appreciation the American way, with cash or check.

Money made contact, from palm to pocket, left Zoli in a haze of continuance. All the pieces were placed together in his mind, fit effortlessly, like paintings into frames fastened forever by four tiny nails. An old friend who lived his nightmare was alive and returned to him; the incredible circumstances that introduced him to the art trade continued to connect him to the hardest days of his past.

"It vas April 27th, I remember ze *datum*," Zoli murmured, a long forgotten misery welled up inside of him. "Zat vas ze last time I saw him."

10

The 7 train in from Queens, where Zoli moved to be close to his brother Laci's family, went underground as it approached the island of Manhattan. Shoulder to shoulder, straphangers endured the modern day monotony while Zoli fought off the sense memory of more excruciating commutes. These passengers were allowed to ascend out of the grit; the subterranean confines of New York were immediately obliterated by the bustle of the American dream. He joined the flow, turned the contours of Central Park, crossed the crowded intersection, on his way into The Coliseum. It stood before him as the pinnacle of American commerce. He had never seen anything like it.

But, over the decade, the neighborhood outside The Coliseum changed, damaged by the economic state of the city; uncertainty drained confidence from the metropolis. The boxy steel-framed New York Coliseum that blemished the west side of Columbus Circle with its drab industrialist exterior and constant care issues held 1,246 conventions in its lifetime. Erected in 1957, the practical complex with four floors of efficient exhibition space large enough to accommodate boats and airplanes represented the pinnacle of industry. By the '70s, the building on the rotary that connected the monied around Central Park with the workers and tourists in Times Square began to suffer from neglect. The complex proved too large and ill-planned to maintain, the structure itself was eventually deemed too damaged to reclaim from its years of mismanagement.

Inside-out, paint stripped, filthy rugs pulled, exterior façade and foundation in need of repair; an asbestos abatement was inevitably deemed necessary by the Board of Health. That was the last inordinate cost the complex couldn't bear. The entire convention center and its attached office block, complete with a residential building, represented the city's blight. Its doors were shuttered in the mid-'80s to make way for a set of glass towers.

A new convention center rose out of the elegant decrepitude that extended out into the Hudson River. It grew out of urban neglect, encouraged by time, and a waterfront worse for wear; it was the first major construction on the river for some time. The city hoped the project would lurch them forward, bring tourism and commerce back to the Baked Apple. A commencement completed. Things got better, Danny wasn't getting mugged as much, neighborhoods regained their presentability.

"Times have gotten better," Zoli thought to himself as he looked to Danny sitting next to him in the back of a Checker Cab; the jump seats that folded out of the of the driver's seat were loose on their hinges and shook in their bumpy procession. Once sketchy 11th Avenue gleamed as a straight shot from the Upper West Side. The taxi averted Lincoln Tunnel traffic; the broad yellow sedan adorned by loads of chrome and art deco detail stayed in the right lane, dropped Zoli and Danny off at the foot of architect James Ingo Freed's newly minted convention center.

Opened in time for the inaugural ArtEXPO, the freshly paved pavilion drew visitors towards a new fortress of crystal and steel, an American Versailles that shimmered in the murky waters of the polluted Hudson it stood over.

Zoli paid the cabbie, turned to straighten out the grey suit he favored for business; a clean white shirt and pale blue tie accentuated the sky in his eyes. He pulled a black Ace comb out of his left inside pocket. Danny watched him run that comb through his hair a million times; salt and pepper fell into place under the palm of his father's hand like Arthur Fonzarelli, he imagined.

Street performers lined their path; acrobats, illusionists, and musicians worked for tips. An African-American kid drummed on a series of inverted pails, each bang resonated through the area, carried across streets and avenues; rebounding double strokes propelled Zoli into a moment he hadn't thought about for decades; each strike, every roll and slam jarred his emotions loose, made him uncomfortable. He could feel the thunderclaps of flak and munitions that beat the Bavarian horizon.

Prayers that were answered in a plume of destruction, and worked to disrupt the finely tuned machine that drove the final solution towards its singular goal, were relived. The sound of trains derailed in the invasion, ships on the Danube that took fire and staggered to remain afloat were burnt in Zoli's corneas. The sight of the glassy calm Hudson River was thrashed by the officers and prisoners that scurried like vermin from the confines of their crafts, of those too weak to swim to the banks of the great river, drowning where they splashed. These memories were tattooed on Zoli's soul and remained ever-present.

The duo continued towards the expansive entrance; flags draped over municipal light poles and posters on passing buses advertised the event with images of Tarkai's ladies.

Zoli smiled at the sight. Not his usual smile, this one was twisted by repressed thoughts and feelings that were left to ferment over decades.

"You ok, Pops?"

He met Danny's concern with a recalibration, his easy ways were always available when family was around.

"I tink, I just tink I'm nervous." He paused, managed to continue. "Maybe just excited. I needs a moment."

He veered off the path, found a spot that overlooked the expansive view. Danny followed. They watched the river's current divide two states. Manhattan waste mingled with Jersey muck; riverside apartments stuck through the horizon like blades of grass caught in a gentle breeze.

Zoli looked at his one and only child, stalled on words hard to discover. ArtEXPO goers came and went behind them, a whirlwind of activity fractured by heaviness of his consideration. "It has been so long, and..." He allowed long forgotten memories to flood back into his consciousness, shuddered while ingesting lost pain. He churned in discomforts reaped, could only manage a handful of false starts before announcing: "He's... he's right in there."

"I know, dad."

He looked at Danny, inspected his recently bar-mitzvahed boy the way he did, placed his hand on his shoulder, ran fingers through his hair, struck still by the semblance of his long lost brother. Jenő's eyes stared back at him. Zoli's kid looked out onto the good life: food in in his stomach, roof overhead, grey cargo pants, haircut fresh off MTV, and new shoes on his feet.

Zoli dreamed in a moment tucked between the skyline of midtown Manhattan and the Hudson, caught thoughts, fanned for details that choked him up. Up to this point, Danny had never seen his father get that emotional. He watched in silence; his father's intensity was contagious, draped every pore of his existence, and was passed down as legacy.

Flashes tore through boundaries of repressed and feared hindsight, images that were rarely far from his nightmares were brought up like acid reflux, burning in perpetuity. Narration by blood, images grew off recollections at 24 frames per second.

Every step they took toward the convention center was a step into the past, every inch forward was slowed by a thickness, reluctance as precarious as quicksand swelled from the inside. It oozed in the anxiety of where Zoli and Tarkai once were.

Father and son no longer stood on the banks of the new world but in contiguous history; all things repeated, relived, pressed together. It was enough to grind the bones of the wary. The inhumanity Zoli experienced turned

Danny's face sour, twisted his stomach, ulcerated tracts, and gave him no control over a habitual anxious cough that would plague him for the rest of his life. The stress had carried over, it was real, it would be there that day and today or every other day. Danny felt it in his DNA.

"Come on," Danny said in a voice so familiar it rippled into the past, called to his father from within the madness. "We can make it."

Zoli saw the pandemonium of the Allied offensive continue within the walls of the Javits Center; light refracted through the glass ceiling caused chaos where there was none. Its glare flashed, caught Zoli's eye, blinded him momentarily, and then gave way to the sight of German officers burning documents, destroying records, and ordering crematoriums to maximum efficiency. Zoli saw guards' interests turn from the Reich to their own longevity. Human instinct kicked in. ArtEXPO attendees continued on around them, hindered their escape. Zoli spun in nerves, blood thrust through his veins, pressure building, boiling at an eruptive pace, past and present spun together in a blur of unease, then stopped. His panic was interrupted by their surroundings, by his purpose.

Danny was dragged along into the abyss of his father's angst, aware and invested in its unraveling. Daylight reflected off the skyline of Manhattan, laid blades of illumination on the two. They entered the wide-open spaces of the new hall, available to the opportunities it contained. Pristine walls of glass encouraged a diffuse glow that rendered the fluorescents by the ticket booth superfluous, an excess of modern convenience.

They waited at check-in, were both given official

ArtEXPO IDs that hung on Javits Center lanyards. They stepped on into the 840,000 square foot exhibition space. Neutral wall-to-wall carpeting tied every corner of the immense room together and sported a pattern that somehow and subconsciously seemed to encourage constant movement.

Dealers, publishers, wholesale frame and accessory vendors, artists, and galleries from around the world converged in aisle upon aisle of commerce. Collectors and the curious crowded around the attractions, tried to get photos with artists. Nagel posters ready for dorm rooms were shown under the same roof as mid-century oils of canvas, works on paper and mixed media, photography, lithography, and the newest in digital printing occupied booths that lined their way.

Zoli made sure to stop and say hello to an associate. "*Annyeong-haseyo*, Mr. Kim." Mr. Kim was the patriarch of the Korean family-owned framing company Dae Ryung. The old man stayed seated, reached out for Zoli's hand. He turned to explain, "I have been vorking with this man for ten years."

"Ten years, is that all?" A broad smile extended over their respective success; the twist of accents excavated a natural cadence. "Time flies..."

Danny locked eyes with Mr. Kim's son; both teenagers, firmly wedged into their legacy, could only muster a polite nod of the head in passing.

They continued across corners that had been transformed; galleries brought the warmth of the European countryside to the middle of the otherwise sterile space;

master works by Monet, Chagall, Picasso and all three generations of Pissarro graced their eye line.

Mr. Rudolf Otto out of Austria was an independent agent who found paintings for galleries all over the world; Zoli stumbled into his Viennese Salon with Mr. Stern on a buying trip drowned in beer and sausage. The business relationship had survived worse.

"Velcome to New York, Mr. Otto."

The well-aged and dapper art dealer got to his feet to meet them. Perfectly placed silver hair, finely waxed mustache, and a tailored grey suit were all in synch with the time on Mr. Otto's sterling silver pocket watch.

"Come meet my son."

"Oh, ze young, Mr. Gluck." Mr. Otto approached, took a closer look through bifocals, tilted from junior to father. "I vas talking to you. Your father was the young man once."

They laughed at years past, gone by in a glimmer; images on canvas were a constant reminder of the way things were.

"Yes, we were all young... Once."

"It is nice to meet you, Mr. Otto."

"And you too, *mein* boy." A pronouncement emphasized by the vigor found in German enthusiasm. The old aesthetician laced dearness into his speech. It molded his intent. "You must bring your lovely wife back to Vienna, Zoli."

"Ve will be pleased to see you on our next trip." They shook hands. "But, we still need paintings for the road, Mr. Otto."

"And, you vill have them."

Zoli completed their business, every landscape, one with a barn, another of the European countryside, that he set aside was close enough to breathe, hard to ignore, and all too familiar. He stood shoulder to shoulder with his son, staring into the past. The farmhouse in the painting was isolated from mayhem. It was cleared out, abandoned. He could still see 10-year-old Itzchak Tarkai trailing behind him and Jenő as they ran away from one just like it. The image of Tarkai's malnourished bones were etched in Zoli's mind, in their escape, and within the brushstrokes of this original oil on canvas.

Zoli steadied his breathing. He gasped between long unfelt and yet specific unease that was potent enough to affect his son's demeanor by proximity. Overcome by the uncharacteristic apprehension, Zoli led Danny through all the required stops, a checklist of familiar vendors and long held associates that drew them closer to the inevitable. Danny slowed to his father's continued concerns.

Zoli and Danny turned a corner, piercing the commotion that revolved around Tarkai's booth; *Ruth*, *Rachel*, and *Tea Time* were among the names of the paintings on display. Acrylics on canvas, watercolors, and bronze figures were all obstructed by the crowd that had gathered around the visiting artist. They watched the pandemonium from a safe distance. Danny filmed the moment on a camcorder, his dad face-to-face with his past, peering across the busy convention room floor.

With fans seeking signatures and conversation, invading his personal space, Itzchak Tarkai shifted uncomfortably in his seat. He signed one newly published book that was immediately replaced by another, then another. The air was flavored by the amassed, grew stale, and drove

Tarkai to his feet. He made way, serpentining through the public, trying to get out; a path presented itself and released Itzchak Tarkai into Zoli's line of vision.

The sight of his old friend from across the room froze Zoli where he stood. It took his breath away; a cognitive dissonance skewed reality, and left Zoli to question his senses.

Flashes of adolescent Tarkai getting taken down by dogs, bullets that brought their escape to an end rang out, tore through the air above their heads, filled Zoli's mind's eye. The German Shepherds that snapped close, deafened all hope, still turned Zoli's blood cold. The churn of loss that Zoli felt so long ago on the family farm and the banks of the Danube and the Germany countryside where he last locked eyes with Tarkai had returned. He measured his fate the same way he did when he watched troops take Tarkai by the arms and drag him into a sea of empty eyes shuffling against their best interests, the desperation of war.

Memories swelled through Zoli, expanded into every available nook of his psyche. It undulated with pain and discomfort.

Half expecting to see the child from the camps, Zoli was surprised to find that Itzchak had grown middle-aged, just like him. With hair grown out, face coriaceous from the Israeli sun, Tarkai wore paint stained khakis and an untucked button down shirt with its sleeves pushed up above the elbow.

"Excuse me, Mr. Tarkai," an introverted art student stepped towards him, impeded his escape with one question. "How do you choose your colors?"

"What kind of question?" Tarkai grinned, half laughed;

a charm that had dried through arid nights came through. He shared a crooked smile, shook his head as he continued in his egress without answering her. "Kids."

He waved his cigarette-wielding hand at approaching admirers, mumbled to himself with a lighter drawn and at the ready. In mid-retreat, he turned to a gallery employee, confined his thick mixed accent to two words: "I smoke."

Free from the crowd, the artist took broad steps, urgency fueled his exit; an escape that would be forever deferred.

Zoli approached, Tarkai turned to glance in his direction, a look that fell past his old friend, got lost in the accumulation, his place within it. The artist's eye-line trailed off to scale the immense walls, searching for details in the high ceilings, considerations that evaporate in the endless depths around him. A hauntingly familiar utterance shattered the unfamiliarity of the space-frame structure: "Itzchak."

Tarkai slowed his retreat; memories replaced the coolness in the artist's eyes; the accent shared took him to another place, far away from the art and the attention. Glimpses of the blood-drenched moon over northern Austria that seared scars into his psyche brought him to a complete halt. The artist turned to look towards the call, caught familial eyes.

The two men inched closer, each inspecting the other's face. Familiar features drew them in; Tarkai, eternally a man of few words, struggled to speak.

Zoli shook his head, recollections muddled his thoughts, welled his eyes. Long restrained and redirected memories rose up from forgotten nooks, abandoned corners. They stood face to face, the totality of their legacies within arms' reach, with arms raised.

"Is that you, Itzchak?" Tarkai used Zoli's Hebrew name, the one that was most familiar to him.

"It's me." They were the only words left to say; the rest rested in their eyes.

A forty-year absence laid to waste, never happened; they looked at one another the same way they did on Frau Baumann's farm in Austria on April 27, 1945. That same desperation charged back as a tidal wave that suffocated with the strength of an all-encompassing force, a rush of feelings that was prepared to occupy every available space of their being.

These two grown men were reduced to tears as they embraced; the hug transcended struggle, traveled through decades, found comfort in the present. The crowd around them had hushed. The usual New York bustle calmed. An oasis was created within the commotion.

Fear and insecurity of that morning so long ago continued to connect the two; they were forever the orphaned Jews subjected to slave labor on a Nazi farm.

"Did your brother make it?" Tarkai asked; his shoulders slumped in the distinct possibility of the worst. "Did Jenő make it?"

Both men were consumed in the bittersweet moment; Zoli's reply was left unsaid, he was there for answers. The silence led them both to the same regret. Forty-year-old bad news infected the artist, a red-hot surge pinned his chest between beats, pinched intestines, nearly toppled him over.

Zoli wanted to bear his weight, but could barely bear

his own. Vertigo ruled; the room spun to a blur, was awash in rewritten histories.

"What happened?" Tarkai said with a whimper. "What happened to us?"

They clung to one another; nursed their trauma, neither able or willing to say goodbye, for the first time.

11

———

With the residue of war strapped to his back, teenaged Zoli dragged Itzchak by the arm, tripped over their urgency. Jenő huddled over them both, almost safely out of plain sight, escaping into the brush.

"We can make it," squirmed Zoli, looked to his brother as Itzchak helped keep Jenő on his feet. They trudged for their lives. Frau Baumann's farm was made an instant distant memory, already another world ago. The nightmare was over. They bathed in the delusion, then woke to a bang.

"ANHALTEN, JUDE!"

One bullet shattered their effort. Defeated without reaction, there were no tears left. Zoli kept Itzchak close. They watched Jenő fall to the ground in front of them.

Smoke stained by blood, soot of charred flesh sailed on the wind like abysmal snowflakes. The infirmed were left with their lives in hand.

Brown shirts pierced the mantle of war, some injured,

all obeying the orders direct from the sadist in charge. Commandant Franz Ziereis breached the burden of destruction, straightened out his uniform; narrow eyes and German chin pointed toward the completion of his final orders from above.

Nazi underlings gathered the youngest of their male prisoners without question, urgently filled a waiting truck with the reclaimed prepubescent workforce. Zoli caught a glimpse of recognition.

Chaim Kemény sat in the back of a canvas-shelled flat bed, seemingly the first of the subjugated to fall back under the thumb of Nazi control.

"ES IST IMMER..." the Commandant spit through his domain, exaggerated goose steps to mark his territory, regain standing. He shot Jews on sight, shopped through the maligned with an erect finger bent unnaturally against the joint, declared, *"...IST DIE ENDGÜLTIGE LÖSUNG!"*

His bark sliced prisoners deep, a scalpel taken to frail bodies frozen in perpetual misery. Humans pinned to the earth by unrelenting disdain, getting passed over; left for dead, the preferable fate.

Zoli ran towards his brother, lost his footing, slid through gravel, tearing up his legs and arms; blood-caked dirt comingled with disease, festered infections. He caught his breath, huddled close to Jenő.

Ten-year-old Tarkai remained tucked to the ground, the child he had been was long gone. He watched Zoli through the clearing smoke and shots fired; the sound of Germans and their dogs grew close around them, around him. Tarkai's wide eyes were stripped of all hope under the glare of Nazi flashlights. He was thrown into the back of the waiting truck as the roundup continued.

"ÜBER HIER! ÜBER HIER!"

The young Jews, delivered to their enemies, cursed God, lost the last of their religion in an instant. Every cell in their bodies was gnawed by surrender; defeat ground their flesh and crawled through their blood, a misery so thick that they barely noticed the bullets that howled around them.

Jenő's fever chased life out of his withering frame, bones poked at his skin, eyes recessed into his skull. Zoli watched the Nazis move, tried to get his brother to his feet, the taste of death more familiar than air left them smacking their lips. Jenő's body crumpled in on itself under the weight of circumstance. The struggle was too much to maintain.

April's early-morning dew chilled them deep, the will to live faded within each cough held silent; Jenő's body fought infection, spitting up blood, each gasp echoing through inflamed cavities, drawing to a difficult repeat.

Zoli placed his hand over his big brother's mouth. They locked eyes; insufferable emptiness poured from their pores, oozed foul. They fought to remain still; feces-tainted, vermin-infested, and consumed by disease.

Nazis swarmed, grabbed whomever they could, lifted the impaired to their feet, threw them directly into a march, left the rest to die where they lay. The weak dropped from exhaustion, starvation, death, were murdered by phenol injections to save bullets. Weaponized labor, Jews were worked to death digging their own mass graves.

Zoli carried Jenő to join the fate of the more than one hundred thousand Jews counted and called for. He watched troops take Tarkai by the arm, drag him into a sea of empty eyes shuffling against self-preservation.

"ITZCHAK!" Zoli focused on the detained, searched through the sea of putrid humanity set on the shores of death, a growing mass headed in its final direction. "ITZCHAK!"

Grief compounded at the sight, drowned in the maelstrom, the brothers were forced to their feet. Zoli moved through the pain to get under Jenő, kept them both in line, on pace; a slow demise, prescribed one step at a time. Days without end, nights without sleep, the terrors of the camp were replaced by the struggle of a forced march; every second was stitched together by the endless death of the overcrowded and dehumanized. Hollow whispers were ever-present, shrouded every step in an infernal promise. The dwindling mass trudged on, glazed over, without an individual human thought left in their heads, complicit in their own mass murder.

Jenő's feet slowed, his little brother forced to encourage forward movement, fighting through the resignation of his own motor functions.

Prisoners, the Jews who were taken from their homes and torn from their families, dropped around them. They were put down or buried half alive at an increasing pace as the days dragged on. Every second felt like an eternity, the sun took its time dragging itself overhead. They huddled close through the nocturne; stars shimmered at 96-frames per second; time was deferred to their collective anticipation.

Any murmur of the Allies or the Americans or freedom was silenced with a bang. Mounds of corpses were left out as a reminder of the inescapable, a testament to the unabated progress of the Nazi's final solution.

No Jew was aware of the desperation that now fueled the slaughter, that the Polish concentration camp Auschwitz had already been liberated, and that the war drew close to its end.

Nazis used the butts of their riffles, heels of their boots to inflict injury and pain onto as many Jews as they could reach, bullets were saved for the front lines, a fevered pace building against the inevitable end of the Third Reich.

Zoli's eyes struggled to remain open. His grip on Jenő loosened. All was lost to the perpetual weight of desperation. Dust and smoke swirled in a torrent of tribulation, a whirlwind that carried over the inch of death that blanketed the Bavarian countryside.

Slowed progress rippled through the thousands in crisis. The uniformly dispirited sensed solace, a lull of anticipation washing over them in unison. Nazi guards took note, not of their prisoners but of the hail of bullets that broke the calm; sources unseen took down the Nazis who stood over the persecuted.

The interned were too impaired to react, froze in place, stress in their bones, breath held tight within tall unkempt grass. Insects and animals scattered; their instincts were free from consequences.

Zoli watched the Nazis take cover, his captors exposed to a barrage launched from over the horizon. The grind of American iron thumped over the landscape; a troop of M18 gun motor carriages, tank destroyers known as Hell-cats for the fight they bring, flattened Nazi ground, cleared a path of freedom through the promise of certain death, their 76.2mm cannons and .50 caliber browning M2HB machine guns rattling the Reich in their advance; a spray of destruction pulled liberation close.

Allied infantrymen filed in behind the destroyers; soldiers slowed their progress, couldn't believe their eyes. The sight of the emaciated and diseased brought them to a nauseated halt. Young troops turned in disbelief, grieved and sick; others were too consumed by rage to react, seethed accordingly while charging to battle.

The roar of their effort kept Zoli on his feet. The two brothers stared at the offensive; a juggernaut of well-armed and well-intentioned saviors cleared a path of righteousness. Many Jews used the last of their strength to watch their salvation, humbled by the active destruction of their tormentors; some managed to cheer as the armada made its way towards the camp of their nearly completed genocide. Survivors praised America. The USA was the subject and savior of all their invocations. They fell to their knees and raised their arms with overflowing devotion.

Hebrew prayer songs grew audible under the spectacle; faith was once again allowed to fill the cracks left by the gravity of their ordeal. For most, it was a test too grave to face when the help that came from above came with their liberation.

Air support flew low to dust the enemy with fire and flack.

The first Holocaust survivors surrendered to the comforts of death, found peace in the prospect of dying free, a relief previously believed unobtainable. Others walked in their own direction, of their own freewill. They clung to the sounds of the distant conflict, the crescendo of bombs on the horizon and Allied planes above. Aftershock rattled the land beneath their feet and signified a new crack to their prescribed misery.

Zoli cradled Jenő through the night. The sound of the scales of war tilting in their direction kept the recently liberated warm with satisfaction, dying breaths comfortably released. Zoli fought to keep his brother conscious, never allowed his eyes to drift away. Jenő looked at his baby brother, destroyed to see that he had grown into a man matured by perpetual death and absolute loss.

Zoli returned his brother's gaze, shared in his disbelief; Jenő was unrecognizable, a shadow of the pillar of strength he once was. The shadow of death drifted across fields, offered all an escape, consumed the willing by the thousands. The wait proved grueling for even the most devout; so many couldn't wait for the help they needed.

A second wave of liberation brought the Red Cross to the scene. Men and women, nurses and doctors, rushed to assist; timetables were set and met, structures were built behind the roll of the Allies' front line.

Supplies were airdropped. American servicemen collected and opened crates, barrels of milk and water were pried open, prepared to accommodate the prisoners of war.

Zoli rubbed yellowed mucous from his eyes and mouth. He collected his balance, moved his brother towards the thump of assistance, towards trucks that hauled food. Troops directed them to dump mounds of sugar and flour on the ground, prepared to feed the poor and huddled mass that failed in its restraint.

The cadaverous dove head first into the sustenance, gorged on the bounty of the processed food that traveled all this way for them, shoveled handfuls of whatever was available into their long-empty intestines.

Zoli guided Jenő towards the plenty, picked up speed the closer he got. His older brother noticed and conjured up his long lost strength, tightened his grip on his younger brother's forearm, and uttered a single Hungarian word: "*Nem.*"

Zoli turned from his brother in disbelief; stomachs gnawed from the insides, lining and mucous long dried and digested, bones and brain proteins hanging on a whimper. Jenő directed their shared glance with his bone-thin finger to the men who lay dead head first in their relief.

"They fed themselves to death, too weak to digest," was uttered and understood in their native tongue. They waited their turn, ate what little fell within reach. "Not too fast, not too much," Jenő said, lost in the absurdity of the request.

The troops filed in, broke off to offer help to whoever needed it. A soldier took little time to collect the brothers. They looked at the young man. His eyes burned with sympathy. Twisted sunlight fell over them, reflected off a cross that hung around the soldier's neck, its reflection bounced off Zoli's stunned person, glistened in Jenő's lifeless eyes.

"You're going to be alright, kid..." It was the first English either of them had ever heard, an American conviction neither understood. "Both of you."

Zoli reached out through a cloud of altered perception,

his brain struggled to comprehend. He touched the soldier's face; he was the first black man he had ever seen.

"I'm David." He thumped his chest with a clenched fist that held his disbelief tight. "*Mein namé ist* Private David Owens." He pointed to them. "You are?"

Zoli craned from the light, took in the fresh air of liberation, answered, "Glück, Zoltan, Itzchak... Zoli."

"Zoli?" The soldier's smile worked its way through dire circumstances, happened to be the precise warmth that the gaunt teen required, an exchange that worked to further alter Zoli's reality, slow time, alleviate grief.

"*Da-veed.*" The kid gave in to the Hebrew pronunciation. An ease granted in the presence of his father's Hebrew name was quickly overwhelmed by weakness. Zoli allowed himself abbreviated pain.

"Okay, Zoli, you're coming with me."

Private David Owens helped both Jenő and Zoli get to the fully trained medics who tended to the neglected; field hospitals were erected, sterile walls created on the ashes of the newly incinerated. An overflow of the would-be-dead found the care they had so long required.

The pangs of war rang out over the horizon, illuminated the sky in brilliant violence, ashes of Allied advancement billowed in clouds of vindication. The countryside was engulfed in a wash of English; unfamiliar people brought unrecognizable hope in the form of modern mid-century medicine and candy bars, an abundance of cigarettes to help lift the spirits of disheartened troops.

Private David Owens walked the brothers through the mayhem, found a sympathetic nurse. "I've got two right here."

Zoli watched the young lady, couldn't believe his eyes: body full of nutrients, curves plump with life, hair and body clean and free of lice and disease. He and Jenő found a faint smell of soap and antiseptic in the air. It locked their attention on her attentiveness; neither were aware of the dedicated women of the Army Nurse Corps that had been close to the front lines since '41 and helped orchestrate the chain of evacuation.

"You're safe now," she said. Her accent was unfamiliar, lacked the guttural force of local languages and dialects. It was thick with the comfort of the American Bible-Belt, empathy that reached out over the Atlantic with an inviting embrace. "You have nothing to worry about." Overcompensated positivity, a grin plastered over her visceral disgust, urged her progress; she took vitals, peered deep into the eyes of slaughtered youth, then made way with a: "God bless you."

A young doctor stepped in, took Jenő's pulse with two fingers, felt glands and flashed a light into his eyes, down his throat. Ulcerated interiors, a discolored tongue pocked with blisters and cracked by dehydration gave the physician pause. He leaned Jenő back, felt his bones and organs through the loose skin that draped over them.

"He's teetering, let's get some liquids into him before it's too late." The doctor was gone as quickly as he came, off to the next hapless soul.

Jenő was set on a gurney, all manner of fluids and medicines injected and applied. Zoli leaned over his brother; their eye contact contorted with cravings for a better world, abrogated by the weight of the moment, loss carried in a single utterance, a plea of, "Jenő..."

They clasped hands, held tight, no words left to express their new found state; Jenő reached out to dry Zoli's eyes, wiped tears he was allowed to shed, then he slapped his kid brother clear across his face. His handprint remained, an inkling of what could be considered a smile extended across Jenő's woebegone face; getting kis-Zoli out of the camps alive was all he had hoped for all these months, it was what kept him alive.

Medical staff closed in with catheters and feeding tube, encouraged bodily calm, healing; analog monitors whizzed and beeped, perverted any positivity with their erratic displays; the sound of construction and churn of the Allied supply line accompanied every moment in the temporary triage center.

"It's ok, Zoli. We'll take care of you and your brother." Private David Owens was available to be reassuring. He locked eyes with Zoli, laid a calming hand on the frantic kid's shoulder. "I promise."

"His organs are shutting down." The staff rolled Jenő into a sea of ambulatory care, large scale suffering on the move.

Zoli tried to follow; Private David Owens was there to keep him in the doctor's care. "Not so fast, big guy."

An available medic gave Zoli the once over, listened to his innards, administered injections and slathered analgesic ointments, an IV line established to replenish vitamins and minerals. Reassurances came solely from the young soldier who refused to leave Zoli's side.

"Just relax, kid. It's gonna be alright." The young soldier led Zoli to a reprieve of clean sheets and encased pillows. Private David Owens released him into comforts he could not have imagined a week before. His pent up despair, the inner churnings that grated his core, were momentarily soothed, allowed to unravel, let him sleep. Wall-to-wall field cots, an orchestra of assisted and shallow breathing, the near dead given a last chance to convalesce.

Private David Owens took leave, backed through the infirmed, disappeared into the fray.

The howls of war, bombs of liberation faded into the dreams of those who made it out of the camps. The sound of each patient's IV drip, repetition of sporadic EKG monitors encouraged tranquility, hypnotized the weary.

Located in southeastern Bavaria, the Feldafing Displaced Persons Camp was partially made out of a school built by the Nazis to educate hate unto the impressionable minds of Hitlerjugend, weaponized learning. Temporary housing and care was given to all who needed it, persecuted people of all backgrounds were given immediate assistance. They came from nearby Mauthausen, off death marches and forced labor, or were refugees of the massacre at the train station near Poing. Seven two-story buildings were appropriated by the US Army. A village of a dozen temporary buildings eventually sprawled out, conditions started out horrid; children slept on wooden pallets, too weak to wake.

Soon after a visit from General Eisenhower and before President Truman's arrival, the American Jewish Joint Distribution Committee (JDC) got involved. Founded in 1914, the organization helped Jewish people through both World Wars, and were eager to continue helping. By September of 1945 they had replaced American military tents and temporary structures with new stone buildings, and together with the American Red Cross they established an emergency medical center with 1000 beds. From then on, the camp was used exclusively to rehabilitate Jewish survivors of the *Shoah* back to full physical and spiritual health. Jews reunited with their people and their traditions. They removed rubble and encouraged community, a respite complete with an expansive view of a nearby Danube.

"Itzchak?" Zoli stirred in a half dream. The medicine, the morphine, the environment overwhelmed the frail, heavied eyelids, disturbed dreams. It started to drizzle, then it poured, cleansed the earth. A cool allowed to drift through his window ran over his recovered physique. The contour of his ribs, lines of cheekbones, were buried under healthy weight gain. He sat up, propped on a pillow moved to support his upper-body.

The smell of normality drifted through institutionalized hallways, a series of corridors that connected patients with nurse stations. A young woman in her early twenties set off through the maze, snow-white uniform and new stockings floated in her progression. She pushed a medical tray into one of the many available doors.

"Hi Zoli. It's me, Gertie..." the young nurse whispered through a smile, her white teeth on full display. Her grandmother taught her that, "a smile was always the best medicine" and that "any kindness worth doing, was worth doing."

"Hello," was some of the only English Zoli had picked up; it was enough. His blue eyes sparkled in Gertie's presence, by her proximity. He wanted to reach out and grab her viviparity, consume it, be consumed by it; his blood flowed in every possible direction.

"I'm going to take these tubes out of you now," she said. Her parted pink lips and long generous smiles were all Zoli needed to consent. He watched her set out military issued medical instruments on cotton gauze. She tilted towards him. "As good as new."

She made her way around, orthopedic shoes tapping linoleum. The scent of her recently shampooed hair drifted across Zoli's nose.

"You were out for some time..." She removed tubes and disconnected wires. He couldn't help but stare. "Don't worry. We have Hungarian doctors; the Red Cross has been doing so much..."

Zoli just shook his head, reality was upside down, everything was lost in translation. His life was left on the banks of the Red Danube. He was trapped in the memory of the last time the family was alive, together. The haze of where he was and what he had gone through kaleidoscoped his perspective, shocked his equilibrium.

Gertie finished up, wiped him down, sterilized and re-bandaged the last of his healing wounds. "Thank goodness you made it out, the stories I've been hearing..."

His body laid stiff. Tension reigned. His eyes half closed. The sickest most gut wrenching loneliness tore his insides out. Scared to ask, Zoli turned with a single question, his hands clenched over his heart, eye contact enveloped every available emotion. "Jenő?"

"I'm sorry." Gertie shook her head, tears hung on lower lids, were released and promptly brushed aside. "I know it's terrible not knowing what happened." Without a means of communication, she puts her hands together in the universal sign for prayer, acted out to get her point across. "The church is in charge of admissions, has a ledger of names, of survivors." She used two fingers to pantomime walking, pointed through walls in the church's general direction. "You will want to go over there after you have been discharged."

The level of confusion in Zoli's face swelled her sympathy. The young nurse was overwhelmed. Zoli's absent adolescences grated against her comprehension, threw her world off kilter. His trauma was infectious, Gertie felt conjoined to it, required therapy. She turned to pull the partition closed, divided them from the other occupants of the large triage; her glance grew shallow, deepened with intent and feeling. She turned to grab a damp sponge out of a small tub on the adjacent tray, motioned to Zoli, "I'm going to give you a bath, ok?"

Quiet consent, a silent understanding, a moment of time shared by two individuals propelled to each other by tragedy.

"Ok?" A sweet affect dripped from her being, draped Zoli in its tenderness. They locked eyes as she moved the hair out of Zoli's young handsome face, shared an authentic smile that blew into Zoli's lungs like gasps of air for the drowning. "You need a haircut."

A baptism by sponge bath, the damp cloth wiped away oppression, washed away the last remaining physical signs of Zoli's struggle. Her eyes followed the length of his frame; farmer muscles barely given time to develop struggled to reform definition.

Dirty water drained, washcloth drenched clean; the

attempt to wash Zoli's trauma away overwhelmed the young nurse. Zoli watched her run her fingers over scars, the wounds that lined his recovery.

She felt his eyes on her; she rubbed all the tension, all the pent up angst and frustration from his being. He closed his eyes, allowed himself momentary relief from the unyielding pain within, a release that celebrated his access to the new world around him with a bang.

Birds chirped, children laughed, the landscape that was once covered by the brutish Bavarian winter and decimated by the ravages of war was now in the midst of being rebuilt and reformed, in full bloom; a bustling Jewish community began to ripen along the streets of the impermanent village. The sounds of Hebrew, Yiddish, and Hungarian filled every corner, and welcomed every person as if they were family to eat and pray.

Zoli was released from the hospital and immediately stepped out into the world that changed around him. The distinctly piecemealed hamlet jutted out of the preexisting complex the way the gypsies had lived on the Great Hungarian Plain. Life reinvigorated in the nomadic community. He would join in the effort, hoisted canvas tarps that broadened the encampment, opened it up to the countryside. Food was shared. Peaches were in season, each juicy bite plastered smiles across faces. Fresh baked bread drenched with just churned butter left to melt through nooks, left golden trails down Zoli's arm. He made conversation in his native tongue and the halting Yiddish he used through childhood, was on a mission.

"I'm looking for my brother. Where can I find the church? Do you know my brother *Glück Jenő?*" He sought assistance where he could, however he could. "I'm from Felsővadász, half day's ride from Szikszó. Is there a list of survivors?"

Questions met with answers and directions. "The church, go to the little chapel by the big church, in town."

He did. The 13th century chapel, left within the 15th century compound the Catholic Church built around it, was on a hill that towered over the displaced persons' camp. Zoli craned his neck to catch sight of a modest steeple within the Gothic angles and intricate details, flamboyant arches and flying buttresses built through recorded history.

He set off in its direction, strained uphill, stood intimidated upon arrival. He looked at the immense cross that balanced on the cathedral's peak. It was the tallest building Zoli had ever seen. The sound of his entrance echoed out, bounced off walls, reverberated through the space, made his presence felt.

A young nun stepped out of a newly built room, stepped to the boy who stood at the head of the chapel's nave; the stained glass, depiction of biblical stories and images haunted Zoli's eye-line.

"Can I help you?" Her soft voice carried through the sanctuary; German uttered deliberately, its commonality with Yiddish was exploited in the nun's over-annunciation. "Are you looking for someone?"

"My brother, I lost him. Is he here? Did he make it? Is he alive?" Zoli begged, a wash of languages that found connectivity out of necessity. "*Glück Jenő*, born 1926." The burden of the unknown overwhelmed Zoli. He continued to plead, "I don't have anyone else."

She led him into the archives, an old room with dark wooden detail, hard benches stained dark and burdened by time; an out of place cabinet built by the Allies gave the camp ledgers a permanent and safe home against the far wall. The young nun searched through appropriated Nazi records, hospital admissions forms, and Allied accounts. Her fingers ran through one alphabetical list after another.

Zoli waited. Each second lasted an eternity.

The young nun closes the last of her ledgers and looked to the boy. He was hunched over, his head buried in the palms of his hands, swirling in vacancy. She peered into his brutalized soul; her own perturbed youth, the misery uncovered and seen first-hand, the life and death of millions of people, all bore down on her. The weight of the accumulated pain clouded her judgment. She wanted to spare Zoli any more pain, prayed to be spared from her own. It was all she could do.

"I am sorry. I cannot find *Glück Jenő*... He could be anywhere, have faith..." She shut the large hardbound leather book; her kind eyes fixed on the forever damaged young man. "This camp is as good a home as any... for now... I think."

12
———

The wind off the Hudson River accompanied the hum from the West Side highway over the flats of Riverside Park. An expansive view of a New York winter opened up from the vantage of the 6th floor of the Schwab House.

Snow-infused light reflected off the river, fell over a napping Zoli; his salt and pepper hair remained uncombed, stood in each and every direction, bath-robe left open to expose his white boxers and ribbed tank top that hugged his well-fed belly. He dreamt in absolute ease of the home he had made for his family in a building that had a story all its own.

In the early 20th century, on the site of a former orphan asylum that afforded ample space, steel magnate Charles M. Schwab built his palatial Riverside House. Construction of the eclectic Beaux-Arts chateau with pink granite detail and a rounded roof pressed by peaked turrets on each corner, dormers on all sides, surrounded by remarkable gardens took four years, from 1902 to 1906, and dwarfed the mansions of his contemporaries. However, inexcusably and unlike the rest of New York City's upper crust, Schwab's house had been constructed on the wrong side of Manhattan.

The Upper West Side was a world away from the more fashionable East Side and their well-to-do peers on 5th Avenue. It was a faux pas that never failed to encroach upon his wife's social calendar and mental well-being; Eurana Schwab grew depressed, became obese, and eventually refused to leave the house at all. Her descent, as well as a substantial loss suffered in the stock market crash of 1929, prompted Schwab to donate his mansion to the City of New York. He intended it to be used as the new mayoral home; however, reform-minded Fiorello La Guardia turned down the accommodations, balking, "What? Me in that?"

The neighborhood changed around the Riverside House; new life was pumped in by vets returning from the multiple fronts of WWII. Apartment buildings went up around the outdated chateau, narrow streets over-crowded, turned blue collar; the top-hat-and-tails lure of this park-side corner was short lived, if it ever existed at all. The grand residence turned into "The Great White Elephant of the Upper West Side." The expense of main-taining the property quickly outweighed its usefulness. Schwab walked away from it, just forfeited the property, and died penniless in a small studio on the Upper East Side in 1939.

By 1951 the dramatic architecture of the largest mansion in New York City had been replaced by the blocky quintessential redbrick post-war apartment complex that was ironically named the Schwab House. Its

633 spacious and extremely utilitarian apartments would go condo in '84.

Over the years the Upper West Side shared the city's economic fate, a rollercoaster ride that took the neighborhood from its early heights to rock bottom and back again. Graffiti-filled nooks of magnificent decrepitude, fallen structures, disregarded landfills, and weathered-beyond-use piers would give the riverfront neighborhood character.

Views through long unwashed windows were dominated by the traffic that revolved around the river; boats, planes, and cars raced up and down Henry Hudson's corridor, the tides of change that had brought Zoli to its shores continued on their unpredictable course.

The momentum of time and history bottlenecked in the present, stirred Zoli awake. He sat for a moment of confusion, a disoriented timeline, seemingly out of place before he eased into his surroundings with feet raised. He sunk back into the mauve La-Z-Boy recliner he had just received from his family for his 65th birthday. The Phil Donahue Show, left on through his nap, winded up and rolled credits.

The apartment that was once too large for the fledgling family now accommodated four adults; its walls crowded with the best of the yet-to-be-sold art collected over Zoli's 35 years in the business. An impressive grouping of works accentuated by a few standouts; a Tarkai city scene gifted by the artist hung in a prime spot above the couch. Zoli's eye-line latched onto it in a half-asleep stare.

Zoli's past melted into the present tense; every moment he had ever lived lived now, here, today. It bunched together in his head, kept muscles at the base of his neck tight, the tips of his toes tingling; a balance of utter sadness and absolute delight, the good and bad eternally entwined. Zoli leaned towards the happiness, but tragic memories that were locked in his subconscious were readily available, and jumped out from behind the curtain without a moment's notice.

"Danny!" his thick accent draped the large room, sailed across the foyer, stopped his kid dead in his tracks. By now, Danny was college aged, making his way to the front door when he heeded the call.

"Wud up, Pops?" was how Danny, born and bred on Gray's Papaya hot dogs and hip hop, thought he had to speak as he entered the expansive living room; blue jeans, t-shirt, and Timberlands rounded out his '80s style.

"Vut up, kiddo?" His father teased, and continued. "I vant you write a letter for me."

"Now? I'm just heading out," Danny replied, his nervous cough not far from eruption; the feeling they'd shared were always available.

"It won't take you long, you writes so good..." Zoli looked at Danny from across the room with a stare thick with history; feelings penetrated, were all-encompassing; the weight of his legacy leveled Danny, pressed him into compliance.

"Just a quick letter to The Phil Donahue Show," he added.

"The Phil Donahue Show?" Danny exclaimed, looking out onto the near bare trees that trembled in the winter that allowed for an unobstructed view of the river and beyond.

"Yes, about how me and Tarkai reconnected..." His eyes

widened as he continued. "Don'ts you tink that's a great story?"

"I do."

The intensity of his life lived whirled between Danny's ears, dizzied his progress, and urged him to a desk set between the La-Z-Boy and a bank of river-facing windows.

"How we both survived and went to Israel and then met after all dose years." Words, thoughts, and feelings combined, "And, he vill be in New York next veek so I vant to send it out soon as possible."

"Okay. No problem," Danny said as he took a seat at his Apple PowerBook 1400; the unseen force of the repressed emotional tsunami that barreled off Zoli crashed into knots buried in Danny's back and neck; second generation survivor guilt filled his frame, affected every word he typed and read concurrently:

```
To The Phil Donahue Show:

I have a great story for you're[sic] program, one that
exhibits the resilience of the human spirit and is a
brilliant example of the strength of a bond forged in the
horrors of World War II.

My father Zoltan Gluck is a survivor of the Holocaust,
living in Mauthausen while just a child. One of the other
children at the concentration camp was Itzchak Tarkai,
who would later become an internationally recognized
artist. They lost touch after the war but reconnected in
1986 at the inaugural artEXPO of the new Jacob Javits
Center. My father had been selling his paintings for
years before they did. The reunion led to an
instantaneous bond, from that moment on they considered
each other brothers.

All the best,

Daniel Gluck
```

Zoli's eyes beamed at the sound of those words. "That iz great, Danny-*kem*..." He pronounced Danny like *Dani*, was known to fall in and out of that from time to time, adding a Hungarian suffix as a term of affection, this one being capable of rendering any person into a loving possession.

"After what you paid for my education, I better be able to write a letter," Danny scoffed, reread, fixed the inevitable typos, spelling errors and grammatical mistakes held over from his years in remedial English, a native tongue most foreign within a home full of immigrants.

The sound of the printer zipping ink on the page broke the hollowed quiet, added to the white noise of the television's blathering, and the hum of the not-so-distant highway that cascaded above the Hudson.

"I cannot believe how long it has been, I can'ts believe everytings I vent through, all the struggles, everyting to get here, to call dis home."

"I know, Dad, it's amazing."

"I know you know."

The facts were glued to Danny's bones, tattooed to his marrow. The thought of sitting on some stoop to drink 40oz beers and smoke blunts in the freezing cold drifted. He poured two drinks from the rolling bar his parents kept in the living room, handed one to his dad.

"Vat, no ice?"

Enough for two, cubes clanked off glass, crackled against the alcohol.

"*L'Chaim!*" They drank. They talked. Danny mostly listened for hours at home or on Cape Cod, in hotel rooms and restaurants, by pools and poker rooms, about everything and nothing in particular. On the road, selling paintings, connected many paths; guilt and awe mixed together with familial obligations that reached back through the hills of Eastern Europe and dragged Danny off on dirt roads laid by fallen empires with fruit in tow.

"There were so many people who made it possible, how many terrible tings had to happen to get me here... to meet Tarkai again vas a blessing I could not imagined." Emotions laced Zoli's speech; perspective left him silent, the giant world reduced to the right now, a long void filled by a swell of sense-memory. "So many I vill never see again."

"Not necessarily," Danny typed a password, waited for connectivity, the shriek of digital communication crowed off the computer's speakers.

"Not necessarily how?" he inquired.

"We can use the internet. Check this out."

"Ok, vone sec..." He balanced his bifocal glasses on the tip of his nose, pushed himself out of his chair, and onto his feet. "I'm gettings old."

"Don't say that, Pops..." Danny said. "You stopped getting old years ago."

"Vat? I looks good for an olderly man," he said with his arms raised, biceps flexed, as he stepped around the desk.

He stood above his son as his modem tore a hole between reality and cyberspace; the internet jumped in through the phone line, the screen danced to the introduction accordingly.

"Vhat's that noise?"

"We're connecting to the World Wide Web."

"Vorld Vide Veb?"

"Yeah, the internet. *Nézhetünk* anything up *ez en. Van egy* digital encyclopedia," he announced in a perpetual mix of English and Hungarian.

The computer interrupted, greeted them both with: "You've got mail."

Zoli leaned in, attempted to understand on sight. He looked to the printer, and asked, "Is this vere ze mail comes out?"

"Don't worry about that. We just have to type in what we're looking for." Zoli looked to him trying to comprehend; the world continued to change by leaps and bounds around him; the impermanence of everyday life was the only thing left intact, a cause of concern and wonder.

"Amazing." He fixed his glasses, adjusted his perception, simultaneously looked at the digitized future while they flipped through pictures of his ever-present past; the cadence of his speech was dinged by miles traveled, marked by languages learned. "Can you look up ze false liberation, 1945 year?"

Cyberspace, crawling out of its primordial ooze of ones and zeroes, was new to them both. Most of the content Danny found was generated by universities, institutions and the nation of Israel itself. He scrolled though links, a litany of articles and papers on the subject. They perused titles, clicked into photo albums, and found historical pictures of the familiar Bavarian landscape by Mauthausen; the selection was on full display when Danny gave his chair over to his dad.

Danny watched him take the seat and stare into the glow of the computer as he continued to toggle through the content, left each grainy image on the small screen for a long moment before moving on to the next. He reached a folder full of dilapidated farmhouses; one after another, war ravaged and teetering, no one but the Nazis left to prosper from the land where these photos were taken. A dismal display. The consequences of occupation took Zoli back through time; he drifted off into memory, entirely lost, glazed over, until: "That's it…"

"What??" Danny blurted out, intrigued. "You recognize this farm?" He zoomed in on the image; pixels shown in the enlargement, the photo lost detail in the process.

"This is vere ve lost my brother, your uncle, Jenő… Jancsi." He drifted into a stream of emotions, chin deep in its unrelenting current. "If we could have only stayed in zat farmhouse, maybe he'd be alive today. Bring him to America like your Uncle Laci brought me… home." Moments as actual as reality lifted up through his stark blue eyes, "There are some things you just cannot forget, Danny-*kem*."

The image printed, Zoli held it in his hands. "This is where we tried to escape, my brother was sick. This vomans and her daughter took us in…' He tilted; they locked eyes. "I told you zis story?"

Danny shook his head to the affirmative, but took his father's lead into the past anyway. "I don't mind."

"Maybe my brother vould have made it if ve veren't found, maybe he vould have survived." Severity draped them both; the repetition of details elevated the intensity of the moment. "That lady risked everyting to help and ve never thank her." He shook his head. "I don't even know if she lived past that day."

A number of clicks, some rudimentary searches

brought info on the farm into frame; a list of owners was available to the public. "You see?" Danny pointed and read, "Günter Baumann's farm was appropriated by the Third Reich in March of 1938. It would be used to feed its military efforts and help fuel the Nazi empire's growth."

"It says all that?" Awed and amused by the rate of advancement, Zoli shook his head and remembered when electricity was a treat.

"Yeah, right here, on this Holocaust memorial site. There's more..." Danny surfed the Net, clicked on hyperlinks, opened new windows. Zoli sat in continued amazement, tried to keep up. "Look at this. After his death, his widow Edith Baumann stayed on the farm and helped 300 Jews escape from the nearby concentration camp. She died in June 6, 1986 and is survived by her only daughter Anja Schroeder..."

"Amazing..." Zoltan whispered, waited for more, stared at the screen, anticipating another illuminative page. "She saved all those Jews?"

Danny stood above his dad, watched him slump over, should-haves and would-haves churned through his insides, saddened his damaged heart.

"Is there anything else?" Zoli broke the lull, sorrow cracked his words.

"Let's see what else I can find." Danny navigated, investigated, overcame the technological learning curve. "Oh, check this out, she lives in Munich, and... It says she's been talking to schools about her experiences during the war... Hey, there's a contact number..."

"Hey, why don't you call her? I think that would be a great idea." Danny, finding an out, wrote the digits out on a rectangular pad, slid them towards his dad. "I'll just give you some space to do that then... See ya," he said halfway towards the front door.

Zoli watched his son go, basked in the freedoms he enjoyed. The hum of the West Side Highway left to blanket his gaze. The sound was a constant reminder of how far he had traveled, all the roads taken to call this city home. Zoli tilted from his river view towards the rectangle of paper. A long minute or two passed as thoughts of what he might uncover shredded through his psyche. He took pause on the threshold of recollection, considered how much more of his past he could bear.

The phone made its presence felt, screamed at him from its prone position; the idea of reaching out to use it welled Zoli's eyes, twisted his intent. He knew he didn't want to know more; sought after pain was like playing with fire, it was the easiest to avoid.

Winter days had grown short, the sun made its final descent into the horizon, spewed thick streaks of fiery oranges amplified into fevered reds across the pollution filled sky; Zoli didn't move much. He checked his watch, calculated time differences, then found a calling card available for long-distance conversations in the middle drawer of his desk. The phone sat by his right hand, within reach, Zoli took a long second to emerge from all doubt with a powerful exhale. He grabbed the receiver, dialed the card code, and waited on the distinctly European ring to end.

"Hallo?" spoken upon answering, distinctively German.

"Hello? Hello? Is this Anja Schroeder?" Zoli pressed the earpiece to his face, "It is?" Aghast, he remained unconvinced even as her answer affirmed his search. "You grew

up on a farm near Mauthausen?" Her English was mediocre, as was Zoli's German, but they communicated none-
theless; he went on to stretch his language skills. "You grew
up on a farm near Mauthausen?"

The momentum of their back and forth took off, snow-
balled into a mutual catharsis. "I don't believes it..."

Zoli listened intently to the other end of his transconti-
nental call, focused on the gruff English carried over from
across the sea. He stared at the escaping sun, its light
grasped onto the last of its blues before turning black
behind the glow of city lights.

"No, no, I am not calling from a school." He broke
into the conversation, took a moment to steady his
resolve, catch his breath before he continued, "*Mein name
ist Glück Zoltan*," he proceeded deliberately. "You don't
know who I am but you and your mother were once very
kind to me..."

The totality of the conversation projected across Zoli's
face; the beginning, middle, and end contorted his eyes in
its peaks and valleys.

"Ya. Ve watched and ve did what ve could, my mother
tried to save as many people as she could." She spoke with
a cadence reserved for her paid lectures, was drenched in
their tandem recollection. She continued on, broken
English with Deutsche accent-marks led the way. "Zey vere
mostly adults who vere able to locate family or friends
close by. Ve snuck them out in the cover of night, in
hollowed out wagon-beds meant to transport food. Ve did
vhat ve could, until..."

A long silence fell over both ends of the conversation,
Zoli ended the reticence: "Your mother let me, my brother,

and our friend hide in your home... You fed us..." Zoli explained. "Ve vere just boys."

"*Mein Gott.* You? You vas there?" she interrupted.

For a man who rarely cried, Zoli was never afraid to show his feelings; a sadness few were able to identify let alone embrace clouded his ocean blue eyes. He was able to connect to his past and present concurrently, was never outwardly burdened by the grief the way many of his contemporaries were. He made sure to steer clear of the depression he saw so many of them fall into, but the sorrow in his eyes and affect in his face overwhelmed him. His good fortune was made bittersweet by the significance of what was lost in the annals of world history.

"Yes. You remember?" The shared past, familiar details, cemented their exchange, sealed it tight in each utterance. "We weren't that lucky. The Nazis found us..."

"*Mein Gott.* I don't believe zis." The tale told jabbed at her insides. "Ya, I remember you and your sick brother, and another little friend." The sentence cut short, caught tears, a silence haunted by the act of remembrance. "That day is ingrained in my mind. The war was near over, Nazis collapsing, the only thing they wanted was to kill the last of the Jews. All we wanted was it to end, to have peace..."

Zoli listened, each word hit him with the force equal to or greater than the pressure felt in his chest; his damaged and stinted heart pounded as Frau Anja continued her story, her German draped in the long haunting *träume* of Wagner's *Wesendonck Lieder*.

"That day they were more desperate. It was over for them. That sadistic Commandant had everyone beside themselves..." Sounds of her shifting in her seat, most likely old and wicker, traveled through the phone, accentuated her discomfort. "I will never forget, the Hitlerjugend scoured the property, and the Jews hiding in the fields were found. That man in charge, the Commandant made sure not to harm some boys, shot others on sight. Himself. It was like he knew where they were hiding. All of you..."

"How did they know? How did they know vhere we vere?" Zoli leaned in, waited, wondered; heavy breaths accompanied careful thinking. The past encouraged to the forefront of their cognition, transported them both by force. "Do you remember?"

Twelve-year-old Anja sat by her kitchen door. She kept watch from behind the curtains, heirlooms held over from the early Austrian empire fell victim to another. The sun refracted through the fumes of battle, diffused and redirected, only the orders of high-ranking Nazis were heard through the aftermath of the Allied charge; their indignant hollers echoed across the integrated recoil, charged to change its momentum.

Nazi SS, uniformed and loyal, yelled at service men, spitting mad inches from their faces. They forced the rank and file to regroup and resume their nefarious duties as the Allied bombing grew continually distant, irregular.

"DIES IST NICHT ÜBER! DIES IST NICHT ÜBER!"

"HEIL HITLER!"

Commandant Franz Ziereis stood firm, watched his men fan out into the fractured countryside. A tall dark haired man with sharp Aryan features came up beside him, warranted the Commandant's attention, and respect. "*Heir Doctor.*"

Dr. Aribert Ferdinand Heim nodded, silent as he knowingly witnessed the near-end to their years of brutality. With a well-planned escape to Egypt in place, Heim continued his experiments, human torture and conditioning, without regard to the subject's life for as long as he could. The capture of countless in the name of science earned him the epithet Dr. Death, as only a few of the patients he experimented on ever left his care. He was reviled and revered for horrors inflicted, lauded by superiors and underlings alike.

Those in his care bathed in the subjugation, fell weak in his presence, seemed relieved to be back in his presence after the Allied bombing shattered their horrific normality.

Anja watched on, couldn't believe her eyes when a young Jewish boy, still in his prison uniform, yellow Mogen-David badge in plain sight, turned to point directly at their farmhouse.

Dr. Heim's eye-line followed his outstretched appendage, darted across the warzone to rush in through the kitchen window. The Nazi's gaze traveled through decades, nearly toppled Anja from her seat, again. The sight of their advance propelled her from her perch; the modern day telephone conversation echoed through the past with a dire revelation. She was that little girl again. They sat side by side.

"It was a *Juden...*" Anja's duet sang through time, twisted across borders, penetrated soft tissue. "I could see the Star of David on his overalls."

"I..." Zoli aged ten years in an instant, life ripped from

his ghost-white-face. His chest tightened at the thought of a Jew leading Heim to them. a betrayal so deep it sent a jolt through his central nervous system; streaks of pin-filled electricity shot through his extremities, a pain that took him back to the most uncomfortable moments of his life. "I don't believes it..."

He laid the phone on its side, could not help but think about how his brother didn't have to be recaptured, didn't have to disappear, of how things could have been. The past and present were eternally entwined in a knot of conflicting feelings: pain and anger, loneliness and hope, fought for supremacy within Zoli's mind, acceptance rose to the top, claimed its victory in his calm resolve.

13

"Did ve ever hear back from ze Phil Donahue Show?"

Father led son south on Park Avenue. The Met Life building created a dead end that accentuated the elevated congestion of this particular neighborhood, contained it to a corner of the city where monoliths grew from prairies of concrete like invasive weeds, drowning out the sky and preventing nourishment for those close to the ground. Engine grease the city used in excess churned through the two-way stop-and-go traffic of the doublewide artery, tourists and locals equally insignificant under architectural grandeur.

"Nope." Danny mirrored his father's disappointment, felt pangs of guilt. He wished he had heard back from The Phil Donahue Show, blamed himself for the radio silence.

"This is such good story." Zoli's familiar accent mixed into nervous banter, built excitement, the flutter of antici-pation escorting each word. Every step through the midtown rat race was fueled by his lofty expectations.

"It vould have been so nice to tell Itzchak face to face."

"Yeah, I don't get it, Pops."

"I don't knows vhat they vere thinking, Itzchak and me in New York. together again." Zoli grew light on his toes as they approached The Waldorf-Astoria.

The city-block-sized Art Deco complex consisted of two conjoined 47-story towers, each crowned by 20 floors of luxury residences above a hotel that accommodated superstars and royalty in perpetuity.

"We can try Geraldo Rivera," Danny considered. "I'll write him when we get home..."

"No tanks you, that guy's a jerk," Zoli scoffed, looked skyward.

For him, the grand hotel epitomized class the same way the name Rockefeller did. His pride upon entry was apparent in his easy progress. A life dragged through the muck, back broken on hard work and forced labor were a constant chaperone on his upward climb, but in the hotel, the resolve of an easy life was available in each step. He glanced over the building's fine detail, its refined presence, pointed out the Israeli flag within a row of others; in the winds above head, the hotel honored foreign guests with a snap of diplomacy.

"I vish you didn't vear those army shorts," Zoli asserted. "I fought my way out of a desert so I vould never have to vear them, and now they're a fashion? You need to dress for the occasion."

"Okay, Members Only," Danny laughed at his father's favorite jacket.

"Vhat?" he said with a smile. "I've had dis jacket for 20 years..."

Men in uniform stood in wait to share a well-practiced, "Welcome to the Waldorf Astoria," as they opened doors for the duo.

"It's sporty casual," Zoli said,

Danny couldn't help but laugh.

Zoli took the lead up the stairs and into the cavernous Park Avenue lobby. A large chandelier illuminated the deep rich colors of the room, warm shades of brown and burgundy, gold trim accents and Deco ornamentation screamed out with design continuity, invited them into an era, an invariable style. Deliberate and precise décor was built around French artist Louis Rigal's large "wheel of life" mosaic they walked over, 148,000 individually cut pieces of tile hand-cemented and perfectly centered on the marble floor.

Zoli basked in the opulence, pointed to the 13 oil murals on the surrounding walls, the ornate molding, gold leaf decorations, and the Art Deco adornments that accompanied them through the landmark. The late morning light diffused through stained glass, fell over their progress.

"It's a good jacket. Very stylish."

They passed innumerable amenities, shopping and services available to all guests and visitors; cafes and bars set out on mezzanines presented the spectacle of New York City complete with wait-service, homemade gourmet potato chips, and lavish interiors that transported pedestrians to another time, even Danny in his camo shorts.

"He said he'd be in the breakfast room by ze grand ballroom."

They continued through the main lobby. Labyrinthine

halls and wide-open public spaces branched out from the iconic clock that anchored the sensory overload and kept innumerable ladies who lunch, power brokers, and tourists on time from the late 19th century on. It marked each quarter-hour with the sound of Westminster Chimes. The nine-foot-tall clock, two-ton mass in brass and marble had sat in the lobby ever since it was acquired by William Waldorf Astor at the Chicago World's Fair back in 1893. Its base bore the likenesses of Presidents Cleveland, Harrison, Washington, Grant, Lincoln, Jackson as well as Queen Victoria, and was layered with innumerable design details, emblazoned by brass eagles with the Statue of Liberty perched on its crest; the overdone, overwrought, over-embellished grandeur towered over them both.

"Jesus, get a load of this thing."

Zoli straightened his posture, proud. He grabbed a passing bellman. "Pardon me, vould you know vhere the grand ballroom is?"

They set off to follow directions through the expansive interior; halls turned lush, dark red wallpaper, patinated dark rich wooden furniture, golden contours, a sumptuous constant.

With doors left open, Danny watched crews expertly transform the empty grand ballroom in a ballet of maintenance and time management; the four-level space featured tiers that climbed walls on branches of nouveau detail, boasted lavish box seats perched above the near synchronized spectacle. Tables were rolled in and placed; movers made way for a stream of stacked chairs set around tables immediately set with cloths and silverware in near concurrence.

"Dude, dad, check this out." They watched together.

A custom made chandelier measuring 16 feet in diameter hung in the center of the room's soaring ceiling. It illuminated the space in its soft glow. The stage, in the midst of being dressed with stark white wedding accouterments, stood as the heart of the celebration, draped in the veneer of affluence this landmark provided.

Satisfied, they continued down the long East Foyer that made the event space accessible to the rest of the hotel and connected them to another large room drenched in the unfiltered glamour of eras past.

"Good morning." Zoli stepped to a young hostess who was there to make sure everyone present was a guest of the hotel. His inner-charm was awoken in her presence, available for the moment.

"Good morning," she replied, a required pleasantry squeezed out by mandate.

"My name is Zoltan Gluck. We are guests of Itzchak Tarkai, darling." Accent and affect leaned pleasant, worked to loosen smiles.

"Zoltan?"

"Yes, darling, and your name?"

"Sarah." Her morning brightened in the exchange. "Very nice to meet you Mr. Gluck."

"Please, call me Zoli." He tried to live vicariously, to make up for a lost youth. "And, this is my son, Danny."

"Danny, yes, hi. Nice to meet you." He turned to his dad, knew what he was up to; Hungarian was the only appropriate language for his retort. "*What are you doing?*"

"Hi." Her hospitality extended his way, in line with the

tropes of the industry, levity lubricated by the sight of their familial exchange.

"Vat?" Zoli asked. "She's beautiful."

"Thank you." Sarah held her smile, it extended through her body, shined through her posture. She caught Danny's eyes.

He hated when his dad did that to him, as often as he did.

They went on to step through a room more suited for a cocktail reception than a continental breakfast buffet with a single omelet station; its elegance was lost equally on the identically dressed businessmen and pathologically under-dressed tourists eating.

"There he is." Zoli spotted his friend sitting alone by the window.

Tarkai wore authenticity in his kind but markedly woeful eyes; a deliberate meditation over coffee and ciga-rettes shattered at first sight of the entering duo.

Comfortable, in jeans and an over-sized long sleeve t-shirt, the kind you buy off the rack not in a pack, Itzchak Tarkai met Zoli with the kind of hug that lingered, told stories, and communicated feelings, history, relief.

Since they reconnected at the Jacob Javits Center eight years earlier, both Itzchak and Zoli had made it a point to keep in touch, visiting each other on the off occasion they were even remotely close to one another. Tarkai's soft spoken man-of-few-words demeanor made phone calls short but satisfying, both able to feel the perpetual twist of fate in the other's subconscious; they knew everyday pleas-antries and small talk were beneath them. They were brothers born from the ashes of genocide.

Danny snapped a few photos of the reunion, trained his Nikon their way. Tarkai towered over Zoli; both tilted in pose. The smiles they were unable to wear as children were now plastered across their faces as they held onto one another, compensation of spirit for youths deferred.

"You hungry?" Any inkling of his prewar life on the Yugoslavian-Hungarian border had been entirely replaced by the effect of life in Israel. Tarkai's strong accent asserted itself on those lucky enough to hear what few words he cared to share. "It's good to see you both." He grabbed Danny's hand with a shake firm with satisfaction.

"Have some breakfast," Tarkai insisted. "There is more than enough." An inside joke on the wants long satiated. They stood facing one another for a moment that lingered on a shared thought, *look how far we've come*, a long lull that trailed them back to Tarkai's table.

"Go eat," Zoli urged.

"Yes, go," Tarkai added. "They have everything."

They watched as Danny stepped across the room to grab a plate, allowed them to move on without him; men bound by bloodshed and suffering needed more than a few moments to themselves.

"*So good to see you brother*," Tarkai said, Hebrew his go-to language.

Both grown and greying men pulled themselves through the desert and made it home; Israel was where they both regained their humanity. Their Jewishness was no longer a blemish to hide but a beacon to be worn in continuity with the struggles of the Old Testament; Abraham hailed a monotheistic people, Jacob established their historical home, Moses led them from servitude,

King David's reign, and Solomon's temple were all connec-
tors of commonality magnified. They were living through
the newest testament, predetermined and holy.

"You have enough paintings, Zoli? Just let me know if
you need more." Tarkai smiled through his eyes. The lush
walls of the large room, the attentive service of the
Waldorf staff, made them both feel like they were lost in a
dream, a reality perpetually endangered by the weight they
carried, suppressed daily.

"Yes, Itzi, thank you for being so generous." Zoli kept a
hand on his old friend, maintained the fantasy. Tarkai
wasn't bothered by the contact; neither wanted to lose the
other in the fray once more. "You don't know what it
means to me..."

"It's a mitzvah."

They turned to watch Zoli's son surround himself in
the abundance they could provide, a halo of excess was the
best they could do to make up for their years of want.

Danny had filled his plate so precisely that there was no
sign of the fine porcelain he used; smoked salmon, eggs
benedict, crab legs, bacon, sausage, croissants and pastries
rolled and teetered in one hand as he balanced a Bloody
Mary with all sorts of stalks and shrimp and straws sticking
out of it in the other. He passed Sarah the hostess on his
way back to the table.

"Oh, hi," Danny said.

"Hello." She matched her guest's enthusiasm. "Looks
good."

"Yeah," Danny smiled, laughed nervously to himself,
looked away, then tried to make eye contact. "Would you

like to maybe get some soft ice cream or something sometime?"

The question missed its mark, fell flat.

"Oh, no," she answered. "I don't think so."

Danny's shoulders retreated into his back, bunched up against his spine, and forced a slouch. He returned from the buffet line, fully loaded and ready to go, comforted by the forkful.

"Eat as much as you can," Zoli and Itzchak thought out loud and in unison. They knew the truth. "Live as much as you can for as long as you can."

Both men reveled in the sight of him plowing through the plenty; fed beyond sustenance. He was an entertaining display for the once starving.

Danny went back for seconds, returned with a serving as massive as the first along with a second Bloody Mary as ridiculous as the first.

All they could do was laugh and eat and love and drink and live, freely.

Tarkai led them back through the long ornate halls of the venerable hotel. Brothers walked shoulder to shoulder. The sharp bite of the Semitic language pinged through the walkway with hard consonants and guttural letter combinations that boiled up from their diaphragms and rolled off their tongues. The conversation was broken momentarily by a reprieve in English.

"Sorry, we speak Hebrew," Tarkai said Danny's way.

"No prob." He was accustomed to and intrigued by his dad's language skills; Yiddish, Hebrew, German, and Italian represented his father's struggled journey and undying resilience, each tongue learned within the duress of a camp or hospital or in the embrace of a kibbutz and in the army of a fledgling nation. An unfortunate litany of new homes that laced his early life left a residue of language in their wake.

Danny followed the sound of their conversation directly into Tarkai's suite, through solid hardwood doors, original finish retouched over the years, never repainted. They stepped into an apartment-turned-studio space; the Israeli artist appropriated every available inch for his works completed and in progress.

Interior refinements and hundred-year-old accouterments were covered by drop cloths. Large acrylic paintings on display redefined the dated space. Lamps that had never been moved now sat on the wall-to-wall carpeting, made way for Tarkai's creations. Canvases replaced the elegance with their own, took on some of the hotel's more notable characteristics: women lounged in the Waldorf's five-star lobby, its monumental clock, under Tarkai's ethereal perspective. His ladies sat in the corners of ornate ballrooms and on mezzanines with views; Matisse-like planes, flat surfaces that presented tables full of fruit, flowers, pottery; cityscapes captured through windows, painted still lives and nudes hung and framed within his compositions. Women sat unaffected by their polished environment; heavily colored eyes and lips took life as it came, without a care. Their all-encompassing ease filled both the viewer and artist with their unearthly comfort.

"My ladies."

Tarkai led them through the room, revealed completed pieces stacked against a wall. A desk tucked into an available alcove usually occupied by Wall Street Journals and corporate raiders, devious investors counting their credit or flush tourists fresh from countries with a favorable exchange rates, was now Tarkai's workstation; watercolors in various states of completion were neatly lined to dry, paint, brushes, and a tin of water at the ready.

"Pick a piece," Tarkai invited in for a closer look.

"Really?"

"Yes, I want you to have one."

Handling art since childhood, Danny jumped right in, flipped through the watercolors in a seasoned, quick and careful way. He took long moments to admire individual pieces, set a couple aside before making a final decision.

"Perfect," Tarkai took a seat, picked up a pen, and scrawled:

TO DANNY

BEST WISHES

TARKAI

6.5.94

Zoli watched his friend finish up marking the lower right hand side of his unframed work on paper. The watercolor of a single lady lounging in a corner seat was nestled in a wash of Tarkai's soul, colors vying for space on a sheet flush with life, fresh flowers illuminated within the four sides of the piece by a mid-century ceiling lamp.

"Thanks," Danny said. He gently placed the gift into the crease of an available legal sized file folder. An exchange of handshakes led to hugs and smiles all around. The kid bore witness, watched survivors drunk on the new world; the levity of the ladies was infectious. They had seen more than a dozen households nationwide light up in their presence.

Good favor faded fast; their proximity, their history, contorted the environment, dimmed the enthusiasm as the visit extended into the afternoon. Zoli broke one of the many long reflective silences. "Are you going to go to the reunion, Itzi?" He laid tender eyes on his childhood friend, and continued, "It will be 50 years since our liberation..."

The balance Tarkai's work gave him daily, that straightened his slouch and brightened his eyes, faded fast. The artist sat disturbed by the catalyst, by a query expecting an answer. The walls of his beautifully constructed reality that kept his darkest experience relegated to bios and press releases was now threatened in the expectant silence.

"Why do I need to go back?" Tarkai shrugged as it came naturally.

"Go back? The reunion is in Tel Aviv."

Soft eyes connected, Tarkai's reluctance was palatable with the all too familiar, the bitter taste of painful memories; languages spoken marked their miles traveled, Hungarian used to cap their deepest regression.

"I know, Zoli, but why do I need to revisit the worst part of my life?"

"We can never let history forget, Itzi, survivors are dying out..."

"Let them, they need to die out, we need to let the victims make way for the victors." He put his hand on his friend's shoulder, continued, "We have come so far, Zoli; not all of us have..." He shared a half formed smile, brought the full arc of their respective journeys into the conversation. "We need to let the heartache go, we have conquered so much to get to this very moment. We need to let it go, like my ladies, not a care in the world; color comes up out of them, Zoli, I do not paint them, the life is allowed to color itself, like we are, old friend." He redirected his attention Danny's way, "You understand? Speak Hungarian?"

"Yes."

"Hebrew?

"No."

"Why not? Learn Hebrew!" The friends exchanged a look, an unspoken need to unify a people deflected by individuality. "And, school?"

Zoli answered for his son. "He's taking time off from NYU. Live a little. Sell some paintings with his olderly father."

Paths preferred by present company led to accumulated adventures, good and bad, sorted out by those who took note and made their own good fortune. Danny was compelled to follow their lead.

"You do what you feel is right for you," Tarkai asserted. "There is no one way in this crazy world."

"Spoken like a true artist." Zoli turned to his son; a familiar mantra never far from his lips: "Experience is the best teacher."

His gaze twisted to the peaks and valleys of life on Earth. Face to face with one of only a few who could relate, Zoli couldn't allow himself to bury his darkest years. "You don't want to see who made it?"

Itzchak straightened out, fought the question, scared of the answers, and stared deep into Zoli. He could see his friend's heart beating, his mind wandering into the past, but could not join in. He lit a cigarette instead.

"Who died a free man?" Zoli continued.

Tarkai's cool façade cracked, the first mark of his mind's recognition of the gravity of the occasion. He blew cigarette smoke, added to the pre-existing haze in the hotel room, before he answered. "We all died in those camps, Zoli. That's enough for me. How many times do I need to die?"

"Don't you want to know what happened? To Jenő? Maybe someone knows... something...." Emotions welled his speech, continued through the sentiment. "Knows about the others? Shandor... Istvan... Chaim...."

"Chaim made it," Tarkai blurted out, a quick reply that reared up from the crevasses of his subconscious; a blister on the face of his entire life burst in one oozy thoughtless moment, a repugnant release of introspection murmured between drags, never meant for others' ears. He immediately regretted it.

"He made it?" Zoli said. His voice caked with concern, curiosity, and amazement. "Do you know what happened?" Narratives raced through his head in a daze of possibilities.

"There's nothing left to remember," Tarkai said with a smoke dangling from his lips. He changed his tone in an instant; brain chemistry shifted, charged in from his amygdala. "I don't want to waste my time thinking about that bullshit. We have our lives, good lives to live. That's it. That's it."

Zoli was sensitive to his friend's reaction, familiar with the discomfort felt by the majority of his peers, tattooed souls who refused to release themselves from the mark. He said no more.

Tarkai lit a new cigarette off the old, let inner demons out in a haze of carcinogens that made way for the works in progress.

14

Despite his best efforts, Zoli's attempts to ignore a dull pressure that started between his left ribs fell short. It lasted for days, hindered his mobility, and stole his breath. All of a sudden, one evening in the bedroom a flight of stairs up from his Provincetown gallery, that manageable sensation gave way, grew sharp, was debilitating. Red blood cells coated by decades of decadence clogged function. His new prosperity, unlimited food and drink, the stresses of business ownership, left a fine film of hardened cholesterol in its wake. Years of making up for lost time were filled with sausage and hard salami, Hungarian style liver with onions and fat, petit filets and Courvoisier, all served with a side of potatoes, rice, or pasta, and plenty of bread with butter, set his heart aflutter, struggling to complete its next beat. HDL battled LDL for supremacy, lost the long war. Zoli's coronary pathways caved to the excess for the second time in ten years, were again entirely blocked. The flow of blood to his heart ceased, damaging muscle in each of its attempts to continue its designated task. His left arm froze, chest cinched from the inside. Agony shot through his system with electrical efficiency.

"HIT HIM AGAIN!"

One shock, then another, the urgency of the EMTs packed in the back of an ambulance was a constant. Sirens streaked down Route 6, charging towards the closest hospital 50 miles away.

Zoli clung to life in their ER, getting airlifted to Mass General in Boston where he was stabilized and prepped for an immediate coronary bypass operation the very next day.

He awoke in a large white room, clean floors gleaming in antibacterial bliss. Light streamed in from a large unobstructed window cracked open for the decency of fresh air. Cracked lips, crusted over eyes, and oxygen tubes were all readjusted as Zoli shuffled upright. Julika was there to place a few pillows behind his back, extend a glass of water for his relief. He fixed his position, looking at Julika.

His wife and partner for the last thirty years hadn't slept for days. Her eyes remained wide with concern despite obvious exhaustion.

"You scared us," she said.

"I'm okay," Zoli strained to speak. "Is Danny here yet?"

"He's on his way," Julika replied. She had started to let the grey come out from under her red dye job six months earlier, and wore a halo of her remaining colored hair close to the shoulders. She adjusted pillows around her husband, fussed to make sure he was comfortable.

The sun set, rose again to the beep of Zoli's EKG meter. Friends and family, a couple of doctors on residency, filed in throughout the day. Cards and flowers were piled on the only available table. Julika's mom shuffled along in her old age, organized the room the best she could throughout the influx and after it subsided. She sat exhausted.

"I don't know how much longer we can keep the gallery closed," Julika worried aloud. "We still have bills, Zoli. I can't do it without you."

"I'll be fine, you heard what the doctor said."

"The doctor said you almost died." Julika was in a constant state of hysteria, trauma set off by the slightest catalyst, and off-the-rail irrational in the face of a real tragedy. "You have to take care of yourself. I can't do this again."

"I'm here. I made it." His voice had come back, his strength inching along. "I'll be back to work in no time, just like last time..."

"Last time you had help, last time..." Julika was interrupted.

The room's front door opened against the pneumatic device that kept it from slamming, causing it to exhale as it released its built up internal pressure.

"Dad," Danny rushed in, headed directly to his father. "Dad."

There were tears in his eyes and booze on his breath; Zoli noticed both as Danny let his newly packed on pounds drop him on the hospital bed beside him.

"Oh my god, dad." Anxiety overwhelmed the adult child from the inside out; constant catastrophizing bound his chest and closed his mind. For his whole life, he had been prepared for the worst. His father's experiences, even through their greatest successes, taught him that life wasn't easy and that it could change at any instant, in an instant. He couldn't escape the legacy, the lesson, no matter how hard he tried. He didn't know it was right there and everywhere the entire time. Danny was inconsolable. He just held on to his father, both arms slung around the old man as he let his emotions take over. Tears flowed, breath was lost, as the worst charged through his head. "Oh my god dad."

"It's okay, Danny," Zoli assured him. "It's okay."

"I'm nothing without you." Danny tried to compose himself, stood up to hug his mother and grandmother, exposing them to his ripped jeans and unkempt person. "I came as fast as I could."

"I know," Zoli whispered.

"You couldn't put on a normal pair of pants to visit your father?" Julika guilted her son. Her mother added in Hungarian. *"You look like a bum."*

Danny turned from them to notice the matching disappointment in his father's eyes. He exhaled, took an opened fifth of Jack Daniels out of his inside pocket, and took an imperceptibly quick swig. They stood in silence, allowed Zoli the peace he needed to reclaim his strength.

Boxer shorts bunched up pasty white thighs; early stage liver spots, monitored moles, and pocks of past skin conditions swirled like solar systems; a long worn white tank top stretched to its limit over the contours of Zoli's protruding belly, under his mountainous snore. A $60,000 custom portrait hung unframed on the wall above his chain-sawed slumber in a hotel room inexpensive enough for both the traveling salesman and those seeking a reprieve by the indoor pool for the weekend.

No matter where in America they were, the Hampton Inn was their home away from home. In their last decade on the road, Zoli had developed a preference for the hotel chain. Whether it was their muted yellow and earthy brown color scheme, the fresh coffee that was always available, or the breakfast, they always booked ahead of time. The fact that they could use any hotel on their route and get the same level of service, same fresh coffee, same clean sheets and bathrooms kept them customers.

Each stop had a lounge area where they had spent thousands of off hours playing chess and monitoring the never-ending cable news cycle within interchangeable interiors. At times, the food outside their hotel doors was the only indication of where they actually were. Bob Evan's Country Kitchen in the Midwest, Copper Canyon Brewery in Michigan, The Buggy Wheel Fine Dining in Ohio, Eat and Park Family Restaurant in the tri-state area of Ohio, West Virginia, and Pennsylvania; Flannigan's Seafood Bar and Grill in Southern Florida and Clams on its panhandle prepared them for appointments like dogs waiting on Pavlov's familiar call.

But for most of the time, the hotel room was their sanctuary. The white noise of the air conditioner that pumped fresh air into the stale room was the only thing keeping Zoli company. The room light was left on. TV low. The second bed still made. Zoli's thunderous nap caught struggle, drew silent, full apnea that prompted repositioning; pillows were drawn in and turned around, comfort found and embraced within climate control.

A knock on the door destroyed the still calm. Four separate attempts to gain entry were needed to jar Zoli out of the depths of his REM; dreams and reality entwined through time, horrors and happiness mingled equally in a dance of emotional equilibrium.

With a slow roll off the bed, eyes half-closed, Zoli slipped his white-socked-feet into black slippers. He took a second to remember exactly where he was, and when he did, immediately made sure the portrait still hung behind him. He straightened it out before answering the next series of knocks with, "Vone minute!"

He opened the door.

"Here's Johnny," Danny stood there with one gym bag full of dirty clothes. His swollen belly and bloated face were no longer a surprise to the family. Their kid had let himself go.

They hugged the instant they laid eyes on one another.

"Didn't have to get dressed up for me, Pops," Danny said.

"Come in, come in." His dad continued with a wink, "Home sveet home."

The kid stepped into the familiar room, promptly grabbed two individually wrapped plastic cups, tore into them, retrieved a bottle out of his bag, and poured out two drinks. Zoli grabbed his.

"To ze road," Zoli held his drink out.

"In that case, I'm going to need a double." Danny tipped his cup toward his dad. They threw their drinks back. Danny went to pour another.

"Vone is enough," Zoli insisted.

"For you maybe," Danny insisted in the moment before

shooting back his second drink. "I'm in dire need now that I'm back."

Danny had run away, or at least he tried. He had gone as far as to drop out of school with a plan to visit all the other colleges his buddies were attending. He went from coast to coast sleeping on floors and couches and bed-hopping from one-night-stand to another.

The lure of the open road was in his blood, so was the familial obligation and guilt that fanned its flame.

"Hey, tanks for coming help your olderly father, Danny-*kem*," broken English adrift in enthusiasm.

"Like I had a choice. At least you don't have to worry about getting old anymore," Danny said to the bottom of his third lowball. "Cause you're already old. Get it? You're old."

Eddie Murphy's face was plastered across the mid-sized tube TV, distracting them both; *Trading Places* was forever on full rotation across both regional and national channels ever since they started traveling together.

"Thank you for correcting my English that stinks," Eddie Murphy's character in disguise said; Danny repeated it in his dad's general direction in the same forced African accent. "Thank you for correcting my English that stinks."

Zoli smiled, old age was the problem he had always hoped for, but growing invalid was the nightmare he shared with his son throughout their time together.

Danny fell on the unmade queen-sized bed he spent the majority of his time on the road on, watched his dad sit at the generic Formica desk, like he always did, phone and address book at the ready.

"Danny, vat are you goings to do about school?" Zoli

asked.

Keen on keeping off the topic, Danny exploited their favorite distraction. "Any appointments yet, Pops?"

A question that launched Zoli into a hustle, bifocals already balanced on the tip of his nose. He flipped through a notepad littered by his unique scrawl, shorthand that combined appointments, directions, and notes.

"Of course, ve have appointment for the next tree days, then home." He looked to Danny. "You coming?"

"Sorry, Pops, I gotta be in Chicago next week."

Disappointment marbled satisfaction; he wished he could venture out once more into the American abyss.

"Experience is the best teacher, you know," Danny dutifully recited.

Zoli stood to his mantra, held his kid's head between his hands; Jenő's hazel eyes stared back at him

"Anyway. Who cares?" Danny rolled to his feet and placed his hands on his belly. "Let's eat."

The Macaroni Grill was the only decent restaurant close to the Hampton Inn, and their dinner there made Danny's return to familial subjugation complete. Neither of them patronized the chain anywhere else.

Danny ordered for his dad from the heart healthy menu. "He'll have the grilled salmon with mustard caper sauce over a bed of sautéed spinach..."

"And, a side of spaghetti," Zoli finished his order, eyed his son for permission, with his one usual argument. "Vat? Of course, spaghetti. We're at an Italian restaurant."

"Dad. You just had a second heart attack like three months ago, dude," Danny exclaimed. "You're lucky to be alive."

They locked eyes, reversed roles, full circle and back again; a display not wasted on the twenty-something waitress who arrived with a complimentary jug of wine as was this establishment's shtick. Her cheerleader curves filled out by staff meals complemented her low cut uniform and cheery disposition. "I'll just run that order in for you two right now," she concluded.

They watched her leave with a deliberate bounce to her step.

"Zat is very annoying."

"You telling me?" Second sips, another bottle, food and waitress served hot to the touch. Danny excused himself after their meal, went off to find the bathroom, but found their waitress instead.

"Was everything ok?" she asked.

"Very good," Danny answered with a distinctive cheap wine slur of his words. He moved closer to her, she inched back, but not quick enough to avoid the palm of Danny's hand on her rear.

"Excuse me?" she reeled.

"No excuses," was the first thing to pop into Danny's head. "I'll be back for you later," he concluded as he turned towards the bathroom.

By the time he returned to their table, Zoli had already paid the bill. "Vat did you do?"

"What?" Danny questioned. "In the bathroom?"

"They asked us to leave." Zoli shot his son a glance. "Did you do something?"

"It wasn't me," was Danny's story, and he stuck to it.

Continuity and familiarity ruled life on the road, appointments with families they watched expand; kids grew into teenagers in the same amount of time it took the duo to fill walls with paintings. They revisited past sales; works that hung decoratively across the nation helped pay for Danny's college and zero out mortgages. For Zoli, the freedoms America had to offer were realized on the road. It was a little different for Danny.

Handy with a fifth of Jack Daniels, Danny surreptitiously took belts from the bottle in driveways where he was left to unpack and repack their minivan, a downsize in semi-retirement from the large cargo truck they started out with. He'd move to help out inside in between tasks; booze, Visine, and breath mints prepared him to earn a growing percentage of the take.

One week's work never enabled so good: Danny's time entwined in family and family business drew him to a panic. He now carried the disaster of his dad's near death around with him like a 1000-pound bag of festering shit tied around his neck. He had to pick up the slack, an act that left him forever running to help maintain the household in which he no longer lived. Even amid rebellion, the road remained a shared effort, an eternal obligation; watching his dad work defined his youth, affected his entire life, and was now his burden to bear.

Zoli took their customers through time; Christian, Hindi, Black or White, Jew and gentile were all welcome to join his tour. The tragedy of his life was never lost on those who listened and listened again.

"You must never get tired of hearing about your dad's life, Danny? You should write a movie about it," was a common reaction. "Or something."

Accustomed to the equation of his dad's story plus an

incomplete film school education equaled something Danny thought he couldn't manage: *How am I supposed to tell such a massive tale, especially one that's so close?*

"Write it? After all these years listening..." he'd reply, only half in jest. He had the vilest realities of his father's life memorized. "I feel like I've lived it."

The guilt of leaving so much behind, the weight of his father's journey, laid heavy on both their shoulders, a generational transference of the tingling kind; for so long, Danny couldn't let his father carry the brunt of his history alone. The destructive force of the Holocaust transcended time and space, infected their family tree at the root, and drove Danny to act out, drink in excess to numb his inherited pain.

"It all happened 50 years ago, almost exactly," Zoli said, drinking coffee or sipping a cordial as Danny slipped unsold paintings into their custom reshaped refrigerator boxes.

Cords fashioned with a slipknot sealed the art in place, Zoli's handwriting marked every container with not only the artist of the current occupant but also the crossed out names of all the works it had held over the years. Every centimeter of the operation was drenched in Zoli's innovations; it bore his soul.

Danny finished up the last box and started to bring the unsold painting out to their ride. Sneaking a sip in the process, he got busted by the daughter of their customer who was happy to join him, then show him her room; the door closed behind them, and reopened before either were missed.

"They are even having a reunion in Tel Aviv to remember ze liberation of ze camps," he continued.

"That's amazing!"

"Praise God!"

Each person reacted to his experiences and stories in their own way, some related to the loss, other reveled in Zoli's ultimate victory.

"Are you going with your father?" one of the clients asked Danny.

"Not this time."

"He vill be continuing on hiz own, taking his time off NYU to see ze country."

"Oh, that's too bad." Chagrined and disappointed reactions to the opportunities missed, customers dressed for the night out couldn't help but assert their opinions. "You two make such a good team. Your father needs you."

Danny collected his thoughts, fell into a distant stare; a lifetime of shadowing his father's aspirations, embracing the labors of both his past and present came out of his pores, twisted his tongue. "I think my dad needs to go this alone, see old faces, miss lost friends..."

"Danny says he need his own chapters," Zoli smiled at the descriptive term. His usually slightly rolled *R* illustrated his enthusiasm in the thought of his kid's yet to be experienced adventures. "That's vat he calls it, chapters."

"Well, my dad had so many forced on him, right? Taken from his home, all the different camps, countries, and you know what happened?" No need to wait for an answer. Danny continued his performance, the road was their stage, and these were his canned responses. "He's learned 11 languages, has stories of heartache and adventure for days, a lifetime of experience that brought him to the most unique livelihood, born from the ashes to live the American dream."

"God bless America," Zoli stood proud.

"That's got to be difficult to live up to..." Midwestern folks sheltered in their cul-de-sacs struggled to imagine a life lived outside their comfort zone, far from drive-thru service and community potlucks.

Later on, after hours, over martinis and stale peanuts, they would count the earnings, calculate costs, and divvy up their cuts.

"You sure you don't vant to come home vith me?"

Pressures held over from youth: the ancient feelings from when he worked his first childhood job and took care of the family business while his father teetered in a Boston area hospital gurgled through his intestines after his first heart attack, the weight of being financially underwater, the impending doom of his parents' unstable childhood. It all hovered overhead, burrowed into Danny's soft tissue and failed to dissipate, so he continued to run.

"You be safe, kiddo."

Danny threw his single gym bag into the back seat of his truck, slammed the door, and turned back to his old man. They hugged like friends, kissed like family, and shook hands like business partners.

Zoli watched his son hop into his Bronco II and take off towards the onramp for the I-75 North, before returning to his room. The hum of Hampton Inn climate control and afternoon television were now his only companion. They lulled him to introspection.

15

El Al flight #4's 13-hour trip from John F. Kennedy International Airport in New York City to Tel Aviv International in Israel was mostly smooth. The heavy turbulence that drew others to prayer, grasping at their seats upon descent, failed to wake Zoli. He remained still as the plane made it to its gate, as passengers began to disembark.

A young Israeli flight attendant made her way through the aisles of the empty aircraft. Her wide curls bounced to the urgency of the cabin check until she reached Zoli asleep in his window seat. She watched him suspended in slumbered reverie, years dreamt away in between hard exhales, his exodus reviewed in full though each sound second, jostled him through the scarce highs and infectious lows trapped in his subconscious.

. . .

It felt like yesterday, a thousand yesterdays ago; allied care was applied and embraced, ingested meals formed muscle on young Zoli's bone-crisp physique. At 16 years old, his strength had returned, coursed through his veins; his pain lurched from his sullen eyes. A vacancy excavated all hope; the emptiness kept him firmly on the precipice, perpetually on edge, in agony. He stood alone in the world, silent, fighting the horrors that reared reminders in nightmares, waking and somnambulant.

Zoli's blue pupils twisted in a bloodshot world. He had trouble remembering where he was, who he was, and how he had gotten there. He tilted upward, looked across a large wooden desk, and saw a young German nun standing patiently before him.

Sister Mary Kessler internalized the acts of her country over the last decade, it prematurely aged her. Her face was wrinkled by concern.

Zoli watched her. She soured to the fate of the countless imprisoned; Jews and Catholics, gays and gypsies, the weak and handicapped filled page after page with endless grief. The sorrow in her eyes was constant; names were read, remembered, reborn in grieved prayers. Sister Mary Kessler flinched at the litany of murders reduced to paperwork; the heaviness of the situation was unavoidable, it chipped away at her faith of a just God.

She looked away; reality was too much to bear.

The Sisters of St. Barbara kept their heads down during the worst of Fascism, ignoring the extent of the atrocities committed in an act of self-preservation. Priests, bishops, and cardinals fell to the force of the new regime. They were killed for speaking out, detained for their faith, and destroyed for their power.

However, after the war, the church was eager to help, to right their wrongs. They worked with the Allies to compile a thorough registrar of the afflicted; dead or alive they'd be in their books.

The Nazis left impeccable records, each name marked precisely, every fate listed matter-of-fact and within the space provided, murder and dehumanization fueled bureaucracy. The coldness of its existence was antagonistic by nature, pained the young nun in her task, in the truth.

"I am sorry. I cannot find Jenő Gluck. He can be anywhere," her slow and deliberate German absorbed by the young man, repeated and repeated.

Zoli stood contracted, feet sunk in their floorboards, weighed down by absolute loneliness; the first he may have ever known. The vacancy expanded, gripped his heart; his aorta shivered cold, blood flowed backwards, arteries clogged in repressed grief.

The nun twisted with empathy, fatalistically took her current station as doctrine. She was commanded the right to protect the innocent from the heavens above, and shut the large hardbound book. Its heavy leather cover retained its shine. Her kind eyes fixed on the lost soul before her; years of war and inhibited spirituality, the utter hopelessness that infected the entire church drenched every word that came out of her mouth. "This camp is as good a home as any... for now... I think."

Young Zoli emerged from the cathedral. Blistering sunlight embraced him in its warmth. Unaccustomed clarity, his eyes struggled to focus, witnessed the altered world around him.

He wandered through the square blocks that made up Feldafing Displaced Persons' Camp, strained in each step and every direction, forty steps and forty strides, an imagined life built by survivors and their liberators that would never be home.

Several buildings, that included what was an elite school for Hitler Youth, were converted and supplemented by JDC erected buildings. The manufactured neighborhood bustled with daily life in an attempt to get back to a normal that was never actualized. The burden of their loss was too great, it was biblical; the refugee camp reminded them daily, it talked to children and elders with hushed assertions, provided downward pressure that kept them dislocated like Moses in the Sinai desert, the end of their journey far from sight, and lived in their faith.

Meals, meetings, making friends, finding family mimicked normalcy, helped everyone recuperate. But too many bittersweet reunions led to tears and a tremendous realization. No Jew was unscathed, each coped their own way.

Zoli watched men not much older than himself gather to shave tattooed numbers right out of their skin. They took blades to flesh, self-loathing dug into forearms, bloodied jabs murderously attempted to rewrite history, kill all feeling. No one was far from someone who died or was waiting to die in an Allied hospital bed. They were all afflicted by the lingering scourge.

. . .

Blood rushed to reoccupy the crevices of Zoli's 66-year-old body. He floated through disembarkation; the introduction of a modern Israel was lost in a haze of pride, adrenaline charged his stride.

The stark white, well-lit halls of the airport baptized Zoli's return. He grew a conflicted smile across his face as an influx of similarly aged men welcomed him back. He couldn't help but scan their faces as they exchanged pleasantries, collected handshakes. He made his way through a crowd of his peers.

The glare of the Israeli morning prismed through the glass ceiling, strobed hysterically.

Zoli retrieved his bags and found a man holding up a sign in Hebrew that read: 50th anniversary. He joined the gathering, conversation and introductions took on a distinct meter, hypnotic modulations joined together, grew consecrated.

Right after their liberation, prayer, relief, and food lines at the Feldafing Displaced Persons' camp had turned strangers into family, they all knew that there was no going back to the way things were; underlying doldrums lined their innards, were inescapable.

Some Jews stayed at that camp until the Germans closed it down in 1951. Others tripped over the first days of the rest of their lives, found paths of their own.

Past the usual greetings, home cooked food, and faces that had grown familiar, young Zoli's daily walks would take him across the entire compound and back again, through its center where one day he caught an out of the ordinary sight.

A young JDC recruiter with a beard and *payots* far-from-regrown after the ordeal, wearing Army pants and boots, yelled from atop an old wooden crate: "This is not our home—*ez nem Magyarország!*"

His attempt to draw in an audience made for a crowd; Zoli inched closer to hear what the guy had to say.

"Is this the life for us? Is this what we suffered for?" A hand on his head kept his *kippah* from launching from his fervor. He grew increasingly passionate the more people gathered. He pointed to Zoli. "You, young man!" Hungarian, Yiddish, Hebrew, were all used in service of the cause. "Do you not want to reclaim our ancestral home, the home of the Torah?"

Young Zoli's eyes bloomed in dreams he never knew he could realize; his childhood and all its anguish would make way for his return.

"Welcome to the Hilton, Tel Aviv. Do you have a reservation?" A beautiful Israeli young woman with big waves of antique brown hair that bounced off skin so subtle and tanned so evenly it resembled fine combed sand; her broad smile tinted by cigarette smoke still gleamed, exuded an ease that turned course Hebrew smooth with hospitality. "And, a passport?"

Zoli handed it over, and turned to peer through the open lobby; doum palm trees dipped in the cool winds that came in off the Mediterranean. Zoli shook his head, couldn't comprehend his blessings, counted the moments that propelled him through history to this moment.

"Imagine to be bar mitzvahed in our own Jewish nation, to leave the hatred we felt in Europe behind," Zoli could still hear the call of that young JDC barker; it was burrowed deep into his story—past, present, and future. "To make our own home in the land of our ancestors, in the land God called our forefathers too."

The call grew faint as young Zoli took hold of his future; grabbed onto the reins of his trajectory, made his own fate.

"Biblical Canaan is our land, since Abraham set foot on its sands and David established it as our homeland..." The sound of a movement lifted into the ether. "Come live your birthright..."

Life in Israel was good for Zoli after the initial struggle. Before entering, he, and many exactly like him, had endured a British-imposed exile at refugee camps in the boot of Italy and on the island of Cyprus. Then, Zoli had to fight for the survival of the Jewish nation-state, nearly died in battle on more than one occasion for his right to a land of milk and honey.

Accountants, teachers, engineers, and world-class body athletes were the individualities lost; everyone was reborn in Israel as a piece of a collective, brought closer to God through the union. They joined together, in a singular effort, on disputed borders, against seemingly insurmountable odds. They shared repressed pain nonverbally, commonalities best forced forgotten. Orphans were bar and bat mitzvahed in large assemblies caught in the dry heat of the desert sun, flashed hot and bright on those expected to build a nation from the travesty of their lives lost.

He connected with people on similar paths; a generation born from the near destruction of a culture was obligated to resuscitate it. It was the reprieve they deserved, a safe haven where they could prepare for their future. For close to ten years, Zoli gained experiences and an education; kibbutz living filled with good friends, army buddies and girls, lots of girls.

A sense of community extended beyond neighborly; incomplete families opened doors, offered apprenticeships, married off their daughters.

Zoli laughed to himself, the memory of finding himself caught up in more than a handful of families looking to marry off their daughters filled his head.

"That could have been me," he thought to himself as he dodged pedestrian traffic on the sidewalks of modern Israel. "I did accept many invitations, and made up for lots of lost time." A flipbook in his mind filled with the collection of dates and crushes that kept him busy. However, the expectations of many fathers rarely aligned with Zoli's. The building of their combined future required babies and he was far from ready to be tied down by fatherhood, but he remembered how happily he entertained their need.

Always the storyteller, he sat in the newly recognized nation, around dinner served and coffee tables to recount parables told to him by relatives, bible stories of Jewish triumphs after long held failures; the cadence and enthusiasm in his voice left more than one of his hosts inviting him back for more. Zoli's piercing blue presence reinvigorated, coaxed smiles long unused. His innate charm was allowed to flourish, took root in liberties he'd experience for the first time.

Israel was where Zoli became human again; immeasurable youths interrupted, uprooted, decimated, were given a chance to believe in something again. They were forever etched into the arenaceous landscape. The hard-fought freedom rewarded the displaced and young with a safe haven in which to lay their long damaged roots. The newly formed government set forth in an effort to reach out to Jews worldwide, located any living relatives lost in the chaos of war. They notified Zoli as soon as they located his brother living in the United States. *Glück László* had changed his name to Leslie Kenedi to sound less German, but he would always be Laci to Zoli.

The two sent letters and telegraphs across oceans and were able to speak over the phone on two separate occasions. A new world opened up, Zoli was no longer alone, not the only Gluck who had made it out alive. Their correspondences peaked when Laci sent his little brother a boat ticket to the United States instead of money for a new bicycle.

The continued and constant pressure on his bachelorhood was more than enough to encourage young Zoli's trip abroad. The sparse desert Zoli called home for ten years would stay with him; for him, it would represent a place where anything could happen, where he reclaimed his youth and was allowed to become a man, live a life of his own before his return to the homeland.

"I came from Ohio," one senior citizen adrift in recollection shared in a room full of others who had made the journey. "How far we have come. I never thought I would see food let alone freedom." It was a thought shared by the aging witnesses of events engrained. No matter where they came from, they all shared Zoli's history. They crossed paths in textbooks and television reports, documentaries and literature padded their collective reflections with reference material.

"*Schindler's List* was like a mirror. I didn't want to watch, but I couldn't turn away."

A wash of accents in different stages of cultural assimilation were lobbed back and forth, each syllable drenched in the flow of antiquity mixed in modernity.

"Right there on the screen for everyone to see."

"I saw it opening night, no one left their seat, not a dry eye in ze house."

"You believe anyone could deny what happened? To us. To Europe."

"To the world."

"The world is still changing."

Zoli interjected with comments that were thick with experience. "Some tings never change, Jews always get the short end of the stick, prejudice continues as it always has..." Sadness filled the attentive, hurt ever-present within the gathered. "In Hungary as a child and even right now, anti-Semitism will always find a home."

Their young Israeli tour guide chimed in, dropped the

party line. "That's why we need Israel. It is where we all belong. It is where we can be safe from discrimination."

The sentiment shielded the old men from horrors committed at their expense, the realities that existed outside the hotels' front door, throughout the Middle East and beyond. It painted over them with two coats of hope that followed Zoli in the week's worth of events in the default capital of Tel Aviv. The international guests boarded luxury buses for the hour long ride up Road 1 to Jerusalem for the final gala of the organized trip.

IDF vehicles were a notable sight on their way, a constant reminder of the persistent unease of the region.

"As you can tell, the struggle is constant," the young Israeli tour guide narrated. Avi stood at the front of the bus; his tight curls and patinaed skin played off the landscape, his accent thick with sand and salt. "Israel's right to exist and govern itself has always been questioned, at risk..."

Avi led his tour group to museums and lecturers, shared little known facts with the returning sons of Israel. He placed their collective struggle out for all to see. "Besides two small Central American countries, the rest of world disrespects Israel's sovereignty when we chose Jerusalem as our capital after we annexed it in the Six-Day War in 1967."

"In '67? So recently," an older man added.

"Yes, I know, we lose track of time, but from then on the world has continued to insist on building their embassies in Tel Aviv instead of Jerusalem, our rightful capital. It was yet another international insult to add to the many endured by the Jewish people..." The room full of survivors related to the endless struggle, its bitter taste remained fresh and familiar. Avi's passion was persistent, his anger untenable; attitude shifted accordingly: "The U.S. Congress only adjusted their error this year, and, on the 50th anniversary of the liberation of the concentration camps, they just announced the Jerusalem Embassy Act." No one knew that it was a promise that would be a struggle to be keep, no embassy had yet been built in Jerusalem.

The trip through the past and obstacles of the present built camaraderie; feelings culminated in the final event held in the hotel's expansive banquet hall.

The crowd shuffled in, the children of the camps were now old men. Young girls kept alive for their vitality had begun to hunch over, dyed their hair. Survivors that endured subjugation as adults had aged exponentially, each year magnified under the stress of continuance, and turned them near invalid. Nurses and family rolled the infirmed through the whirl of activity.

Boys who trudged through malnutrition, the worst dehumanization, walked shoulder to shoulder suffering from the luxuries of old age; arthritis, diabetes, and heart disease slowed their progress.

Zoli carried a palm sized video camera around with him in hopes of recording the event for his family. However, the emotions of the reunion leveled the camera towards the floor; audio recorded the exchanges that tilted it in the first place.

"Brother, good to see you."

"Every day is a blessing."

"*Abi gezunt!*"

The pleasantries shielded painful realities; tearful introductions caught on tape as the misdirected lens continued to bounce with enthusiasm, focused on everything but the gathering. Carpet and feet panned by, the liberated free to comingle, their shoes heading in directions of their choosing. Conversations caught were a collage of new concerns and old nightmares, and inescapable political discussions.

"We're here, let's talk."

Photo opportunities were exploited and televised, reporters and politicians staggered into the hotel like an intrusive wave of lava, took turns taking turns, made speeches. "50 years ago, Jews were once again led out of captivity, left again to wander in Jewish diaspora, but by the grace of God many of you before me were led home, brought to the holy land..." Other speakers took the opportunity to lead the amassed in prayer: "*Sh'ma Yisra'eil Adonai Eloheinu Adonai echad...*"

Zoli sat at a table full of Mauthausen memories, introductions full of faulty recall made their way around the table. "Zoltan Gluck from New York City, originally from Hungary. My Hebrew name is Itzchak Ben-David."

Liquor lubricated, led to levity, drew out connections. Men worked on recognizing brethren whose paths they may or may not have crossed, connected names to experience in the exaggerated embrace of encouraged reconciliation.

"I was at the quarry, what I saw... I will never forget."

"How could we forget?"

"I was in the munitions factory." Attempts to reconnect to their history ended there, set silent, reflective.

"And now we're here." Years, journeys, families, and regret rolled into each utterance.

"What a way to come together. Fifty years into our new lives. The things we saw. People we never knew we met... all here."

"It's a *brokheh*, a blessing to sit together like this... with old friends."

Zoli waited for the right moment, asked, "Does anyone know Itzchak Tarkai?"

"The name sounds familiar."

"Do you mean the artist?"

"Yes, ve were in the camps together. He said he vasn't going to come, but I vas wondering if he did."

"I saw his work in the gallery off the lobby."

"Imagine that. How many artists, poets, intellectuals were lost?"

"Does anyvone know if he's here?" Zoli added.

"I'm sure someone would have announced his appearance, no?"

"Yes, he has made a name for himself." The conversation made its rounds, every one seated at the circular banquet table compelled to add to the discussion.

"We bought a piece of his on a cruise ship. Was it the smartest thing to do?"

Zoli atypically shied from sales pitched, stayed on topic, lodged in time remembered. "How about Chaim Kemény? Or any of the other boys who worked on the farm at Mauthausen... Tibor, Istvan... my brother... Jenő... any of them...?" Silence fell, statistics surged through their heads. Zoli broke from dejection. "It'd be nice to see someone I remember... know that they made it out..." Words led to faces twisted; they were all reduced to the children who agonized under the thumb of Nazi maleficence; that feeling didn't just linger, it was always there. Zoli found strength in an audience that could relate, continued in a whisper. "Ve were under the vatch of those sadistic pieces of garbage Ziereis, Heim. I vish I could cut them all out of my mind."

The Nazi commandant's name sent the table into a collective recoil, some went as far as to spit on the hotel's wall-to-wall carpeting in disdain.

"I vish I could forget those bastards..."

"May they rot in hell."

"Ve can never let anyone forget vhat happened to us, vhy it happened, how it could happen again," Zoli said. "You never know vhen another powerful man, or men, vill come around and persuade the veak minded to follow their vicked lead."

"It is a different time. The world is a different place."

"Things are not as different as you think." Zoli recounted discrimination witnessed, from the time of his youth to the Jim Crow South through to the Skin Heads that harassed him and his wife in Budapest. "Maybe it has happened. Ve never see it coming. Hitler vas elected, remember?"

His stories washed the table in the essence of their respective lives; minor differences filled out by shared discomfort, familiar prejudice buried in plain sight.

They fell into a lull, loosened ties, unbuttoned shirts, as ruffled pants shifted uncomfortably in firm banquet hall chairs.

"We should think this way?" Why worry about what has not happened?" one of them questioned.

"Anything could happen," another added.

"They do happen..." Zoli's idea caught on, his incredulous audience couldn't help but understand. "It is always happening."

"You can never tell how a person will act when they have been taught how to feel, not to feel," one of the older attendees added. "And that is something we have all been victims of, as Schopenhauer asserts..."

"Bullshit!" An interruption, point of contention, a purely emotional response to an entirely emotional moment. "Bullshit!" This was a betrayal too deep for the mentally and physically scarred to comprehend. "Bullshit!" They were addled by experience, comforted by denial. "How can you say humanity hasn't grown from what we went through?"

Excitement and alcohol pushed and pulled all strings, the attendees held prey to their unrelenting emotions.

"We have. The world... I don't know..."

"It's true..." Zoli's sad eyes reflected the feelings surrounding him, undeniable truths were the hardest to swallow. "It vas vorse... They divided us..."

Banquet staff ordered to bus table brought back uneaten meals; reunion conversation spoiled many otherwise insatiable appetites.

"Everyone knows that Jewish Kapos betrayed their own people to save their own skin."

"They turned a blind eye."

"Who turned a blind eye? We were liberated. You were liberated."

"I can still hear the American bombs... closer... closer." The discourse devolved, individual emotions and images resurfaced; smiles extended, the thought of the Nazis getting what they deserved brightened the moment. "Boom."

Zoli remained on point. "I talked to a little girl who vas there, now all grown, who helped us back then. She saw Jews vith the Nazis, not Kapos, not prisoners, not soldiers, but Jewish children stood shoulder-to-shoulder with them. She saw it vith her own eyes. Said she vould never forget." His audience remained stoic, unmoved. "She said they helped round us up, those children led them right to vhere ve vere hiding."

"This is just another story." Anger poked at Zoli's assertions.

"Is it? Zey found us, so many of us..." Zoli's usual calm fled the moment. "How do ve know vhat happened?"

"She hides her involvement, her shame. It's the human condition."

"The way we do?" a statement dressed like a question inserted from the round.

"We can't, so why go back? Who needs to revisit the pain when it's already inescapable?"

After a lifetime, murders and mayhem before prepubescent eyes continued to disturb the reactions of the silver haired caucus; they all knew what the other was thinking, feeling.

"My brother died because ve vere found, ve vere so close, he could have made it..." Zoli felt his words.

Grown men held back tears as glimpses of family they would never know impacted them where they sat; chest pains, anxiety pills, and cocktails were distributed as needed, grief their only untreatable symptom.

"He vouldn't have gone missing..." Zoli looked up and

into a mirror of emotion; lives altered in unison drowned in pain unrelenting. "I don't even know vhat happened to him. He could have been looking for me." Pathos cut through the poorly circulated air, weighed heavy on present company. "I traveled so many miles over so many years, no accomplishment felt complete without him there... vithout knowing vhat happened to him..." Zoli looked out at his brothers born in servitude, found unspoken understanding, and continued on. "After all these years, I just vish to know."

16
———

The smooth sound of a high speed rail system hummed to the expansive view of the Israeli landscape; Zoli lulled in and out of slumber. Topography as diverse and distinct as the young nation drew him lucid, caught between the real and remembered.

The disquietudes of war stood hand in hand with the countryside, both ever-present, embedded in every inch. From Crusades to Caliphates, conflicts were marked by changes in the atmosphere. Religious and ideological shifts always at odds, kept a whole nation on edge as it waited for the next paradigm to drop.

Zoli took it all in, focused on the familiar terrain that zipped by, a nickelodeon running at 24 frames per second through pages of history; lectures given in the hotel's many conference rooms in the days leading up to this trip rang fresh in his mind, added narration.

"On November 29th, 1947, the United Nations General Assembly Resolution #181 aimed to implement borders;

the British Mandate of Palestine was to split the Promised Land into two states. A Zionist paramilitary organization LEHI, founded by Abraham 'Yair' Stern, defended the fledgling Jewish state from another round of institutionalized prejudice. They were not going to give anything up after the horrific appropriations of the Shoah." Pure disdain, intellectual aversion, utter outrage carried over into the speech of hardliner. "He wasn't the only one unwilling to abide by U.N. rule; Arab leaders refused to give any land over for a Jewish state. They insisted a Palestinian state not exist alongside a Jewish state but rather on top of the Jewish State, instead of the Jewish state. Both sides were fixed in their ideals..."

The room was full of those with vested interests, facing a historian with the answers to the gaps of their lives lived, as had been documented in all manner of historical and educational media and literature, major motion pictures.

"Yair went as far as to twice attempt to ally himself with the Fascists. He hoped they would join the fight against the British occupiers of Palestine, and expected them to transfer all Jews from Nazi territories into the Promised Land." Slideshows and newsreels displayed Anglo occupation; curfews, and martial law failed to stymie the movement. Longtime enemies opposed the same foreign terms. There was no peace, lines were drawn.

"The English Navy blocked the flow of the *Ha'apala* immigrants from Europe," one of a number of lecturers would add; grainy black and white slides projected in a slow and clunky progression. Pictures of ships, and camps, and Jews locked helplessly in the struggle.

Zoli sat through talks that rendered a life enduring all

the camps from the Mauthausen to Feldafing, to internment on Cyprus, where the rush of immigrants had been
diverted by England's naval blockade, all before facing the
challenges of returning to his ancestral home; the pages of
history, he learned, now called it the *Aliyah Bet*. He was
there, it was his Exodus. Zoli stopped hearing words, saw
no presentation, as he glanced off into time.

With hopes of seeing the land of their forefathers, anxious
to be so close to home, 16-year-old Zoli was swept up in a
charge to the bow of a small cargo ship. A vessel unsuited
to carry passengers accommodated a crowd. Refugees
swayed en masse to the pulse of ocean, glimpses of the
homeland appeared through the haze of waves broken
against closed borders. The British Navy circled, closed in,
invaded space. Seawater crashed against the small craft,
spilled over its hull. Men, women, and children on the
verge of freedom held tight; Jews battled the force of diaspora, were willing to endure.

Lectures mixed together, realities tacked to Zoli's mind,
visions of English battleships intent on rendering the
needy nomadic pressed up on all sides of his mind. He
could still feel the mist of crashing waves against his face,
hear the creaks of structural integrity vibrating underfoot,
of wood planks buckling. The ship took on water. Their
collective struggle was far from over.

"After Yair's death, LEHI swayed left on the political
spectrum, declared support for National Bolshevism,

eeeeh." An exclamation for the significant, a young Israeli PhD was excited to continue, hands flailed. "Their efforts culminated in a series of attacks against British occupiers that rendered a great deal of LEHI's leadership imprisoned. A well-orchestrated plan was devised, a prison break that consisted of fighters in disguise and supported by stolen British military apparatus, including military vehicles armed to the teeth and ready for action."

This was all news to Zoli, all he knew was that he had to wait to fight for the Jewish homeland in an English run internment camp on an island sequestered by the Mediterranean; ancient impatience danced to the sound of the presentation, forgotten experiences, disturbing photos, and first-landings clips on grainy 16mm film stock that painted history in flickers of black and white.

Another lecturer had all the dates at the ready, timelines and maps used as visual aids. "On May 4th at 4:20pm in 1947, a date chosen to coincide with the UN's general assembly discussing the future of The British Mandate of Palestine, the operation to free their brethren from the British commenced. From inside and out, the Acre Prison was hit simultaneously at its weakest point. They blew a hole into the building, vacated the prison of its prisoners, Jews and Arabs alike freed to fight for what they claimed as their own."

Mile after mile of contested land sped across Zoli's eyeline, lodged into the top of his head. Gunfire and bullets percussed through daydreams. His mind drifted on topic.

"This as well as other offensives gave the Yishuv Jews, the Jews who were here before Israeli independence, hope. A distinction that had been made since the late 20th

century. New momentum continued to damage British prestige on the international stage." He continued, slow, deliberate, always pro-Israel. The weight of the audience's attention set the tone with sable intensity; a few caught snoring were promptly shushed as lessons continued. "The embarrassment also sped up the formation of the UNSCOP Committee that took a hands-on approach to deciding who would govern the disputed territory. After many visits to the land, and exhaustive discussions over its future, the UN put Resolution #181 into the books. It divided the land between the historical occupants of the region; after 5000 years of wandering through a proverbial desert of hate and prejudice, the Jewish people were finally home in the midst of a battle with new neighbors displeased by OUR very existence."

Men and women mingled between events, made time to reflect, to adjust to the official history of their own lives. Wonder passed from one to another through each date learned for the first time of events lived through so long ago.

By May 24th, 1948, the underground resistance was disbanded and rebranded as the IDF; 18-year-old Zoli had no idea what auspices he was fighting under, only knew what he was fighting for. His light blue eyes turned heavy through his progression. From victim to victor, the tumult on both sides of war had taken a large chunk out of the good looking young man, and was replaced by the twist of ancient discomfort.

"ITZCHAK!" Field Commander Ariel Sharon, the future Israeli Prime Minister, used Zoli's Hebrew name in the midst of battle; bullets streaked, explosions turned

vehicles, smoke billowed in their efforts to reclaim land. The language was rough like the landscape, elegant in its connectivity, the harsh highs and solemn lows like dunes shifting forever in sand. *"MOVE YOUR BATTALION! GET OVER HERE!"*

"YES, SIR." Zoli raced to his commanding officer, shedding the past for a triumphant future, rising through the ranks of the IDL that went from flouting British control to fighting for its U.N. mandated borders, and then some. With a rifle strapped to his back, Zoli awaited orders.

Gunfire cracked the horizon from a distant, single source; conditions worsened, sand storms brewed. The sun fought to crack clouds of granular fragments that swirled off dunes in gusts that howled like feuding deities. The young commander lowered his binoculars; eagle eyes looked out, locked on target. He issued an order. "Take that bastard out..."

Zoli immediately dropped to the ground, shimmied into position, hidden in the endless sea of sand and stone, cacti and succulents the only sign of life in the arid landscape. He lay in a prone position; heels flat on the ground to steady his body in line with the British rifle conveniently left behind by occupying forces. He measured distances, squared his shoulders, placed his mark in the crosshairs of his scope before adjusting for wind. His blue eye closed to focus, long exhales soothed nerves as Zoli put his finger on the trigger; flesh pressed against metal clenched, squeezed, steadied, released.

The barrage of sniper fire kept Field Commander Ariel Sharon's unit locked to their position; a group of young men, convinced from above that the Jewish State hung in the balance, waited on edge to get back on the offensive.

They were determined to secure the strategically critical city of Latrun; Operation Bin Nun was Sharon's opportunity to gain significant ground; both in land and in politics. They were sent to initiate the battle, hold ground and cut off supply lines until more troops were made available. But, Sharon seized an opportunity to exceed expectations, knew he could overrun the enemy from his outlining position, expected to use the desert to his advantage. He ordered his men to flank the enemy, when they got caught in sniper fire. They took cover and waited on Zoli.

His one shot rang out; a bullet twisted from the barrel of Zoli's gun, traveled unobstructed to silence the threat. Zoli checked the outcome through his scope, then jumped to his feet, and stood at attention. *"Yes, Commander!"*

The unit broke ranks, momentarily dropped pretense, acted their age while congratulating Zoli on his shot with pats on the back and the meaningful clasping of hands, prayer never far from such a mitzvah. They would end up accomplishing the mission, securing the land, and controlling the region.

"Field Commander Sharon's reputation for appropriating and keeping land had spread through the IDF. His unit within the Alexandroni Brigade, the 72nd Battalion, consisted mostly of young Holocaust survivors and was key in obtaining victory in the Arab-Israeli War of 1948." Israeli strategy, and early battle plans were projected, pointed to as reference. "Sharon's questionable tactics won many a confrontation, the results of which were highly respected, and helped him rise through the ranks of the military. Despite his hard line and disregard for orders, he would fulfill an ambition that took him to the pinnacle of Israeli power."

The ring of his life-turned-to-history flooded Zoli's senses. The view out of his moving tour through the Jewish towns that popped up between the shoreline and Road 2 punctuated the efforts of his youth.

He glazed over in thought, all the battles, all the death, were worthwhile. Were they worthwhile? He drifted through the entirety of his journey, considered, "We have a safe place to call home, the sacrifice we all made was for the greater good. We will never be exterminated like Nazi garbage again."

His service to the nation resonated within the senior citizen; determination remained apparent in his straightened posture, pride. Never forgotten events continued to flood in through the landscape, were tucked behind patches of hoodia gordonii succulents native to the area; their orange flowers littered the pasture in various stages of bloom, looked pink in the glare of the desert sun. The familiar heat pressed against Zoli's face through large windows; cacti needles tilted defensively in the direction of the moving train.

Zoli remembered steadying his rifle, how he had grown into his uniform and rank, and his history of masterful gunshots, like he had never left.

Well-trained and well-fed, Zoli's broad physique squatted into a kneeling position. He took a second to scope the immediate area for a rock large and flat enough to shield him from the evasive succulent's obtrusive needles. He steadied himself against the rock, pressed his eyes onto the scope, draped his finger across the trigger, set to fire when...

A force barreled him backward. Taken off his feet, back first into the sand, Zoli focused on the bullet that careened off the rock he just placed against his chest. Enemy fire had ricocheted, redirected to knock the helmet right off of his head. He lived to tell the tale.

Continued dedication, determination, and an unwavering sense of duty propelled Zoli to the rank of captain. He was placed in charge of a full battalion; their performance was his responsibility.

One evening he had gone to inspect the perimeter of gained territory, interacting with soldiers on patrol, peering out over the starlit horizon for unexpected movement, imminent threats. He moved from position to position, quickly and quietly under the undulating heavens when three shots broke the silence; a sound wave danced through the desert, disrupted sleeping birds. Bullets pranced under open skies and over restful lands directly towards Captain Zoltan Itzchak Gluck.

The next day Zoli court-martialed the soldier on guard who he charged not with shooting at a superior officer but for missing such a close target. The delicate balance of Israeli sovereignty would fail to exist with shots that poor.

Zoli shook his head, grey hair kept long and combed back loosened, fell in front of his aged blue eyes; his white eyelashes, full eyebrows and unmanageable accent were remnants of his lifelong rollercoaster ride. He cracked a smile at his good fortunes, at the absurdity of his youthful actions, the bravado of his life reborn. He remembered how reckless he once was: fights for grenades nearly detonated in hand during training exercises, races on military horses through the Sinai that ended in a tangle of broken bones and open gashes, motorcycles and military vehicles maneuvered to within an inch of their capacity, young soldiers leaping over canyons when they weren't dodging bullets or snuffing out Molotov cocktails. Zoli had teetered on the precipice. He took his life into his own hands; it was the first thing many young male Holocaust survivors needed to do, live on their own terms. Zoli would never have all his wheels on the ground again.

He looked out at homes planted, towns nurtured, a population that reestablished its birthright. Zoli caught sight of families with children playing in a land protected out of necessity. Threats seen, experienced, and unimaginable lurked in the everyday, were felt in each innocent laugh, all family reunions.

The sight of what he had fought for continued past his eye-line; the moving train barreled through the years.

Zoli saw the foundation and formation of his Israel; the land Abraham was led to was his to defend. The fragility of its being was and continued to be hard to escape. Soldiers did whatever they could to protect their borders, guard their endangered sovereignty.

They continued to fight for lands contested for the last 5755 years. Its right to exist was all that mattered to the emerging Jewish government. It operated under edict that they as a people had claim to their historical home; it was a need magnified after narrowly escaping genocide. A Semitic sanctuary was established through antiquity, politically and biblically significant to the Jewish people from the time of pharaohs and onward; generals marched on the tenets of the Old Testament, assigned providence to military actions. Zionism ignited the flame, fueled the fight; it enveloped a nation then became its culture.

Ariel Sharon's surly disposition, his continued call for conflict, and total dedication to the armed forces and aspiration for more ended Zoli's military career; Zoli decided that his life was going to be for living, not for fighting.

They reveled in the camaraderie, young and brave fulfilled their calling, fought shoulder to shoulder; kids moved towards their prescribed fate. Zoli was in the push, called the shots, was an exceptional officer, but could never escape the daydreams of his lost youth on the Great Hungarian Plain.

His time in Israel buzzed by like the landscape, a blur of activity bridged into a singular entity. Communal kibbutz living offered him a familiar day-to-day, the predictable monotony of farm life was a welcome relief at the tail-end of his precarious exodus. The land he had fought so hard for was now giving back to its people. It was a place where they could contemplate their loss and heal, together. For some, it was a place to forget and start anew.

17

————

Zoli's train slowed, his mind drew to the present. He looked out onto the HaShmona Railway Station in Haifa, one of the older still remaining British structures in the port city. It was where Zoli had first landed in '47, fresh off his last detention, freedom birthed from the Mediterranean.

The city had grown out of and around crumbling English infrastructure; Israeli pride and ingenuity took up where Zoli's efforts left them. The modern city flourished in Sisyphean prosperity.

Zoli couldn't believe his eyes, wiped sweat from his brow. Desert heat lifted off roads, made way for scattered clarity. He was amazed at how the English factory town had turned into the Silicon Valley of the Middle East; IBM, Intel, Philips, Microsoft, Google, and Israeli tech companies Elbit, Zoran, and Amdocs would all have outposts close to Haifa's University. The adage *Pray in*

Jerusalem, Play in Tel Aviv, and Work in Haifa, stood apparent in the visible signage.

Zoli serpentined through the interior and exterior elements of the Bauhaus style transportation hub, its blocky but functional concrete detail. He breached its confines, was immediately embraced in the soothing incline of Mount Carmel. Its peaks pitched, verdant hillsides rolled into the country's third largest city, opened up to the sweet blue horizon of an available sea.

Zoli remained still, appreciated the expanse. The urban development, the satisfying view of Do Beach, its boardwalk, and cafes were all full of life, Jewish families with children, so many children, free to enjoy the land of their forefathers.

Zoli signed deeply, thought about the fragility of peace; it tainted the picture-perfect composition, prompted anxieties retrievable from the population's collective consciousness. He was just 89 miles south of Damascus. Up until the Israeli-Jordan Peace Treaty sponsored by American President Bill Clinton on October 26, 1994, all of Israel's neighbors sought to wipe the entire country from existence, from history. However, things didn't feel much different a year later.

Zoli scanned the crowd, turned towards the sound of his name.

"Zoli!"

He searched faces, examined the determination in each Israeli's gait, pride pronounced in each liberated footstep.

"Over here, old man." Tarkai walked towards Zoli with arms outstretched; his cigarette dangled on a second thought from his bottom lip, affixed with arid resolve.

"Itzi." They met with an embrace; comfort that they needed as children experienced now as adults under the familiar glare of the Judean Desert, neither in a hurry to release the other from the reprieve.

"It has been too long." Zoli fell into Hungarian, rippled back from adolescent conversations.

"What are you talking about? I just saw you in New York." Hebrew was Tarkai's language of choice; travels influenced both their accents, stained their speech with an almanac of experiences.

Their hug lingered.

"It is good to see you, brother." Hungarian dropped for Hebrew, a progression most familiar, from one home land to another.

Tarkai's smile said all. He pulled back, took a last puff, extinguished his cigarette in an available trash receptacle, and turned to Zoli.

"Come on, I want to show you something."

He pulled Zoli away from the train station, like the two boys they never were allowed to race towards a pleasant unknown, towards an old Israeli army jeep.

"Just like the ones you drove in the army, right?"

"I cannot believe it," Zoli reacted as he saddled up to the vehicle. The impact of past and present comingling was palpable; a cumulative history glowed off their relationship like a beacon had pedestrians stop and stare. Men of their age represented the past that the present was built upon.

They climbed into the vehicle; a flash of familiarity surged through Zoli; a young man's smile crossed his lips. He buckled into the passenger's side seat, turned to Tarkai, took it all in, then spoke. "You didn't come to the reunion."

They locked eyes.

"What would I want to go to that for?" Tarkai excavated a smoke from its pack, placed and lit it between his lips in a single well-practiced move, took his time taking the next of many long hard drags. Smoke lingered in a haze that cleared out of the roofless vehicle. Tarkai continued, "Haven't we given enough?"

"Yes, maybe we have." Zoli watched his old friend start the jeep, its AMC 3.983 liter 6-cylinder petrol fuel injection engine shook its reinforced frame, launched their progress through the streets of Haifa.

"Ok, I can drop my stuff at the hotel before dinner, maybe have a quick shower, change..."

Tarkai turned to stare at Zoli. His cigarette dangled by sheer will from its familiar perch. He shook his head, a boldness punctuated Tarkai's good-natured-assertion. "You're staying with me, brother."

"No."

"I have room in my studio."

"You sure?"

A smile developed between the two; a connection drawn from the depths of camaraderie, an understanding that came naturally and without effort.

"Why didn't you tell me before I booked a room?"

They shared a laugh; the money lost was worth the story.

"This is better. You'll have your own apartment."

Basement light from sidewalk level, windows collected sea air, a fine film that diffused light, obstructed a line of sight. The untreated luminescence washed Tarkai's studio in an ethereal glow. Time stood still; canvases opened windows unto the past, present, and future, plied all four walls, were stacked in piles, and filled every available inch of the space: Ladies in Haifa take tea by the sea, lunch at the vineyards, drank wine in in the bars and cafes that lined the neighborhood; Sarah, Rachel, Josephine in place, enveloped by an abundance of texture and depth.

"Not bad?" Tarkai turned to ask with a crooked smile.

"Amazing," Zoli replied.

Nomadic tongues danced through time together; Hebrew made way for Hungarian, Yiddish injected through exclamations, English made its expected appearances as they traipsed across subject matter, business and pleasure; moments never mentioned screamed the loudest, they churned under the surface and were actively redirected.

Tarkai retrieved a reserve pack of smokes from a convenient crevasse, a force of habit brought him to light it as he pressed tubes of color onto an infinitely used palette; signature hues dried in layers on the flat board, years of paintings commemorated in a swirl left by the process. His brush glided through fresh colors, streaked in stokes transferred and arranged.

Zoli couldn't help but peruse the works in progress, riffled through watercolors ready for frames, paintings that had been worked and reworked, never finished; a fold out cot tucked into the corner caught his eye.

"Youz kiddings me?" The 66-year-old shot his friend an askance glance.

"Like you said, it's only for one night..." Cigarette half-smoked, paintbrush in hand, Tarkai walked and talked sideways. "You stay with me." He spoke unconsciously; his full focus remained on his mistresses. The words that came to his mouth were instantly forgotten; the artist was transported, eyes glazed over with peace of mind, lulled in a perfect distraction. "Yeah. Yeah. We talk all night."

"You smoke all night."

"Smoke, drink, talk... paint." He said, taking a drag, acrylic pooled at the tip of his applicator, peaked and at the ready, waited on inspiration alone.

Zoli watched his friend move from one painting to the next, bursts of magenta accented existing compositions, instinctive brushstrokes added to the majesty; into the mind of the distracted painter, time and place faded into the background, all lost in the movements of Tarkai's most-natural impulses.

Hours passed, light faded.

The sun set over water, its blaze raced from the horizon, clung to the heavens, extended out towards the southernmost shores of Eastern Europe. Salty winds twirled over the city, extended out over a dinner party on a familiar patio, like stepping into one of Tarkai's paintings. Remains of a home cooked meal were set out in a composition torn directly from any of his canvases hanging around the world, conversation reserved for present company.

"...I just don't think they're ever done," Tarkai finished his point.

"He needs me to tell him when to stop." Rachel Tarkai anchored the evening; often a model for her husband, her desert accent was laced with laughter, moved their rapport forward. "What? I'm serious. Believe me."

Her wine-fueled levity drew smiles over empty plates and refilled stemware. Haifa's lights danced through the night, bounced off the adjacent Mediterranean.

"They wouldn't ever be finished if I didn't come and tear them out of his hands. It's like he escapes into each one of those scenes, gets trapped in there..." She shot him loving looks that could melt steel, a uniquely Semitic balance of caring, indifference, resolve, love and guilt.

"I could sell any piece in your studio with a phone call," Zoli announced to the bottom of his emptied glass. The blood brothers looked at one another, clasped hands, smiled wide. "If you vould let your girls go..."

"Should I be jealous of 'your girls?'" The expected playful disinterest and imperturbable strength of an Israeli was evident in her conviction. "We'd starve if it were up to him."

She began to clear the table; Zoli got to his feet, quick to help.

"No, please, you are our guest," she insisted.

Too late, Zoli lined dinner plates and dishes up his arm, balanced cutlery and water glasses with style, techniques well-practiced throughout his years in the service industry. "No problem."

Wine, conversation, and more than enough secondhand smoke filled the air, stretched long into the night, and left Zoli exhausted.

"I must wish you both a good night." He checked his watch, left with a smile, kissed Rachel; sincerity traveled through the words: "What a great night."

Itzchak insisted on walking Zoli into the midnight streets of his city. They took their time through great developments, new neighborhoods. Tarkai pointed out the growth of his nation one block at a time.

Back at his studio. The painter worked his way through

the space, the dim lamp light set up in a way to illuminate the pieces he intended to tinker with through the night, a habit difficult to break even with a friend in from overseas.

Zoli prepared for bed through blades of illumination with eyes on works in progress. He sat on the edge of his bed and watched his friend in action.

"This is something else," was all Zoli could manage to say.

Tarkai was in tune, one with the task at hand; he smoked mindlessly, painted enthusiastically, silent the entire time.

"So, great, Itzi..." Zoli adjusted himself, failed to find the cot's sweet spot. "So, great to get to see you..."

Tarkai was entranced, danced from brushstroke to brushstroke, movements that were hidden in the final product.

"I do wish you could have made it to the reunion."

Tarkai slowed, stopped, stared at what he'd done, how far he'd come. His progress was all expansive, took up every inch of his eye-line, all of the wide open studio space. Acts he employed to keep the pain of his early life forgotten.

Zoli filled the silence with Hungarian, "There were a lot of people there..." His choice of language took them back to the ever-shifting borders of their childhood.

Tarkai turned away from the conversation, continued to add layers of colors and light to his perspectives; positive emotions and ever-present ease created and exaggerated in perpetuity. The work embodied his need for relief, distraction, a collective sigh. Tarkai allowed his art to speak for itself, layers of protection from what haunted him most, his subject matter being its antithesis, conceived to counter all retained and repressed insecurities.

"So many olderly people..." Zoli laughed, continued in English, "Everyone remembers everything differently."

Zoli chipped away at the wall Tarkai had built around himself.

"Did I tell you I found the family who owned that barn?"

That barn—all Zoli needed to say to perturb the artist mid-stroke; an out-of-place line marked a painting in testament of the conversational transgression.

"None of them remembered anything like what I heard from Ms. Schroeder..." He looked to his friend. "I'm talking about ze little girl who vas there that day. Do you remember?"

"Zoli, please..." Tarkai broke his resolve, tilted with a swing of his hands that non-verbally asked his friend, *Why talk about this?*

"You know I talked to her on the phone?"

Regrets clung to spines, clenched tight, shockwaves surged through marrow, tingled toes, and bled on the inside.

Forever a man of few words, Tarkai grunted murmurs, gurgled discomfort from deep within, defiantly turned back to work.

"Ve vere on the phone for an hour. The tings she told me..."

Tarkai couldn't paint anymore. He stepped to clean and place his tools aside. No smoke, no wine, no brush; just a flood of feelings misdirected for decades allowed to tear through ancient walls erected in Tarkai's subconscious.

"Zoli, why go back there? Look at us: my home by the sea, yours on a river. Look how far we have come..." Paint on his pants and shirt, he bent to retrieve the good stuff from a cabinet tucked under rolls of unused canvas.

He turned to hand his friend a glass raised, eye contact; sips turned to gulps that were promptly topped off. The paintings kept good company, men surrounded by women who met every situation with a flirty composure that played against Zoli's festering concerns.

"People sometimes ask how I can paint such colorful, light subjects after so much loss." Tarkai drank, went for a smoke, lit it, talked with it; a flaming red point made with each jab. "I say how can I not." He took broad steps through his studio, fed off his efforts, symbiosis complete and apparent, as he continued to explain himself. "I paint to celebrate the beauty of the world, forever young girls, hard-ons on canvas, nothing worth forgetting, everything within reach. You have that too. We're lucky."

"I am still there. I am right there," Zoli mouthed, an inadvertent admission.

"What are you talking about?" Tarkai was scared to ask.

After reeling from his confession for a second, Zoli gave in. "It isn't a memory, Itzi. It never vas."

"Zoli, what do you want?" was the polite way for Tarkai to try and end the conversation. He threw up his hands, red paint slashed color stained walls. "What is the point?"

"I am there now is ze point." Zoli was locked in, eyes on to his friend and on their past.

"You're crazy," Tarkai insisted, red paint continued to fly in in the face of his every assertion, acrylic was sent in all directions. "Why are you taking me there with you?" He continued to splash his angst against finished and half-finished paintings, the polished concrete floor, the mini fridge, file cabinets, countertops, ceiling fan, and the cot Zoli was meant to sleep were all splattered red. "I don't want to go back." The artist's proclamation closed in, blinded him. He could no longer see straight, his arms flailed in his effort to come up with his next words. He was in a panic, at a loss, spatter sailed as he tried to talk, couldn't talk. He had fallen out of his regular cool, confronting his past left him seeing red, everywhere red, everything red. "I can't."

"You vere there." Zoli stood toe to toe with his friend.

"No."

"You are there vith me now"

"No." Tarkai's escape ran out of room, the walls of time closed in on him. His arms fell to his side, his eighth cigarette of the night bounced off his floor, stepped on till extinguished. "What are you doing?"

The lingering mania that was long at rest in their yesteryears flooded the space between the two, mixed with smoke to create a noxious mix harmful to both body and soul.

"I don't know." Zoli paused to think, pause was what they had, every moment to themselves was a luxury that was never taken for granted. The pain was fluid in each of Zoli's words. "Jenő made it out of the camps alive, he made it." The truth, the possibilities swelled his progress, he slowed to the unknown. "If what I heard is true... we could have..."

"But we didn't!" A sharp interruption from an agitated man, Tarkai jumped at the thought. He caught himself before he was overrun by an impulse; centered himself before he continued. "He didn't."

A tiny crimson globule sailed off in the unnerved exchange, it caught Zoli on the cheek, so small he didn't notice. It streaked red down Zoli's face.

"Those people, that little girl and her mother, risked their lives to help us." Zoli struggled. "They sacrificed everything they had left."

Tarkai turned from the truth, his back spoke for him.

"Do you know what happened to them?" Zoli begged. "Do you remember anything?"

"They lived, they died." Tarkai blurted out. His bravado repelled angst for a long as it could, not too long. "They were going to kill us all, Zoli, all of us," Tarkai declared. "Nazi bastards ruined it for everyone, we know this." Arms outstretched, he stood confident in the assertion that followed: "Do we need to go back?"

Zoli looked at his friend. The darkest moments of their lives were fresh. "I need you to remember."

Tarkai stirred in a heaviness, finished his thought: "I don't want to go back." He fended off his long buried burden, a pressure deep within that pounded pounds. He allowed his most guarded feelings to sneak through the cracks of his manufactured defenses; hard thoughts were said out loud, the brilliance of their surroundings was affected by the weight of what came flooding in from the past to manifest in the tears of grown men.

The two of them fought to contain the layers of grief and depravity experienced.

Zoli stirred from their memoriam. "I can't anymore. How could I live with such betrayal, never thought I had to, maybe it was better vhen I didn't know..." Whiskey whirled his momentum, amplified his disdain. "Especially to a man as cruel as Ziereis. How do you move on from that?"

"It wasn't Commandant Franz Ziereis who wanted those boys..." Tarkai added in a whisper not meant to ever be heard.

"Vhat?"

A moment stained, a paintbrush dropped, tilted askew in regression, slow-motion as it hit the industrial floor with the full weight of the moment; a small red pool left to dry like blood against the polished concrete.

"It was Chaim," Tarkai said, avoiding eye contact. He turned to pour himself another drink, continued. "It was the Doctor. Dr. Death he would be called..."

"What are you talking about?"

"That day, Zoli, the last day we saw each other..." Electricity charged through Tarkai's everything; a tsunami of memories tore off his psyche, urged him into its painful release. "They got me, Zoli, they got me... I was beaten, they only spared me when that piece-of-shit doctor got there."

The hardest parts obliterated the artist's senses, he stood silent, took a look inside, at the loss, his loss; the moment lingered, was broken only by his tobacco addiction, smoke that settled his nerves.

Zoli waited for his friend to continue; a Pandora's Box opened wide, its festering insides apparent and abysmal.

"He brought me back to Mauthausen, to his residence just outside the walls, a cold repurposed castle." Tarkai's words crumbled between heavy drags, each pull worked to give Tarkai an out, an excuse to not finish his story. With his brother-in-catastrophe present, he deferred repression for the opportunity to share a most gut-wrenching secret, relieve himself of its weight.

"I never told anyone..." Tarkai stammered.

"I am here." Zoli reached out to him, drawn to speaking Hebrew. "I am here for you, brother." The following seconds felt like an eternity; Zoli watched Tarkai confront his own story before he uttered another word.

"That sick Nazi treated us like his pets, a home full of desperate animals all looking for their next meal." Tarkai shook his head, infuriated, spit as he proclaimed, "He fed us, bathed us, gave us new clothes, played a sick game... "

Zoli hung on his friend's next impulse, expected anything. Tarkai locked eyes with his friend with a severity as hard as the floors they stood on.

"Pet us."

Tears welled in the stoic men's eyes. They reverted into the little boys they were. They grabbed one another, consoled each other through each atrocity measured to the millimeter.

"And, I wasn't the only one, I was just the newest one..."

Every murder and every hardship, all the abuse and degradation, every moment spent in those inhumane conditions was present.

"Chaim was there, others too, all boys doing what they had to." Tarkai chain smoked, lit a new cigarette with the old, unconsciously shook his head in an attempt to lose memories just verbalized. "They did whatever sick things that monster asked them to do, and they loved him for it..."

The disgust was apparent, revulsion swirled in the mix of adverse reactions, Zoli was aghast at what he heard. Blood rushed from of his face, he turned deathly pale.

"Zoli..."

The painter braced himself; a haze filled his lungs, clouded the room. The nicotine that calmed his nerves also veiled his face. Tarkai took his time conjuring his words, and speaking them.

"I was next... those sick old bastards had a harem of boys to abuse and I was going to be next ..." A frigid cold shocked his posture; he contorted in hindsight. "What could make men so sick?"

18

———

Franz Ziereis enjoyed the prosperity of the German Empire, the second German Reich, as it existed through the first decade of his life. His youth was filled with the comforts afforded by incredible economic growth. Under Emperor Wilhelm I, the homeland thrived, grew rich and strong. Employment and the standard of living were at an all-time high, industry soared. The bar was set, there was work for everyone, and all whom lived under that prosperity thought it would last forever.

A hegemony was in place; 27 constituent states; territories, kingdoms, duchies, grand duchies, principalities, free Hanseatic cities and an imperial territory were all unified by the time Emperor Wilhelm II took his father's place. The nation states under Germany's auspices participated in collective affluence, in the unprecedented efficiency in manufacture and design; factories thrived, railways were built to connect the expansive empire. A thump of pride coursed through its populous.

Heinrich Ziereis provided for his young wife in the foundries that helped fuel German expansion. With the work that drove the economy in hand, the people knew they were all a part of it; every man, woman, and child felt like they benefitted from the boon. Heinrich worked his hands to the bone and earned the promotions he thought guaranteed him an enviable life.

Workers enjoyed health and accident insurance, maternity benefits, pension plans, and public biergartens for their service to the crown. The mirage of freedom extended into the state run press that lauded and overrepresented the party line of one vote for every man in a Reichstag. In actuality, the powered elite propagated this sense of involvement for all men in order to combat revolt. It turned out that strong industry and successful social programs were enough to keep the population preoccupied, docile, and content. But, empires prefer to fall from within anyway.

Wilhelm II's foreign policy, ineffective leadership, budding welfare state, and poor military decisions plunged the great nation into its first bouts of insecurity; its borders, the economy, and social order were all jeopardized by a flippant leader's whims.

Heinrich Ziereis's young family grew out of its infancy directly into the unknowns of world war; the fate of their stability was to be determined by the waves of death that drowned a continent and forever changed the standing and security of every citizen within Imperial Germany.

Abuses in the home and at work were the status quo; German people required the best from each other, punishments and subjugation to the state, to superiors, parents, and royalty was expected. Children received reprimand with a sense of duty, without complaint, taken as an oath for a better Germany that matured with the strongest military in the world.

The Crown, captains of industry, and the common man lost their identity. Industry shifted to a military footing; their innovations now armed and supplied nationalist efforts, defended the rightful superiority of the German people, but the effort was daunting. The world stood opposed.

All Ziereis wanted to do was provide for his family, a need that was obliterated by the conflict that would define him, that took him to the front lines; trench warfare, endless bloodshed, perpetual slow deaths were difficult on the homeland.

The German Empire's power wore thin with cut supply lines and stalemates on multiple fronts, millions left dead in the hand-dug ditches of European battlefields; families starved in their own homes; a generation grew up without. Death was a way of life.

After their defeat, the monarchy was abolished; their fate sealed, international opposition overpowered them and left a vacuum where the powerful kingdom once stood. The poor forgotten masses, veterans struggling to survive, and proud Germans whom had lost it all turned their vigor towards the wealthy, blamed royalty and "Socialist Jews" for the destruction of their prosperity.

The obliteration of the German ideal left a population churning. They drowned their sorrows in overflowing steins of their threatened way of life. Bier halls were rebuilt out of necessity, gave those with nowhere else to go the distraction they needed.

Home-life, homeland, every person diminished within the pitiful remnants of the once great empire; a devastating culture crash buried Germany under the weight of foreign mandate. A desperation permeated the culture, affected all it crossed, became status quo.

Little Franz Ziereis heard his father's cries; rage-fueled tears tore through his return; drinking to forget rendered a national pastime. The desperate man of the house took his frustrations out on his wife and child. He used large wooden spoons or glasses emptied of intoxicants to flout his worthlessness on their backs. He stood over the bed of his child, delirious; lights off, doors closed, power and control temporarily regained in the hides of those closest to him. It was the only power Heinrich Ziereis had left.

Inspired by the Russian revolution and its outcome, the German people took up arms, stormed the streets; a year-long revolt obliterated the remnants of the monarchy.

The Weimar Republic established itself in the summer of 1919, a social democracy that sought to include all citizens. However, over its short existence, the Republic could not ease mounting economic pressures. The country plunged into prolonged bouts of hyperinflation and depression, a loaf of bread for a month's worth of wages.

Germans were once again without food, but there was always plenty of bier.

Crying over his beaten wife, the woman he insisted he still loved was left in an inhuman twist of bones dropped like a ragdoll on a little girl's bed.

Heinrich Ziereis drained the last of his schnapps,

searched for more, winding up with empties hurled in an unrelenting furor; Franz was often the only one left to face his father's wrath. He threw himself between his parents; his mom's blood streaked across his arms and clothes as he laid out over her.

"Leave her alone!"

"The world is a horrible place, no one cares about us, no one cares about you..." Heinrich tried to steady himself, off kilter as he stepped towards his compromised family, "And, I have to come home to this?" German spoken gently in contrast to the gravity of the situation. "How can I be a man with a home like this?"

"Stop it." Frau Ziereis stirred conscious with the command, the last of her strength designated to protect her child; an effort proved ineffective.

The drunken fiend grabbed his boy by the arm, held him close; conflict tore through innards, rage spit through eyes, inconsolable.

"How can I live like this, boy?"

He threw the 8-year-old Franz against the wall, kicked his wife in the ribs; evacuated breaths wiped objections from her lips. "You gave him this life. You wanted this child." Tears continued to flood up from contracted rage. "There is nothing out there for the German people. They raped us all..."

Young boys that were to be the future of the fatherland were now a constant reminder of the failures of the newly formed republic; they were idolized and sexualized for the benefit for all involved.

Heinrich included his boy in the impuissance, in the delirium it fed. He brought him along to different meetings and rallies; their unholy relationship braced by the mold of German stoicism, aligned with the pain of his peers, the troubles of his national family.

Entertainment distracted the populous; cabaret nights and open debauchery grasped at any remnant of lost abundance, turned heads away from their collective problems. Sex parties grew out of poverty, people played god when there was none for them to follow; it was the reprieve needed, Heinrich could no longer see his bleak reality.

All the German people wanted was to ascend to their rightful place in the world, to reclaim the respect they had earned but remained far from sight. They drowned themselves in hope for the improbable; Germany would never be great again, they collectively worried.

But then, in an instant, the *Machtergreifung*; fire destroyed the Reichstag, brought the representational government controlled by the wealthy to the ground. Out of the ashes rose a single democratically elected leader who stole power and kept it by fulfilling brutal promises; a litany of aggressions that were required to bring about Deutschland's mythical potential.

Hope spread through the country; Heinrich took his family to stadiums and parades, reveled in the regained momentum of his nation and its leader who set the economy ablaze with a push in military manufacturing. Reinvigorated by the possibilities, Heinrich threw his right arm out at a 45-degree angle, fingers held at eye level, pointed to the sky with a howl of "*HEIL HITLER!*"

Father and son caught the wave of consensus that blanketed the nation, a shawl on a cold Bavarian night. They learned the problems that haunted the nation were not the fault of the great men and women of Germany but of foreign manipulators, immigrants who stole their jobs, and the Jews.

Heinrich was proud to have his son join the ranks of the *Hitlerjugend*; parents stood straight, tears of joy welled eyes, mothers said their last goodbyes to children about to be transformed to better serve the Third Reich.

Franz found compatriots in the Hitler Youths; so many of the *jugend* experienced the same unspoken hardships at the hands of those they trusted most, a love that pained them in identical ways, and brought them together in their twisted understanding of love and respect.

They learned of their superiority, their rightful station in the world, from the annals of history; they were convinced that the vicar of the Germanic god himself ordained their efforts; exceptionalism forgave them of all their sins.

Franz Ziereis took the mixed emotions of his youth and balled them up in an explosive mix of camaraderie, sado-masochism, and pride for the Nazi party. For the first time in his life he felt like he belonged, was allowed to be true to himself.

Boys developed the bond of commonality, born in constant contact. They spent days in classes studying the history of their great Reich. They had every meal together, shared common bathrooms, showered in plain sight; no stalls offered a collective space for them to decompress, wet games of youth played by fit Aryans drenched in the bubbles of their retained superiority; the only love they would ever create belonged in shared sleeping barracks and pooled in the drains of their descent.

Within the still calm of lights out, in training camps erected far from distraction, Hitler Youth met their match. Boys consummated relationships the only way they had been taught how. They normalized trauma by creating new memories, redefined parameters; a grand release stained *Wehrmacht* issued linens.

Camaraderie blossomed through a rewritten history that gave them everything, righted all their wrongs. The collective posture of a people straightened, and the world took note.

Germany was given the honor of hosting the Olympics in 1936; Hitler was named *Time Magazine*'s Man of the Year in 1938. He took full credit for bringing his nation back from defeat and subjugation.

The people believed their leader; Franz Ziereis excelled, brought the weight of his insecurity into the ranks of the Nazi file. His particular brand of kind cruelty set him on the path of leadership; he was thought to have had a way with friend and foe alike. He went straight from the Hitler Youth to the *Schutzstaffel*, the paramilitary branch of the SS, a force that differentiated itself from the *Wehrmacht* that continued to abide by the Treaty of Versailles.

Ziereis's twisted childhood sprouted ersatz emotions, unable to differentiate between his inner grief and the woes of the fatherland; his stolen youth and abuse coated the furthest regions of his manipulated mind.

He fought for the sovereignty of his country with recognized valor, his stake was personal; the pain fueled the foulness of his actions, fermented atrocities that proved successful only in terms of their collective plight.

Ziereis was in control; the little boy who braved the fall of the German Empire and the trouble thereof was no longer available, was replaced by a soldier.

Hitler flouted international restraints and developed the German military beyond the limit of 100,000 troops. The army, navy, and air force of the *Wehrmacht*, resurrected from earlier reichs, were turned into a modern fighting force designed solely for the offensive restructuring of the globe.

Ziereis convinced himself that the discipline he dished out was how he cared, the way his father cared for him, abuse wrapped carefully in compassion. This disconnect served him well within the cogs of the war machine. It was a dirty little secret left out to air dry for all to see and accept.

In 1939, Ziereis happily accepted his post and rank of commandant at the death camp Mauthausen, but was forever soured by the fact that his father died before he could witness his son's ascension to such a grand station in life. Ziereis made sure to bring the lessons learned in his youth with him to the camps; tough-love propelled him to the heights of military esteem, built him a reputation he held close.

During his tenure, Ziereis was influenced by like-minded Nazis intent on an Aryan world. By 1941, Dr. Aribert Heim, a protégé of the infamous-in-his-time Dr. Josef Mengele and known as Dr. Death for his own horrendous deeds, had joined the ranks of the camp. Along with fellow sadist Dr. Oskar Dirlewanger, they devised the cruelest scheme of labor-induced death that would further subjugate an already hopeless population.

With progress well-regimented, command requested young boys to work appropriated lands nearby. By 1944 Hungarian Jews were flooding in; some were fated to die working, used up and turned to medical waste, others were hand-selected for their specific needs. Ziereis's doctors had pick of the litter.

For years, Ziereis's camp worked slave labor to death, they were sent to manufacturing jobs on an empty stomach, churned out goods and supplies for German companies like Bayer, BMW, and *Flugmotorenwerkes*. Slaves fed the *Wehrmacht*; an evil empire rested on the productivity of forced labor.

Ziereis ruled over the swath of land in southern Bavaria, off the banks of the Danube and in buildings built to fit his needs. He replaced the helplessness of his youth with the immense power of his position: head held high, chin up, beyond reprehension.

Taking daily strolls through vast fields, Ziereis enjoyed watching the emaciated work for the good of his people. Each boy represented a success, however, each death was a blow to his workforce.

Ziereis insisted he was taking perfect care of his young farmhands. "They could be working the quarries," he yelled, frowning at soldiers who threw food to his collection. He took the act as an insinuation that he was doing otherwise; a perverse inherited adoration left the commandant eternally confused. "They cannot see how we love our Jew boys, how we take care of them. They could be working in some factory or dying in the quarries," he explained to Doctor Oskar Paul Dirlewanger. Low to the ground and hunched over in his uniform, Dirlewanger didn't need convincing, his pocked face ever attentive, bald head tilted as his cohort continued, "You know they mean everything to the Reich."

"Ya, they feed us, build for us." Dr. Dirlewanger twisted the commandant's loving irreverence, fed on what was provided. "We love our dirty Jews."

19

___

Cattle cars unaltered hauled human cargo, stained by blood, man and bovine. Chaim Kemény came in on the rail from the border of Ukraine and Hungary. Born in *Munkacs*, later called *Mukacheve* under Soviet rule, he was one of the younger boys to have made it to the farm. His thick brown curls and pretty face drew Dirlewanger's attention from the moment he saw the child waiting to die. He had soldiers dispose of his remaining family, allowed the boy to marinate in helplessness before the twisted doctor offered him salvation on the farm.

Jenő held Zoli close, their clothes reduced to rags, breath never recovered. They bounded to a loose line, Nazi soldiers spat in their faces. Jenő watched what was going on ahead of him, noticed Nazis separating young boys from the rest who were ordered to their deaths. They inched their way down a hellish queue, waited on their end; they stood before the ghoulish doctor for the first time.

Dr. Dirlewanger's breath preceded him, even under a

literal cloud of the most despicable acts, his stench created an aura most-foul; it polluted every inch he broached, all he laid his hands on.

Jenő noticed Chaim shivering next to them, lost in a daze, little body consumed with shock, unable to feel or function. Affected by the sight, Jenő told the Nazi doctor that they were all together, pulled Chaim along with them

"What is the age?" pronounced Dr. Dirlewanger, not understood by Hungarian children. Kapo Adams was available to translate.

Jenő remained attentive, attuned to the Nazi's selection process, answered for the youngers. He insisted that they were all strong enough to work, a lie partially believed. Chaim's irresistible innocence encouraged the final decision.

Dirlewanger happily separated the two from their protector, Zoli torn from the last of his family. The doctor reveled in their desperation; Commandant Ziereis was present to enjoy the spectacle, the power. "Dr. Heim will be pleased with our new Hungarian stock." They never missed an opportunity to play savior, and went on to tease the collected, with eyes on Chaim. "Maybe you little chickens can even have some bread…"

After months on task, the already broken and down-trodden were well-trained. Zoli scurried to work, evaded attention. He snuck a glance at Chaim in time to see him finish the heel of bread that was tossed to him by the young soldier from the other side of their chain-linked existence. He tilted from the sight, honed in on the food that laid abandoned in the dirt between them.

"I'm sorry," Commandant Ziereis said to himself as he

took his place above Chaim, his full Nazi uniform kept clean by the comforts of rank. He casually held a cattle prod in his right hand; lifted with the force of his convictions, he brought it down in a series of sharp swings that snapped flesh. "This is what's best for you! Do you want to die of starvation on your feet building engines or mining for stone with your bare hands?" The Nazi's intensity lightened, a smile of rotted teeth made an appearance to accentuate an offer in the making. "Or you can stay here with me?"

Chaim wanted to cry, needed to cry, but had no more tears; aged by an insidious routine, life was wrung out of his slight frame, he could barely feel the lashings that followed him from task to task. Worked to subjugation, culminating in a low point, the boy dropped in the waste that collected on the most unholy soil of the pig's pen.

Swine closed in; snorts of hot breath tempted their appetite, their teeth grinding with anticipation. They were dissuaded from their meal only when Commandant Ziereis came to endear himself to the Jew-boy by swatting the beasts from their intended meal.

"I will not let anything happen to you. You are safe with us." He extended a hand, helped the boy up, worked his impressionable mind with malevolent kindness. "You are safe with me."

Zoli was there to watch guards retrieve Chaim's lifeless body. They carried the boy out of Zoli's eye-line, and further off the farm in the direction of an appropriated Bavarian castle refitted as officer's barracks.

Ziereis's quarters were spacious, boasted high ceilings and arched windows that flooded the floors of this private domicile with natural light. Creature comforts unheard of outside his walls were enjoyed in wartime abundance: liquors, fresh fruit and bread, milk and butter. Ziereis took every advantage.

The commandant insisted on raising his glass, called for the room's attention with the usual German pomp. "I would like to welcome all of our renowned guests, two noted doctors have paid us a visit…" A spattering of self-aggrandization stopped hard when he continued, "Dr. Heim the esteemed protégé of Mengele himself." Moments were given, praise dealt accordingly. "And, Dr. Dirlewanger who led criminals to the frontline to prove his methods effective is already a thing of legend…" A rousing applause surprised the hunched over, over-thin, rotting corpse of the man honored. Dirlewanger straightened his glasses, took it all in, but, of course, let Commandant Ziereis finish his praise. The celebration never ended, crescendoed. "We hope he will do the same here. With his help, we will have our prisoners rebuild what they have destroyed. They will thank us for the work we give them. Dirty Jews will pay for what they have cost Europe and the world."

"*Heil Hitler.*"

"Bravo."

"*Ist korrek!*"

They basked in institutionalized like-mindedness, agreed that they had earned the right to recalibrate, reassert German dominance.

Nazis flourished in the brutality on which they were raised; revenge and retribution were flowers that blossomed on the annihilation of others, grown out from the manure of Nazi self-righteousness.

Brutalized boys were given the reprieve as promised. Ziereis provided them with whatever they needed; food, water, a clean bed, and companionship. A taste of normalcy soothed the shell shocked. Ziereis held the key to their sanctuary and periodically dished out a brutal reminder of the fine line they teetered on.

"I could send you to die, if you prefer, work in the quarries with numbers tattooed on your arm," was an option extended, repeated tenderly in the midst of his most horrific indulgences. "No. I keep you clean, no markings, well-fed..."

Adult men took turns taking hours bathing and pampering the guests. They sat on the edge of the tub, brushed hair, directed children into compromises beyond their manipulated understanding.

Young boys were trained to depend on sin-filled tenderness; food and a place to sleep, sheets free of fecal matter and disease, clean clothes and a permanent reprieve from work was reserved for a select few; children most indoctrinated and favored by the commandant were more than just slaves, they were pets.

Ziereis was in complete control of his world; his twisted affections had flourished in good company. His collection depended on what he was giving them. The commandant basked in their appreciation with arms wide and eyes closed. By the end of the war, he and his cohorts received what was expected without having to ask. Their guests were entirely attuned to their needs, wiped-clean of their own concerns.

Ziereis took nights alone to bask in his ascension, in accomplishments achieved by few. He created a happy home for himself; a seemingly endless supply of replenished youth to feed on, servitude shipped in through a train depot entirely under his charge.

Aside from the medical pretense on which these accommodations were justified, there was the cruelty of the two doctors who experimented on the innocent in the name of science. Ziereis considered what he was doing as humane. Proof of German superiority. He was an *Übermensch* capable of molding the world around him, beyond good and evil. His ascension from a starving child to the master of his domain in the course of a single lifetime filled him with self-righteous self-satisfaction.

A large pit fireplace warmed the cool Bavarian night. Far off winds blew in over the wide-open landscape, rattled shutters, knocked antique windows. The tides of change penetrated Ziereis's enclave, his personal space, his kingdom.

He looked up from the pages of an often read copy of *Thus Spoke Zarathustra*, for all and none, placed the work by Friedrich Nietzsche on an adjacent end table. His cool calm was fractured by the crack of explosives falling from from the sky.

"Vas es das?"

Ziereis charged from his accommodations, greeted immediately by underlings awaiting orders as others took cover.

"VAS ES DAS?" he yelled to the sky above, questioned any available deity, the gods of Aryans old. Nordic heroes who shared their glory would certainly heed Ziereis's discontent. *"VAS ES DAS, SHITE?"*

The commandant stood on the threshold of his crumbling empire; it tumbled like a house of cards in the wind. His fear of losing it all was buried under rage.

"*DIES IST NICHT ÜBER!*" he screamed. "*HEIL HITLER!*"

His men were compelled to parrot his assertions.

A barrage of munitions fell on the landscape, SS ran for cover, officers were slain mid-step; clouds of gunpowder masked an imposed stillness, created a dreary calm in its place; silence teetered on the faint sound of the next impending strafe. Commandant Ziereis's commands fell on chaos; Allied pressure grew all-encompassing, tore through Nazi treachery at will.

Ziereis wondered out loud, not loud enough for others to hear, about the only thing that ever gave him any peace throughout his entire troubled life. "*Vas über meine haustiere?*" Thoughts of his loss drained color from his face, the entirety of what was at stake slumped his shoulders, welled his eyes. "*Mein kleiner, mein kleiner Juden...*"

Marches designed to wear Jews to their deaths slowed. The prisoners who were left unattended were too weak to escape. They waited for death with hands held open.

American airplanes churned close, P-51 Mustangs retro-fitted with Rolls-Royce designed engines were built to better the German's Luftwaffe fighters, thumped the sounds of the United States over Nazi occupied lands; innovation drizzled gunfire from M2/AN Browning mounted machine guns fixed and fired .50 mm shells at 850 rounds per minute in a run designed to make way for bombers closing in behind the initial sting.

Desperation set in. Ziereis knew his unfortunate orders, straightened himself out before relaying the contingency plan: *"TÖTEN DAS JUDEN."* He spat conflicted, turned for all to hear. *"ALLE VON IHNEN!"*

He watched dutiful men shoot Jews on sight; a soldier took aim on the small and weak about to fire when Ziereis stepped in. The commandant stood above the spared, an unholy smile infected his face as he ran his fingers through Chaim's thick curls.

"Everything will be alright," he forced the course German language tender, continued that way. "It will be as it was, pet. I will make it so."

Chaim's eyes smiled with relief, ease circulated through his shaken bones. "Whatever you want," were the only words Chaim could utter.

Ziereis turned from the comforting moment, ordered his men to find the members of his workforce, and to make sure that they be taken to the safety of his private bunker.

"Spread out and find my boys!" Ziereis relayed to his subordinate; his wishes permeated the ranks. Troops fell in line, regained form, and fanned out over the rattled countryside, trusted to make Ziereis whole again. "Kill the rest."

Jenő's eyes welled with the collective struggles of all Jewry, all the prejudice, all the hatred, from the times of pharaohs on to the present; his breath grew shallow, their fate in hand. "They'll find us here," he whimpered.

Young Anja reeled from the kitchen window, nearly fell off her stool.

Zoli and Tarkai shared a glance drowned in misery. No good options were left for them as Jenő struggled to stay alive.

They ran from the safe haven with no memory of

making the decision to do so, tore through the backfields of what was once the Baumann's family farm with what little strength they could conjure.

Anja and her mother watched their escape through the frame of the backdoor; a commotion grew close.

Their front door was torn open; Nazi commotion instantaneously filled the farmhouse with its wrath, devastated the two Baumanns in its disregard; walls and furniture, precious baubles and tapestries were destroyed without thought. Mother and child held one another, when, they tilted to see Ziereis and his pet walking through the search and seizure, hand in hand.

Flashes and conflagrations, explosions of light accompanied carnage, produced noticeable shadows; grotesques of negative space stretched over blood soaked land, mixed with the ridged silhouettes of malformed trees; branches reached out like fingers, stole children, returned the select few to the lowest levels of the available hell. Zoli remained close to his brother, buried in mud and misery, lost track of the rest of the world, and were spared the brutality of Nazi desperation.

The final solution was hastened; Jews were reeled in for the slaughter.

Ziereis's collected were holed up in his gothic residence, illuminated by the flicker of candlelight; walls creaked to shifting tides, floors quaked with a percussive predictability that fueled anxiety. Men of all ranks congregated in halls of decadence, past leisure swept under the imported Persian rug and replaced with abuses designed to empower the doomed.

Young boys stood in various states of undress, some

naked, all clean and waiting for what they were there for; baths were the comfort they all needed. Smoke-drenched, morphine-plied, and officer-filled rooms waited on still soaked boys to emerge from their forced baptisms. They were turned inside out, with nothing left of themselves to destroy.

Nazis dried them with available towels; crooked smiles directed to the next in an assembly line of final devastation; one child after another was lost in the inevitability they faced, half-eaten.

The line shifted, parted ways, revealed young Itzchak Tarkai in his undergarments. He trembled with his privates grasped between his two hands as Dirlewanger laid eyes on him for the first time.

Dirlewanger's bone-thin fingers rubbed against young exposed skin; his wretched aura expelled a noxious film that enveloped those set out for his taking, consumed in a mélange of the loving and lascivious.

"I will not let anything happen to you." Words didn't match actions. Dirlewanger reached out for nine-year-old Tarkai, recycled sentiments from his own troubled youth. "This is what's best for you."

Tarkai stood petrified. A long torment stretched through his silence, etched into the boy's subconscious; he was forever unable to detach from the pressure of this exact moment.

Dirlewanger continued to feign caring; a smile born of sinister intent projected softly out to the pale, rail-thin boy. "*Kommen hier, mien klein juden,*" said as the Nazi's prurience made contact with fractured innocence.

Tarkai reeled, an impulse he regretted the instant it

came over him. He straightened himself, steadied for a reprimand, and waited. He waited for the worst. Dirlewanger's initial disappointment contorted into focus, then dire concern.

Echoes of artillery boomed in the distance, traveled in their direction.

"DIES IST NICHT ÜBER!" Ziereis ordered. *"HEIL HITLER!"*

But even before Ziereis could rally his men, while Dirlewanger stumbled with his pants around his ankles, American shells met their mark. Booms threw soldiers aside, took down the 100-year-old walls around them. A hail of 76.2 mm bullets followed; rocks and mortar mixed to dust.

Explosions ripped through the terrain, earth rearranged by mayhem, blasted structures, stations lay in ruin.

Tarkai was launched out of the way. He found cover under a half overturned table, avoided debris, falling bricks, and shattered glass. He shifted, focused, and caught a last glimpse of Dirlewanger trapped under the rubble; he watched the Nazi gasp for his last breath under the weight of his own excess.

Those who moved could; Nazis scattered. Tarkai took his first steps towards Stars and Stripes. Swept up in immediate assistance, he caught sight of a single boy standing on the precipice of another imposed commencement.

Chaim stood in soiled undergarments as his world came crashing down around him; he mourned the only comfort he had ever known as an uncertain future charged in with a fury. It nearly brought the little victim to tears.

Commandant Ziereis had branded them all, for life.

20

Time caught up to Zoli, the totality of his experiences bottlenecked in semi-retirement on the beachfronts of southern Florida. The Hungarian community in New York turned snowbird, collectively spent increasingly more and more time away from the debilitating winters in the city. Goulash Alley of Second Avenue had slowly transformed into a yuppie enclave; Magyar butchers and Hungarian restaurants were almost entirely replaced by banks, sports bars, and sushi joints.

The remaining members of the First Hungarian Literary Society migrated to their sister club on Hallandale Beach Boulevard. The southeast tip of the United States was close and familiar to Hungarians who had traveled for work and leisure over the years. In the past, the seasonal Floridian economy balanced the year with summers in the Catskills. Recently immigrated Hungarians looking for work in the '60s and '70s flocked to coastal cities, beach living close to racetracks and never-before-experienced nightlife. Cuban flavors and cruise-wear culture were thoroughly enjoyed.

An exuberant Eastern European population developed from that early rush for the warm life: Russians, Ukrainians, Romanians, Serbians, and the Polish would eventually all be represented in the aisles of local grocery stores and flea markets. Teli salami, Hungarian paprika, imported liquors, and candies were available and most comforting. Restaurants and cafés were littered with languages familiar, misplaced communities were resurrected in the humidity. Distractions were embraced in the movie theaters at the Aventura Mall and at the poker rooms that began to sprout up around them. Jai alai was always popular. Retirees sat shoulder to shoulder with the out-of-work. Social security checks mixed with unemployment benefits in medium sized pots at one-two hold 'em tables throughout southern Florida.

Claiming as much of the good life as they could for themselves, they all carried stories of familiar miseries and comforting victories. But however great the success, however nice the view, resilient nightmares lingered through each day. Every thought, every action, was affected by the trauma of youths stunted. Deeply imbalanced by sights experienced, they now, in the autumn of their years, saw anti-Semitism everywhere. Any story, every joke, the news, an offhand comment, political move, or skewed glance was talked about, analyzed, reiterated, and scowled upon. Hatred had stained their insides, painted the world accordingly.

They earned their right to complain, survived more than just the worst. Zoli and his seven card partners sat around a green felted table at their club; closed off, with few windows, fluorescent light glazed every inch of the space. goulash and bread, *töltött káposzta* with boiled potatoes, *paprikás csirke nokedlivel*, and some bland heart-healthy options no one wanted to order sat on various rollaway side-tables as they gambled. Ate. Drank. Gambled. And so on.

"You read about this new trade agreement?" one octogenarian yelled out in a mix of accents that had long been sharpened to its Queens College edge. "They won't be happy till Israel is gone."

All the action, every outrageous bet and bluff was designed to quiet their existential cries; Edvard Munch's nightmares tore at their skin from the inside. They couldn't ignore it. It had festered over decades, was ever-available. Ancient animus left a residue that ripped any inkling of closure apart. The kids who faced the unspeakable were resurrected in retirement homes. Their grief permeated through all the good, and the bad, and the anti-Semitic.

They saw prejudice everywhere, in everything, made sport talking about it. It was a guaranteed part of nightly conversations, and daily concerns. The world had changed around them, not within them. After all the years, the threat of starvation remained, empty plates were the status quo, anything left over was taken home, never wasted.

"He said, 'No sauce'..." was spit out in a huff by Laszlo Schwartz, known at The Club as Banán, banana in Hungarian, for his signature gameplay. He splashed the pot. "Raise! Five *banán*!"

Over the last forty years in the United States, Banán

had been one of Zoli's closest friends, their collective experiences were ripe with familiarity. They sat at a table full of grey hair and type 2 diabetes. Only one woman among the gamblers, Agi, the Hungarian abbreviation for Agatha or Agnes, could keep up. She had that killer spirit, an all-in mentality. "Twenty more," she asserted.

A pause in play, senior citizens hung on Banán's next word, his charisma potent enough to captivate rooms full of school children in Germany where he had been invited to share stories of his youth in the camps. Earning some minor notoriety, he even met the Chancellor of Germany herself; self-importance fueled his confidence, kept him talking.

"So I asked, 'How bout some water?'" Comic timing never in short supply, his audience scoffed at the anticipated end of the story. "The idiot tells me 'No water.' Believe that? Because I'm a Jew. Have you ever heard of such a ting?"

"Can we play?" Agi bellowed, failed to turn attention, continued with volume raised. "Are you calling or vhat?"

Lotto, keno, cards, and dice. These guys loved to gamble, always had. Their lives were a gamble, longshots through the long haul. They were now cashing in on borrowed time.

Agi boomed in a yell that was her conversational voice. "Come on!"

A flurry of bets made it around the table.

"Yes, but it is a problem, anti-Semitism, that is..." Zoli couldn't help himself, smiled with his eyes as he interjected in his usual mischievous way. "Some people even blame the sinking of the Titanic on ze Jews. Can youz believe that?"

"The stupidity of some people."

"Damn anti-Semites."

"They should rot."

Discomfort made its rounds around the retired, prompted scowls, vexed the older, rowdier, and most gullible of the group. Zoli watched on amused, his good nature intact as he played into their anger with feigned outrage, egging them on, lining them up. "But, I tell them it vas an ice-berg... not a Gold-berg."

The joke hit its mark, reactions abounded; most of the guys didn't remember hearing it a thousand times before; Ishtvan didn't get it, took it to heart, not quite the same since his much younger girlfriend moved back to Hungary with all his money. He waved his fist in the air. "Prejudeeest!"

Agi remained impatient, anxious over the weight of her hand. Her eyes darted from pot to her card then at the players, all distracted and ripe for an easy call. Drifting conversations and mediocre mental and physical health were among the reasons she was able to make a living playing cards, and she wouldn't be the first nor probably the last to use club winnings as a sole source of income. So, she forgave digressions. It was part of the process.

"But, Zoli, why joke? We all know how serious the problem is." The involuntarily bobbing of a liver-spotted baldhead punctuated the concern, fine hairs haloed in the fluorescent light thickened around ears. The old man took a moment to remember whether or not he had anything else to add, turned to his light nosh instead. Unconcerned, he smacked away at his supper, dentures clacked loose between spoonfuls.

They all knew that victimization continued; it stuck to their bones, flowed in their marrow, was passed around the card room through the ether.

"Leave me alone, I'm a retired man now," the old man yelled at his soup.

"Yes, we're all retired now," Zoli mussed.

"Retired my ass. These tings stick around," Banán interjected with a podium ready bellow, his Jewishness penetrated every assertion. "We live with this, Zoli. You should see how these kids listen to my story. I relive it for them. They cannot believe it... Raise! Ten *banán*." His chips hit the pot, an easy toss that projected confidence in his hand, poker faces a thing of their past. "They're going to make a movie about me, the producer of *Cats*, you know, from the Winter Garden Theater. A big shot. He vants to do it."

"Why must you always have to raise, Laci?" griped near-effeminate András; his high-pitched voice and ineffectual whine stood out within the gathering of hardened refugees. He threw his cards into the muck; one flipped over in the sloppy fold.

The jack of spades was laid out for all to see; its sword held comfortably and casually through the back of his own head.

Fixed incomes washed out in the tide of Banán's big stack, the sight laid another sensation over their buried burdens. The thrill of gambling cured symptoms, never the disease.

The deck moved over. Erno grabbed hold. Debilitated by stroke, he mumbled out of the left side of his mouth, shuffled two decks together, had them cut by András on his right. He shook through his deal, fourteen cards to each of the eight players seated in the round. The deck was left in the middle of the table, its top card turned to expose the six of hearts.

"And for the money..." Erno added to the conversation. Banán shot his long-time card partner a glance, side-eyed as if secrets were being spilt. He sat in his wheelchair and reminded everyone: "You do it for the money, Banán."

"Yeah, so vhat?" Back on his favorite topic, "I'm like a national treasure over there. They all want to hear about what we went through. There are so few survivors left that they have made a list of us over there." He took pause to tear into some bread, sloppily getting soup to his mouth with an uneasy arch of a spoon. A liver dumpling made the load as Banán chewed open-mouthed and continued, "Remembering what they did to us is, it is very important to the German people." He washed the sentiment down with room temperature soda water that was on the table before they even got there. "They feel very guilty and bring me photos of their grandfathers in Nazi uniforms. Their burden is great. Eh? We look back to learn and to lead, Zoli, right?"

"Life is like a *tzibele*... you know vat a *tzibele* is?" Erno chimed, in his own world, with hands trembling out of his control.

Play continued undeterred. The seven other players ignored Erno and focused on a game with elusive origins. Some romanticized the notion that Poker Rummy, which is what they played, was developed in the French prisons during the time of the revolution.

Newer members who were familiar with the Chinese

game of *Khanhoo* saw similarities between the two, insisted that it had more in common with their game than the French version. It was an argument that never failed to prompt instant irritation among the older players. The only thing they could all agree on was the fact that it found its way to the Club in New York via French Moroccans in the late '70s. That was that.

These eight friends had been playing together every Monday, Wednesday, and Friday from practically the moment they first met. The number of hands played together would be near impossible to calculate; one of them once asserted that they'd have to consult NASA to get even close. The game they played was just as complicated.

Two decks were shuffled together, jokers set aside and later doled out as the 14th card for each player; two are forced to fold if six have acted before them, the rest are required to make an initial bet or fold. It's the first of two betting rounds in a race to accumulate sequences of at least three cards of the same suit or three- or four-card sets of the same numerical card value. They took turns picking off the stock pile. Erno's accustomed digression faded into the room's white noise.

"A *tzibele* is an onion." Erno looked around, somehow managed to play his hand, and went on, "And, life is like an onion... many layers..."

"Come on, let's play," was a constant. Agi's impatience told the strength of her hand. Her opponents were too distracted to piece her tell together. "Are we going to bet?"

"Banán..." Zoli grounded the shared space. He was happy for every moment he'd had; his blue eyes flashed under wide-open lids. The boy he was pressed up against his innards. The pressure that lightened over the years was replaced by a corneal blockage and repressed heartache. His remaining senility staved off the escape offered to so many of his peers, the blessing of an inevitable reprieve loomed. "Haven't ve suffered enough? All I vant is to laugh, to live, to have grandchildren, play cards, drink cognac, maybe a girlfriend here and zere." He looked at his newly dealt cards, a garbage hand folded post-haste. "You vant I sit here and only tell stories about vhat I vent through? How it keeps me up at night, gives me pain in ze chest?" Everything was a question. Questions were answered by questions, not a single answer in sight. "To tell you what I have learned since?"

"What's new, Zoli?" Banán barked across the table, jarring all but Agi who remained focused on the game. Crumbs launched in Banán's continued delivery, "What has happened since? You tell me."

"I told you vhat happened..."

Banán shrugged.

Zoli's shoulders bunched. Tightened muscles and difficult memories entwined. An excruciating reflection inflicted physical pain, heartbeats skipped beats, then another. "I told you *alter kockers* everything that happened. Don't anyvone listen around here?" Zoli said with a voice raised by frustration.

"I remember, Zoli," Agi croaked, laid out her winning hand, pulled in a massive pot, the conversation strained by the sight for a second.

"I don't know vhat's ze point. Youz old farts starting to loose your minds."

The deck was passed. New hands dealt.

Zoli inspected his, led out with the required bet. A trail of folds laid out behind him. "I tolds you how I found my friend, there are boxes that should never be opened, can never be shut."

"Yes, yes, we all lost everyone," Banán exclaimed, abrupt and out loud, a natural crescendo in the boisterous flight of the Jewish language: "*Der mensch trakht un Gott lahkht.*"

"*Abi gezunt!*" was the appropriate and expected reply. A few old guys followed Banán's utterance, mouthed the sentiment, but Zoli's health had changed.

Heartbreak atop heart disease, a failure of moving beyond the what-could-have-beens, daydreams and night terrors entwined with inescapable regret. "Every time I look back I am hit by something new, I can't get out from under it. I told you about the skin punks in Budapest?" Only a few of his card partners remembered, he went on anyway. "Or, my neighbor in Provincetown claiming I didn't own property I bought?" He waited for a reaction, got none. "People are villing to be on the side of lies, all over again. That will never change."

"Skin heads, Zoli, skin heads," Erno added in his one-sided speech.

"Things have not changed as much as we hoped. I drive through America, think about my life, look into my life, and I look around America and think... I DON'T trust any of you. I have seen vat is out zer."

"*Es vet gornit helfen!*" *Nothing will help*, Erno added; his friends watched Zoli connect to what they've all felt.

Anchored in the pit of their stomachs, the cancer twisted through their entire lives. *"Es vet gornit helfen!"*

Zoli made sure to connect eyes with each of his friends at the table; men stopped eating, looked away from their cards, listened to their brother.

"I see anti-Semites on the streets, next door, and remember being betrayed by my neighbors, teachers, and... friends back vhen I vas a child. I vonder if another charismatic leader could lead everyone back into that mess, into another slaughter, vith simple promises and brutal actions... I don't know, maybe some country, some state... are ready for those ideas again, ever since I first vent down south, they just don't point their prejudice mainly at ze Jews, but it's ze same ting."

"Some tings never change."

"It is Poland all over again."

"It has already started. The world is fucked," Banán interjected in his usual way.

"A breyre hob ich?" Erno uttered into his cooling soup, an abundance of attention given to the act of steadying his spoon upon approach, smacks of his gums and the clank of loose dentures marked anticipation, and laid background to his mouthing of: *"Abi gezunt!"*

"Everything is rosy on the outside, but inside it's... rotten," added the ever-bitter Ishtvan. He held an apple out as an example, took a bite, disappointed to find it crispy and delicious.

"It only got vorse."

"Eh? What? Zoli, how could it get worse?"

"Ve can't forget, ve cannot move on, vhen ve look back ve have to learn, the truths ve don't vant to hear, to think about." Zoli took his time, a long pause to the sound of cards reshuffled. "I did go back, I heard the same horrible stories over and over again."

"Ve have heard them all."

"Ve have lived through it, Zoli."

"Ve live vit it every day."

"You can't think that way. Life is too short."

"And getting shorter."

Conversation flowed around the table faster than the card game, and only slowed in the muck of reflection.

"What's the point of even talking about it?"

"You just told me to talk about it."

Banán shrugged.

Zoli shook his head, turned quiet with contemplation. "In Provincetown, at my gallery, there was a skunk who lived under the building..."

"A skunk?"

"Did he say skunk?"

"Yes, a skunk... Turn up your hearink aide," Zoli insisted before continuing. "I named him Charlie. I don't know if it vas ze same skunk every night, but there vas a skunk in my yard like clockverk. He was my friend." He laughed at the memory. "We had an understanding..."

Card play made its way around.

"I agreed to let him live there. He agreed not to stink up my business. Ve vere the vones who had to live with zat, vith the skunk. It would never go away, and it vas out of my control..." Zoli took a moment to rearrange his cards as reflection set in, before he concluded, "And now I don't have to live with that burden anymore."

"What are you talking about?"

"A skunk?"

"Can you please play your hand, Zoli?" Agi roared.

Zoli looked at her, tilted back to the table, and laid out two sets and two sequences that used up all of his fourteen cards.

He raked the pot to the groans of his longtime card partners. Life was good.

21

After 40 years in the art business and 32 years in Province-town, Zoli decided to semi-retire and sold the Federal-style home he had turned into his gallery. The decision was helped along by his years spent as an outsider on the very tip of Cape Cod.

The old-time Portuguese were wary of wash-a-shores in to make a buck; they distrusted any new face, especially ones as foreign as the Glucks. They were among just a handful of Jews whom made it to land's end.

As soon as the gallery turned profitable, as soon as Julika and Zoli began to feel the force of the American dream, the family who lived in the near identical Federal-style building a few doors down started what would be decades of constant harassment. The malice transcended generations.

The discomfort of Zoli's youth was conjured in the animus of his American neighbors; his abutters seemingly did everything in their power to stifle the Glucks' prosperity. Economic anti-Semitism is how Zoli defined the relationship he had with his neighbors; the more he acquired the worse it seemed to get.

Zoli bought the waterfront property across the street from his gallery. Two buildings on the .09-acre piece of land were conjoined to a public right of way and town landing. He planned to add 177 feet of living space to the 288 square foot cottage that sat on Provincetown Harbor. After a three-year wait, he finally obtained the Chapter 91 license required by the commonwealth for the existing property. It was approved by both the Department of Environmental Protection, and signed by then Governor and would-be presidential candidate Mitt Romney.

Embracing the freedoms promised by the Statue of Liberty, Zoli led his poor huddled family, and proceeded by the book. Out of his comfort zone, and wary of large interfering government bodies, he worked hand in hand with the town's Conservation Commission and Historical Committee. They collectively came to a plan that respected the waterways of the Outer Cape. Zoli agreed to the conditions required by the Harbor Commission and the Harbormaster in the name of preservation. He also agreed to pay for and maintain the American beach grass that was to surround the property and provide dinghy posts for locals and tourists alike. He bit his tongue while accepting government mandates. In his mind, he was just one step away from appropriation; deep down he expected to lose everything the way his family had in Felsővadász.

But, once again, the unexpected was expected; it didn't take long for it to arrive. Zoltan Gluck's success was met by the accustomed objections from the people whom he had lived closest to. Different nation, same degradation; discrimination was piled on by those he had hoped could be more neighborly.

The patriarch of the aforementioned family a few doors down married into the wealth of property ownership, defended his new station in life; nothing was going to propel him back to struggles of contract fishing. He clawed his way through the greater Atlantic across fields of kelp and seaweed, after innumerable backbreaking hauls, to actualize his dream of respectability on Commercial Street. He dragged his way over over the breakwater, across the beach, sliced himself on seashells and driftwood, to stake his claim in the foundation of an old Cape Cod family, to make something of himself. And then, Zoli appeared from nowhere to do the same. The lack of context drove those who thought it was just luck mad.

It was a lunacy Zoli recognized from childhood; he saw the mob at his father's market, the winds picked up the sentiment in Hungary and carried it through time and across continents to land squarely in the actions of others. His neighbor hired a crew to illegally build on Zoli's land. He lived with an out-of-place telephone pole for a week while Zoning, Building, and Historical Committees had to inspect and converse about the implications and legality of the out-of-place structure. They put Zoli on trial, made him prove where his property lines were, blamed the victim before putting in an order for its removal.

The sole objective of providing for a family was once again disrupted by unprovoked bigotry, small town bureaucracy that seemed to be fueled by innuendoes immune to fact; Zoli had felt it in one form or another throughout his time on Cape Cod, making only a handful of friends within the wash of ornery locals, drunken fishermen, and endless tourists. Hippie culture and hippie happenings, Portuguese and painterly histories all eluded him and Julika both. They were perpetually bound by the insecurities of their formative years. They pined for the Hungarian community, way of life, had no interest in assimilation. They raised their son Hungarian with a live-in grandma who, after 40 plus years in the United States, couldn't speak more than 30 words of English, and never regretted it.

Along with the usual oft-spoken discrimination, the old man down the street continued to encroach on Zoli's piece of the pie for the rest of his life. He invited his friends and fishermen to move their lobster pots and dinghies out of his gift shop's parking spot, where he had allowed them to be, and onto Zoli's beachside property where they were not permitted; no Chief of Police, no Harbormaster, no kind neighborly interaction could ever rectify the continued disregard over the sovereignty of his property line.

The old man's prejudice, as prejudice goes, was highly infectious. It would be inherited, along with the vast piece of prime real estate, by his only daughter. She picked up the bitter gauntlet after he passed away, wielded its power with the same ignorance her father taught by example. Overly protective of her substantive inheritance, she would never marry and seemed to only derive pleasure from the misery of others—as well as at the bottom of bottle. The gift shop remained her base of operation, where she carried on her father's tradition. She went as far as to rent a manure truck and park it in front of Zoli's gallery, refusing to move it until ordered to do so by the Board of

Health, and only after they threatened to pull her business license.

Apples rolled close to their roots on the very tip of this peninsula, everything turned around as you twisted out onto the arm of Cape Cod; West turned East to the uninitiated, up was down, left/right, in and out entwined.

Throughout the decades, neighborly animus perpetually transported Zoli back to 1944; thoughts of the unprovoked disdain that led to his family's deportation and extermination connected to the reality he perceived around him. Zoli couldn't help but feel as though, once again, the person down the street represented a real threat to him and his family's right to exist. It made the otherwise picturesque setting unbearable.

This ancient and daily anxiety found reprieve in the innumerable moments he had caught on Cape Cod: watching his son grow up on the beach, make lifelong friends, share large meals of local fish, mollusk, and crustacean, sitting on the front porch of his gallery, drink in hand, people watching. Zoli would never forget riding through the streets of P-town; memories riffled like a nickelodeon, cascading decades, from fishing village to artist colony and beyond, with Hell's Angels and Dykes on Bikes playing equal parts in its remarkable legacy. He rode on in his straw hat and sleeves torn off an old button down worn mostly unbuttoned. Little Danny was always in the kiddie seat, ready to take it all in. Zoli's kid was still friends with the one-year-old they would see doing the same with his pregnant mom. A couple months after that, she gave birth to another one of Danny's oldest friends. Zoli watched his son grow up with the two brothers, Anson and Chad, in the northwest breeze that cooled hot summer days, envied their vigor, their freedom. But Danny had grown up in Provincetown; his lifelong connection showed.

Zoli was caught between the inner churnings that had haunted his every decision and his conscious mind that tried to make sense of it all. He was torn between the two when another issue arose that required direct action. Zoli attended meeting after meeting for the chance to make his case. All he wanted to do was clean up his beach and rebuild his cottage to code before it got swept away in the rising tides. The cost of maintaining the structure was beginning to outweigh its usefulness.

Provincetown Town Hall sat in the middle of all the action, right on the main drag of Commercial Street. It grounded the town's infamous eccentricities with its historic charms. The structure was built in 1885 and was filled through time with paintings by various local artists. It was as much a museum as a municipal building; Hawthorne and Hensche, Moffett and Oppenheim's work hung around every corner, oil painted reflections of the tranquility of the Outer Cape, the hard work of its settlers on full framed display.

Zoli took his time passing the works. They represented the ideal he had hoped to present and preserve for his family. Fishermen bringing in food for the family, a lone cottage on water's edge, and dunes that stretched into the setting sun teased his progress.

The Judge Welsh Meeting Room had filled with board members and townsfolk there to decide the fate of Zoli's construction project. Danny was present. He stood close to his dad. They watched neighbors, aligned to malign, insist that the Glucks didn't even own the land their 288 square foot building was on.

Their assertions bowled Zoli over, propelled him squarely into his stolen past; flashes of familiar mob mentality, mass havoc, and subjugation led him to withdraw his application.

Zoli and Julika didn't need much more to be convinced that selling out was right for them; they thought, while concurrently and entirely unaware of the bylaws that dictated procedure, that contractors and administrators, inspectors and fire chiefs, neighbors and judges conspired to ignore their needs because they were Jews. Bad luck and misunderstood restrictions were misconstrued as personal attacks, opinions were as sharp as spears and had twice the reach.

"Dad, we can't just leave P-town," Danny pleaded. "I don't mind living in there, and who knows what we can do with it in the future. And, who's going to buy a flooded cottage on a littered beach anyway?"

Zoli listened, interjected. An uncharacteristic edge laced his speech. "I don't know vhat you can do vith it, Danny. The building is ready to float off into the ocean. And, and... ze neighbor..." Not much more had to be said.

They spent their last season drenched in the soft embrace of their gallery, salty air coddled the whole family. Danny had moved into their rundown cabin as soon his parents considered it unsafe to rent. Zoli sat on his perch on the hill above the town landing and watched his son's life from afar. He saw him have fresh experiences outside of the gallery, a first glimpse of other interests that crept into his son's life. Danny had taken a job on a local whale watch boat and worked as a videographer alongside his local lifelong friends. They chased girls, went out drinking, had cookouts, played Frisbee, and chased girls some more. The grew up in the northwest winds that blew in from Canada, crisp air that carried sunsets that lit twilight in streaks of hot orange and hazy purples caught on cumulous clouds, reflected off the surrounding waters.

By the end of the summer, Zoli had a thought. It came to him daily, stretched back into the season and further into the past. He was adrift in feelings tucked away and unexplored, unanalyzed traumas manifested as fear and anger; the repressed anxieties battled with the positives, the life he was able to provide his family, his impending retirement. He shared it all with Danny, they'd talk for hours on the front porch of 398 Commercial St. watching the gulls float on the winds above, the gift-shop-lady harassing pedestrians and paying customers alike. "You can't walk this way, sir, this is private property," she'd yell from across the street, audible from where they sat.

"Youz don't need ze headache," Zoli stated the obvious.

"Dad, we can't just leave P-town, gotta keep something."

"Ok, Danny," he said. "But, no vone needs neighbors like dis."

"She's an anti-Semetic, vitch," Julika added, an accurate accusation. The gift-shop-lady did actually come from a long line of witches. Her lineage could be tracked back to before the Salem trials.

The mess of dumped kayaks, lobsterpots, and bureau-cracy would remain long past their last days on Cape Cod. Julika and Zoli were happy to leave it all behind. Even though they knew better, Zoli felt public officials and his neighbors would have readily loaded his entire family on a back of a horse-drawn wagon if they could. Those concerns were left on the very tip of Cape Cod.

The evolution of Provincetown continued without them; old timers and the fishing-class were slowly replaced. New blood and openhandedness turned the town rainbow; collective eyes looked into a future of prosperity shared, where everyone belonged.

Then, much later, on December 3rd, 2015, close to a decade after Zoli would pass way, at another meeting in the Judge Welsh Room at Provincetown's Town Hall. It was Danny's turn. He had worked within the guidelines of the town's Historical Committee, incorporated design notes by his dad's "favorite guy," artist John Dowd. The wide-eyed up-and-comer Zoli knew had become the quintessential Provincetownian and sat on the historical board at the time. Danny took it as a good omen. It wasn't the only one. The Conservation Commission was also stacked with people familiar to Danny, locals he grew up with, worked for, saw throughout his life. They guided him through the environmental planning of a site that had fallen under protected status, suggested kayak racks that would keep abandoned boats off of protected beach grass.

After a five-year orchestration, at a meeting dipped in winter's chill, Danny's effort would be met by the same claim of non-ownership by the gift-shop-lady. He had hired a lawyer to set her straight.

A new neighbor up the street went to the trouble of flying in from Palm Springs, twice, to object to the plan that had been agreed upon by a litany of agencies and signed off by the Governor of Massachusetts. He stood before the board, Danny, his contractor, and on closed circuit TV to complain about how the added noise would disturb the adjacent restaurant, upset that Danny's plans weren't presented to him even though they were available to the public via town hall. He expected Danny's contractor to come to him and to all the other neighbors for permission first.

The board had to redirect his concerns, they weren't there to talk about unrealistic expectations, or the restaurant.

Letters were read, opinions shared, and over a single board member's disapproval, the Zoning Board of Provincetown, Massachusetts voted in favor of the project 4 to 1.

By 2017, Danny would construct what his old man dreamt of building twenty years earlier.

22

By the late '90s New York City had witnessed the beginnings of its Disney-fication. Times Square had transformed before. The golden age of lights, martinis, and the high life played on in archival photographs. Dance halls and show girls, big bands and early musicals urged action and had set the tone. Boys back from the front forced kisses on unsuspecting nurses in celluloid perfection. But, the theaters that once showed nickel movies crumbled to accommodate 25-cent peep shows. Porn theaters with bars between seats to deter helping hands stood in place of once respectable establishments. The decline was all-encompassing; kid-friendly Play Land Arcades became gang havens. Hustlers and prostitutes replaced the New York ideal.

All that texture, all that raw human emotion from the neighborhood's most memorable eras, high and low, would slowly vanish into chain restaurants, franchised and advertised. It dissolved into toy stores and theme-driven mega-marketing opportunities, its charms were run off by dirty-costumed characters out to inflict donations from the crowds. A buck per photo *with you and your stupid family* summed up the city's commerce driven metamorphosis. New York City was in the midst of a once in a lifetime transformation for the third time in the last half century.

The West Village, East Village, Alphabet City, and even Soho retained some of the grit of past decades, for a little while at least. The Giuliani administration did what it could to rein in the debauchery in an attempt to attract as many tourist dollars as possible—or something like that. The lure built the city up from where it had fallen. The streets were once again safe to walk, scrubbed clean by foreign currencies exchanged at favorable rates.

The curved and cobblestoned stretch of Bleecker Street was once again filled with cafés and salons, book-stores and boutiques. The clientele was a mix of the urban chic and young professionals who enjoyed the extended revitalization of the once rough and tumble city. Little thought was left for the artists and hustlers that had attracted them in the first place. A new breed of urban explorer filled the streets. They armed themselves with innovation instead of instigation. The hustle, however, remained forever New York.

Danny had gone straight from the pressures of high school to the responsibilities of bringing in the family's income. Lost jobs and strayed goals freed up time to help his father continue his trade, visit customers nationwide.

Happy to not have the anchor of running the gallery in Provincetown around his neck, he knew that, like his dad, he had more than one chapter to live. He'd have to lose sight of the shore before he could find anything unfamiliar.

But, at this moment in time, it turned out, no matter how hard he tried, he'd never be able to stray too far. Compared to Zoli, his experiences felt paid for and small. The shadow he lived under had no end. Before long, he'd be fifty-fifty in the art biz and soon after that he tried to go it alone. Danny's parents hoped he would bring his new wife into the business once he got the hang of it.

Danny attempted to streamline what his father had created, thought it was an antiquated business model. He reigned in spending as it cut into his bottom line, stopped buying art outright. His father's reputation allowed him to consign works from galleries and artists, collections turned over for resale were the cornerstone of the business. Nevertheless, even with an abundance of works available to him at no cost, Danny couldn't recapture the charm of his father's enterprise.

He drove out of Zoli's new home base in Florida to make it around the United States with a quarter of a million dollars-worth of other people's art stacked in the back a Dodge Caravan. He retrofitted its slight interior with wooden shelves installed in the humidity of a typical spring day on Hallandale Beach, each piece slipped into place with its price printed atop their cardboard sleeves; $10,000, $12,500, $45,000 in place. The vehicle's value soared as Danny filled every crevice the minivan offered. Both driver's side and passenger seats were required to scoot up entirely, knees to chest, in order to accommodate his inventory.

The pressure, the responsibility, the value of what was locked up in the minivan was enough to keep Danny up and at the window all night while appointments without his father lacked the magic customers had grown accustomed to. He would return to Florida with all of his inventory, unable to move a single painting, still burdened with the expense of returning all of the consigned artwork to their rightful owners, resenting every second of it. Danny was given the tools; he just didn't know how to use them.

Danny tried to revitalize the business the only way he knew how. He went from gallery to gallery, hustled New York style. He worked the downtown art scene, set up a stand by the Union Square farmers market, and tried to sell mass produced prints to frame stores, but nothing clicked. He stood alone within the crowded streets of old New York, discouraged. Sales slumped as the art his father made so desirable grew stale under Danny's conservatorship. His inventory swelled as interest remained stagnant. He lacked the authentic connection to the works he had access to; his lack of passion, the underlining resentment, and uphill battle were ever-present and soured his sales pitch.

A spring breeze blew over Danny, traveled the length of the island of Manhattan, and crept through the concrete corridors of the Upper West Side to land on his parents. Zoli's hair shifted out of place, was promptly coifed.

"Are you excited to see our home country?" Zoli turned to ask his Korean-born, New Jersey raised, daughter-in-law, Elizabeth Porter-Gluck, known to her friends as Lizzy.

"You know I am, Zoli." Her enthusiasm was infectious, good will on full and perpetual display. Her expressive eyes teemed with positivity, love secreted from her pores. She swung thick locks of pure black hair back behind her shoulder, cinched it behind her ear. She placed her palm on Zoli as she fixed her shoe; her smile never wavering. "I'm ready to get my paprika on."

"I can't wait for you two to meet my art dealer friends," Zoli continued. "Maybe you can pick up some new pieces for the road."

Lizzy straightened her dress as it flowed in the wind, caught gusts that rushed up side streets, built momentum in avenues, and buried a cringe under her smile. She knew the difficulties Danny had faced taking over the business and of his dreams of an alternate reality where he could pursue his own interests instead, but played along anyway. "Sounds great."

"Now, if only your husband can get here, we can go," Julika said with a laugh that was cracked by nerves.

They waited on the sidewalk atop the incline of Manhattan Island, bags and carry-ons at the ready, staring south down West End Avenue hoping to spot Danny, praying to any available deity, the almighty Universe, that Danny was already in a cab and well on his way.

"Ve're going to miss our plane," Julika shrieked. Her voice was shrill and full of anxiety, chain-smoke was all she could do. "I don'ts believes it."

"Julika, relax, Danny had some business to take care of," Zoli intervened, was more than aware of where his wife's constant catastrophizing could and had led. "Ve'll make its, plenty of time." He lied to support the peace, injected humor into all discomfort. "Ve can always svim."

The joke missed its mark; seconds continued to pass with percussive persistence, a countdown accompanied by Julika's jitters. None of them could stand still.

After the long agitation, Zoli's eyes lit up as he caught sight of his son racing across West End Avenue. Lizzy was the first to meet him with a kiss. They locked eyes, communicated nonverbally.

"No one is buying," Danny answered her unspoken concern.

"Danny!" Julika interrupted with an accent that laid her impatience out for all to see. "You're going to make us miss our trip. Ve're going to lose it all..."

"Sorry, sorry. You won't even believe what happened."

"Don't you vorry. Ve aren't going to miss anyting." Zoli was always quick to hold the newest Gluck in his arms; Lizzy's vivacious youth retained, held close. The extent of Zoli's life was forgotten in moments of happiness, in front of the Schwab House, with his growing family, the Glucks reborn.

"What you hugging her for?" Danny joked, moving to separate his dad from his wife as a cab slowed in front of his outstretched arm. "Okay. Okay. That's enough, Pops."

"I'm just so happy for you two." The sentiment shared, the hug was extended by another affectionate squeeze.

"Okay. Okay," Danny had to remind him, get them into the waiting car.

"The Continental," Lizzy said with the accent Christopher Walken used on SNL, a caricature of Zoli's European charms, complete with: "Courvoisier?"

Her nature was exposed with gracious ease, beauty by authenticity, a certainty that cultivated connectivity. Her firm but gentle way was inescapable and was fortified by the mettle woven into her Korean DNA. She fit right into the Gluck family.

"Did you call ze gallery to make an appointment, Danny?" Zoli asked. "I vant to make sure to make ze introduction."

"Um," Danny stalled, looked squarely into his wife's eyes as he continued. "About that..."

Lizzy's straightforward, down-to-earth manner was instilled by her conservative immigrant family; her intensity, sharp intellect, and innate business savvy was an anomaly not only in her household, but also in the slow-paced suburbs of New Jersey where she grew up. A mix of strength and understanding, humor and outright silliness, were filled out by a series of trials faced and conquered. Chiseled by contradictions till balanced, her allure softened the eurocentricities of the Gluck family in a way a child psychologist soothes a room full of hyper kids. A strong independent woman, on her own and taking care of herself since high school graduation, Lizzy didn't need a man to take care of her. She once told Danny that it didn't matter what a guy did as long as he was happy doing it. It was that sentiment that would eventually set Danny free and allow him to be the man he was always meant to be.

"I'd marry a garbage man as long as he loved it," she'd said.

"I may hold you to that," Danny half-joked as he would soon decide to leave the art business behind to become a writer. She supported his dream and they would move to Los Angeles so Danny could pursue a career writing for the movies.

"Yes, yes, very nice, but vhen do I get my grandchild?" Zoli said, mid-conversation.

"Dad!" A look was followed by a shrug from either side

of the bulletproof Plexiglas that separated the interior of the taxi into halves, and have-nots.

"Danny!" Zoli matched and mocked his outrage.

"We're working on it, Zoli." Lizzy could do no wrong, her words floated through Zoli like the smell of fresh baked bread in the mornings of his youth before the war, a pure joy of seeing his son with such a serious and beautiful young lady penetrated every cell of his being, left him fulfilled.

"Yeah, Pops, practice makes perfect. If you know what I mean?" They shared a sense of humor, "And, I know you do."

Zoli shot his son a playful glance.

Julika remained uncomfortably anxious, fought the urge to tell the cab driver what to do, unsuccessfully, hysterically. "This right, this right. Oh my god. Where are you going? You're going to make us late."

Lizzy excavated her PDA, checked emails. Zoli watched. She took him through the steps of opening and reading a message, the advancements of modern technology.

"Amazing. Like in ze TV." His eyes were wide, astounded by how far into the future he had lived. "I never thought I'd see anyting like zis, it's like from a UFO." Zoli believed, always wished to have been an abductee, continued to marvel at his actualized fantasies. "All in your hand?" He tilted from her smiling face to the Blackberry mobile device that sat in her palm.

Lizzy worked hard, enjoyed having the best toys; her thumb instinctively balanced the small computer's roller-ball within items on its screen, pulling up messages, phone logs, her address book. Zoli adjusted glasses perched on the crook of this nose, got close, nearly pressed against the 3.5 inch 720x720-pixel display screen of the futuristic intrusion, amazed.

"Unbelievable how far ve've come," Zoli mused.

Throughout the smooth check-in, boarding and take-off, peanuts and an unexpectedly good in-flight meal, with lots of drinks, Julika prepared "the kids" for the whirlwind tour of their birth country. She had the entire trip scheduled out; restaurants, museums, childhood homes, road trips, old friends and long lost relatives packed every day of their visit.

"We ate plums from the branches, as many as ve vanted. I remember getting sick from eating so many, I couldn't help myself, I was six and hungry." Zoli drifted off, practically feeling the acidic burn of the peel on his tongue. The sweetness of its flesh dripped over the chin-side of his remembrances. "There were so many, a whole field purple from the..."

Unfocused memories made clear, darkness swelled to life, gleamed purple when brushed by the right angle, an old morning light. Plump contours and thick skin confined the plenty, delayed rupture. Fruit plucked from branches were saved or discarded, left to rot back into the earth, all over again, then again.

"Abundance," Danny finished his thought for him, joined his father's trip into the past, as had become a force of habit for the adult child.

Zoli anticipated and rearranged stories long committed to memory, each reflection bent to the present moment, were held together by twine made of time, pain, happiness, loss. An overlying relief and well-earned ease smoothed out the bumps of a well-worn life. The diabetic-friendly icing on his cake.

"Watch out, Budapest, here come The Glucks!" Danny teased. He grabbed Lizzy the way he did. They laughed. They kissed. They lived.

Zoli's attention squared on those closest to him. A smile sprouted across his lips. He led his family into the old country; any and all the trouble of past trips and his early life horrors faded into his Americanized accumulation, shielded by a tree of life that was in full, pungent, boisterous bloom for all to see.

23

With no time to acclimate, jet lagged and hung over, an itinerary refined over the last twenty years took the family straight to Jancsi Neni's kitchen. Deep in the hills of Buda, the restaurant that Julika's family had gone to for special occasions while she was still just a little girl before the war had turned into a tourist trap. They began cutting costs, garnished their home cooked entrees with frozen potatoes and recycled parsley, watered down drinks and western accouterments, and added as many tables as they could. But, some of their dishes remained authentic, transportative by the way of taste-buds. The softball-sized *túrógombóc*, steamed cheese-curd balls topped with sour cream and sugar, rolled about the plate and remained a crowd-pleaser. They made Lizzy exclaim: "Oh, we're coming back here."

The night went on as most of their nights in Hungary did, eating and drinking till it was all gone. A second opened bottle of *pálinka* sat next to its empty cousin. The Lizzy-initiated nightcap was enjoyed in their hotel room at the Gellért Hotel. A cheese plate, dried fruit straight from the market, confections and marzipan were set out for the picking by a window that opened up on the Danube.

Lizzy floated on the lights of *Pest* as they danced in the river's currents. She swooned to the tint of the European waterway; its heart pumped blue through the ancient artery in a steady flow of endless possibilities. Danny stood close to her. They leaned on one another.

Zoli's heart gasped at the sight of the next generation, looked from them to the wash of their view; a moment that drowned him in good fortune.

A fresh perspective was injected into the Glucks' habitual visits back to the old country, every sight and memory developed new joy; the opera house, The Gerbeaud, Parliament, and Heroes' Square were institutions seen through new eyes.

They walked through the Mihaly Munkácsy retrospective at the National Museum, laughed about the small piece they spent too much money on and weren't unable to sell.

Lizzy sidled up to Danny, her soft skin pressed on mine, the scent of her shampoo lulled Danny in familiarity. She pointed out a biography of the artist, commented, "He was a carpenter before making it in the arts..." She leaned in, eye leveled, continued, "Just like your dad."

Bakeries and cafés that held historical and personal significance, the *Dohány Utcai* Synagogue, were layered in the revelry of their latest visit.

They showed off. Julika even gave Lizzy a glimpse of how good her life was before the war. She brought the family to the large country home she grew up in, the fact that her home remained broken up into four apartments as the communists had left it was a non-issue.

Days of tours, nights of booze, paprika laced meals and menus, sun up then down, every minute was occupied. They went to visit their only remaining relatives living in Budapest. Eva and Tibor Braun lived in the same prewar apartment building Julika visited when she was a child. It was where they hid. They used the false papers Julika's Uncle Béla had arranged for the entire family. They were able to stay by telling the communists they intended to raise their future families there, neither ever married nor had children.

Zoli watched the old couple, enjoyed their company. Their European existences marked a path that could have been his, Zoli thought. He inhaled the distances traveled, the way he had come so far, as the generation that never left Hungary playfully called their guests, "fat Americans," and, "swollen Jews."

"What does that mean?" Lizzy asked.

"I'll tell you later."

The trip to Zoli's hometown Felsővadász required Danny to go to the local police station for an International Driving Permit. Then they rented a car from an independently owned and operated company out to harangue tourists with false state mandated requirements, petty scams, and hollow promises, upsells designed solely to remove people from their American dollars.

Dew clouded windows, headlights illuminated a fog that lifted off the river. They shared maps and routed their way through the Hungarian countryside. Zoli planned one stop for the way back.

Before Zoli left New York he met Banán at some out of place desk in the back of some random Upper East Side realty office. He sat there waiting for Zoli. A manila-folder was already laid out for him.

"Tell them Schwartz Laci sent you." He made sure to look Zoli in the eyes before he continued. "I am a very important person over there. They love me."

That day, Zoli went on to chat with people and proprietors at the last of the Hungarian meat markets on 2nd Avenue. He betrayed his life diet by sampling some fresh *májos pörkölt* straight from the pan. He hadn't had any Hungarian style liver with onions since his second heart attack almost killed him.

Hungarians congregated over food, ate standing up among the shelves of Hungarian imports that lined the aisles of a store that was running out of time. The European café across the street that was always teeming with Hungarian refugees every day, especially Sunday after church, was now a Starbucks. Hungarians still loitered there as often. Cheap coffee and long reminiscences mixed with the young professionals whom had claimed the neighborhood as their own.

Zoli made an appointment within the halls of the Hungarian Consulate General on 52nd St., was met with enthusiasm, led to back offices and archives. Persistent anti-Semitism encouraged the consul to accommodate the needs of the Hungarian American Jews. Hungarian nationals dressed for business sorted through available information, physical files, and still growing computer databases for the names of any and all of Zoli's possible relatives.

Long lost histories were added to Zoli's persistent search of an elusive cessation, each discovery pertinent in his repressed need to resurrect family.

The effort paid off, a single connection found. His mother's sister's name flashed on screen. Highlighted white letters blinked before Zoli, reflected in his sky blue eyes, and added weight to his small family.

Erzsi Tepper made residence in Miskolc as recently as two years prior to Zoli's efforts. The town was the distant hub Zoli's father traveled to back in the day. The last city before an expanse of farmlands that stood through time, grew with empires, and transformed by communist efficiency. Ample apartment buildings and grid like urban planning made the ride into and throughout the city straightforward, only a few old-world eccentricities and dead ends were endured before they rolled into the first gas station Danny saw.

They followed directions to a Soviet style housing block, an extremely tall and unusually wide structure with an imposing façade pocked by tightly squared windows, half sized and in various states of disrepair, some opened by panes shattered and ignored long ago. A few accommodated smokers or old ladies able to find enough space within the small frames. They got comfortable in well-practiced reclines held tight. Their hair put up in kerchiefs, uniform in their inaction, all stuck in the same place, in the same time, for as long as their knitting remained within reach.

Zoli stepped excitedly over sidewalks cracked and turned to debris; broken bottles and discarded cigarette butts mosaicked his march towards the entry way, a pattern of pollutants found in the disillusioned citizens of a country reeling from the void of a failed political system. These accommodations were held over for them from communism; de facto prisons that retained their captors even after the gates had been left wide open.

It was a sight to be had, a monolith left to commemorate a fallen bear towered over Zoli's progress. He ventured closer to the building's directory.

The family lingered close, watched Zoli scroll through listed occupants. He slowed through T without a Tepper in sight. The disappointment overwhelmed him, took the color out of his usually rosy completion. He leaned back, gave himself over to the undeniable force of gravity, teetered away from the bleak reality of his withered family tree.

"It vould have been nice to talk to someone who knew my family..." slipped from silence in a murmur corrected, "I mean, is my family."

The depth of the situation connected with Lizzy; herself without blood relations, abandoned in Seoul in her infancy, adopted by a family in New Jersey within her first year. She couldn't help but reach out to Zoli, they all did; despondence shared, draped them in the warmth of new communion.

"We're your family," Lizzy added, always putting others' feeling before her own.

"Who are you looking for?" was bellowed from above in Hungarian, broke their introspection; an echo over time tore through space, drew their attention upward, into the past.

They placed an older woman a few stories up. She

leaned out of her window with two arms propped against the window. Her body pressed up against the cold facade, discomfort pronounced in her pose.

"Erzsi Tepper!" Zoli replied. He cleared his throat, repeated himself with a full howl. His native language obliged. "My mother's sister Erzsi Tepper lived here."

A long devastating moment formed as the old woman wracked her brain to place the name. She turned to someone inside her apartment, then turned back to address the waiting Americans.

"I'm sorry." An unfortunate silence leveled their conversation, lingered. "She died about six months ago. She had no children. No relatives."

Optimism flushed from Zoli's face, was drained into a collective pit of disappointment, into the shit of his youth. Zoli held tears back as he said: "I was a relative."

Zoli played the ideal in his mind, a loop of what could have been; a reunion that tied his past to the present, old relatives and new daughter-in-laws entwined in a moment that would never happen.

"You got us, Pops!"

They laid hugs on the old guy. A smile extended across his face.

They got in the rental, and within 15 minutes they were driving through the grand nothingness of Zoli's childhood. Flat plains and open spaces dizzied city folk equilibrium, all signs of civilization were left in their rear view.

The main highway turned into county roads, slowly crumbled to dirt paths. Dust extended to the hamlets that hung on the northwest corner of the 52,000-kilometer-wide Great Hungarian Plain.

Newly erected aboveground phone and electrical posts led the way. The car lurched off the beaten path, toward distant town centers. A spattering of activity within the verdant expanse was pointed out along the way.

"Pull over here, to zat farmhouse!" Zoli yelled urgently, startled the carload. They laughed together, excitement and anxiety rolled into one.

Danny slowed up, stopped at a property line marked by overgrown crops.

"Zis vas my grandmother's house..."

A long breeze that had lingered over the property for generations took its turn over the car, seeped in through cracked windows, and chilled the occupants to the bone. They sat silent, waited for him to continue; thoughts of getting out of the car were stifled by Lizzy.

"Daniel." She held Danny to his seat from behind and whispered, "We're in the middle of nowhere, like, literally in the middle of nowhere." She buried her fingertips into his shoulder.

"Uh, I know. I drove through nothing to get us here," he quipped back.

"I'm not even getting service." Cultures crashed and compounded as an old lady made her way over from the nearby house. Danny rolled down windows to accommodate her approach. Lizzy reacted: "Danny, what are you doing? Roll up your window." She shook her head in disbelief, "I can't believe this."

"What are you doing so far from home?" Rural Hungarian croaked into the car, the smell of onions and garlic on each utterance. A voice toned by adversity, generations of alcoholism, and a pack a day shifted everyone in their seats.

With the sun at her back, beams of light blinded the family. The old lady remained silhouetted, glimpses allowed as she shifted with curiosity. Her face was constrained by a babushka worn tight around her head, tied under her chin; it accentuated wrinkles formed by time stilted, in effort, by an endless and unavoidable struggle; her bulbous nose cracked by drink, craters of broken skin brought near. She leaned in to continue her visit, admired the car's creature comforts, modern marvels.

"This is where I was raised..." Zoli pronounced in his native tongue. The declaration resurrected old feelings. The gleam of a lost childhood caught in Zoli's eyes, rose from the landscape like the wheat in the fields he pointed to. "My grandmother lived right here."

Lizzy whispered to her husband, "What's up with all the old ladies?"

Years of his father's stories, shared pain, detailed reflections of horrid facts led to a single explanation Danny had come up with: "It's a nation of widows, a lot of men didn't make it past the war, past communism."

"Your home?" An odd sensation came over the old lady, an unfamiliar feeling that forced her to take a long pause. She had experienced joy and sorrow, jealousy and anger, but never a return like Zoli's. Life in these parts remained simple, predictability was the only force majeure, set solely by the crop cycle. She shook her head, disbelief trumped all, but made way for: "The last child to grow up here from back then was little-Zoli."

"*Kish-Zoli,*" is what Lizzy heard, words that she

watched her father-in-law repeat to himself with the correct Hungarian spelling: "*Kis*-Zoli."

They watched Zoli drift into the childhood etched in the landscape. He ran through hindsight, tore through the hills with his three older brothers. Jenő minded the youngest of them, at his peak strength, on horseback, with health and happiness intact.

"That's me," he shared, solemnly with a glimmer. "I am little-Zoli."

He locked on to the elderly farm lady's disbelief; they laughed at her amazement said their goodbyes, and continued their way towards the center of town. The dull beige import rolled through a burg left to fester, past streets and homes unchanged; every inch remained true to Zoli's recollection.

"Up this street," Zoli said, assembling the pieces of his childhood in real time. "Turn right at the fork, here, here."

By now, the late model Japanese import drew townsfolk from their respective homes; word had gotten out, people came to greet the anomalous visitors.

Parked and trailed by the curious, kids who had never seen a new car before, the old who wracked their brains to recognize the old man who had to have been a little boy the last time they laid eyes on him, had all gathered. They watched Zoli lead his family in a walking tour of Felsővadász.

Lizzy hung tight, was dipped in the complete inverse of the universe as she knew it; dirt roads, thatched roofs, farm animals wandering in the streets, and toothless villagers commanded her unease.

Zoli continued through the streets, amazed, amused.

"Nothing has changed." He bounded toward a house on a hill. Green paint peeled from its exterior, it stood victim to the tumult of time and environment. He knocked on the front door then waited a second before he trespassed, craned to peek inside. The living room that hosted his birth was visible through half blinded windows.

He turned, heaved over-stimulated, motion sick as he swung full circle. Peace was thick in the country air; the family connected with its ease, and collectively waited for an answer at the front door. Patience melted, Zoli couldn't help but feel as though no one had been home since he left fifty years ago.

Zoli twisted toward a familiar view that had greyed through the decades, and seemed so small; the well of his youth remained intact. Its stone base erected in the shifting ground, run askew by the roll of change and locked closed to protect what continued to be the property owner's only source of fresh drinking water.

Zoli led his family through town. They evaded pigs, poultry, and the handful of pedestrians who trailed their march down dirt roads. The more townsfolk appeared the less comfortable Lizzy got. She may have been the only Asian person to have ever stepped foot in this part of the country since Genghis Khan's armies returned to Mongolia —at least that's how she felt.

She hopped back into the car as soon as she got the chance, as soon as the weary and prematurely aged towns-folk gathered. They existed in black and white, permanently boozed into place, wondering who their visors were.

Zoli returned home, to an unchanged world, the place where he would have remained in a life undisrupted;

glimpses connected the past to present, reality fluttered like fantasy, faded paint and disrepair the only thing that separated the two.

"You looking for something?" a country callused man in his mid-to-late-sixties asked, spit grass. His soiled tank-top and distended liver matched house and home. He eyed Zoli, moved to loiter against the poorly maintained fence that stood between them.

"Just looking," Zoli replied. "I grew up here, until…"

The stranger's face contorted; missing teeth, gummed intensity, a tilted head to help place the face all slammed against a wall of recognition; bile, regrets, shame, regurgitated through the peasant's status quo simultaneously; a rooster's untimely crow turned heads, it had come home to roost.

"1945," the date, a point, the festering hole in the chronology of Zoli's youth, made clear,

He watched the guilt of a child boil over, strength mustered from the kid who watched his friend's deportation, now faced with a question he didn't want the answer: "You are Glück?"

A slow turn, inquired look; Zoli gave the peasant the once over in his peripheral, "Yes, it's me, *Kis*-Zoli."

The name struck the booze-addled failed farmer like a bullet fired from one soul to pierce another. The target barreled over in generational regret, unable to identify the feelings he redirected, nerves bound by the drunken happy that numbed all regrets except for the ones that drive up to your front door.

"Oh my god, it is good to see you… It's me, Csaba. Remember? Remember me?"

Zoli did. He saw.

Boys jeered and cheered as the Glück family was carted out of town with the one other Jewish family; seven-year-old Csaba was among the revelers. They were all confined in the embrace of a hatred that begat hatred.

"Yes, I remember."

The same face, years later, was enthused to see Zoli, practically relieved to have him alive and in his presence.

"Come in. Come in for a drink? A little *pálinka*? You have time?" A usually empty gesture was drowned with meaning, apologies buried in invitations. "You have time! You have time!"

Zoli looked over, noticed Lizzy in the car with the windows up and doors locked; the sun grew heavy in the sky, kissed the horizon in a gouache of oranges and reds painted on the canvas of his past.

"Next time," Zoli said. He was struck by a satisfaction he never realized he needed, a sensation he never knew he hoped would come his way. A bittersweet victory stemmed from life that would have never been without his family's expulsion.

"That could have been me," he declared as the ladies slept in the back seat. Zoli held a mirror up to revision: What if he remained, with his family, at home in Felső-vadász, forever?

They drove through the night and back into the twinkle of a glowing metropolis Zoli could have only dreamt of as a child.

24

Incandescent bulbs burned amber, ornate fixtures laid their warmth over the interior of the Gellért Hotel. Zoli and his family basked in its sanctuary, warmed within by Bulgarian whiskey and Hungarian wine, resumed their vacation. The experience collected in their journey was smacked aside by the stark reality of a life lived.

"My grandmother used to bake fruits fresh from the fields in cakes and pies. She made fresh jams and compotes." Smacked lips and enticed salivary glands shared a Pavlovian response to the thought. "They were so sweet. I can still taste it on my tongue."

"And you used to make *pálinka* with Laci," Julika chimed in half-English, half-Hungarian.

"Yes," laughter encouraged fond memories. "He put a shotgun into my hands to protect our moonshine, I vas nine-years-old at the time." Conversation redirected to Lizzy's fresh set of ears, "My broder had a very big business, he vas the envy of everyone."

"Yes, I know, Pops."

"I vas talking to my lovely daughter-in-law." The moment hung on a gleeful memory, a smile shared with his son's wife, turned on the totality of Zoli's bleak childhood. "And, what did it get him?"

They continued to eat and explore the city divided by the Danube; Lizzy's introduction to Eastern Europe was filled with all the usual stops, over eating and indulgent drinking folded into every experience. She bore witness to the overcompensation of two youths that went without, all grown up with hard-earned cash in hand. Lizzy was run ragged by the excesses of Julika's itinerary.

"Just give us a day for the baths," Lizzy had to beg.

Their old friend Gabor was still the concierge; it was beginning to feel like he always would be. He interrupted a Gluck family caucus with phone in hand, an unexpected interruption laid forth in the language of their collective youths. "Excuse me, I hate to interrupt."

"No bother, Gabi." Smiles were exchanged.

"I have a call for you, Zoli."

"For me?"

"An American."

Zoli took the phone from Gabor, sheepishly placed it against his ear. "Hello?" He listened intently, "Yes, yes, that's me.... That is amazing. Here in Budapest?" A few more words exchanged over the call, Zoli reacted accordingly, "Yes, I would be honored to..."

He motioned for a pen and pad that were immediately supplied by their friend the concierge. Zoli jotted down an address, a phone number, the name of an organization. Eyeing his family through the conversation; Zoli answered his call, "Ok. I vill be there." He hung up, looked to those closest to him. "It vas an American organization here in Budapest to document Holocaust history and interview survivors. Cans you believe dat?"

"How'd they know you were here?"

"I forgot I called them. Banán gave me their number." He heaved a heart heavy sigh. "They want to interview me on camera while we're here."

"You gonna do it, Pops? You have to do it," Danny asserted.

"I vill," Zoli avowed. "I am."

"You have such an amazing story, Zoli," Lizzy chimed in; she secretly hoped that the reprieve would allow her some time at the thermal baths and spa. "You have to share it..."

And, he did.

"The survivors gave us their testimonies so that we would tell the world and educate future generations twenty, fifty, a hundred years from now and beyond. The testimonies go beyond what you can find in a book, beyond what you can see on a blackboard, beyond what you can type on a tablet."
-Stephen Smith
Executive Director, USC Shoah Foundation

Zoli adjusted his bifocals, focused on the quote displayed on the outside wall of the temporary Budapest branch of The Shoah Foundation. Danny went along, just the two of them. Zoli steadied his nerves. They entered.

Students from the University of Southern California

were waiting; a diverse but somehow familiar looking group represented many degrees of separation from their shared Jewish roots, a few native Hungarians were hired for administrative duties and such.

"Mr. Gluck?" a young lady said as she approached Zoli. "Thank you for coming in, please, this way."

"Thank you, darling."

Zoli was happily led into a makeshift studio; lights and camera set up in front of a chair set against a backdrop. Zoli took the seat.

Professor Karl Bardosh, a thin man with angular features and limited stature, wore a suit made of black pleather, donned a hat befitting an eccentric auteur, a film-maker. He had worked with innumerable pillars of Hungarian cinema before emigrating to the United States to attend the American Film Institute and was now back in the homeland to direct these testimonials.

"Very nice to meet you, Mr. Gluck." Bardosh was joined by his students, production assistants working for class credit. "Are you familiar with the Shoah Foundation?"

"Just what you told me over the phone."

"Very well." Bardosh had his help adjust equipment so he could continue. "The Shoah Foundation was made possible by a grant made by Stephen Spielberg in 1994..."

"Spielberg, the movie maker?"

"Yes, he made all this possible. He even found us a permanent home at University of Southern California in Los Angeles." Bardosh took a seat off camera, across from Zoli. "We are in Hungary to collect stories, record the past, uncovering history in the strangest places. We just found a wealth of papers unearthed during a renovation of a nearby communist era apartment."

"What did you find?"

"We have never seen anything like it." The professor was visibly excited by the significance of their haul, leaned into the conversation. "A total of 6,300 documents from a 1944 census were torn out of a wall by the new owners."

Americans interested in reconnecting to their lineage bought condos with great views of the Danube, Parliament building, and beyond. They mostly planned on keeping the old-world charm intact, but the addition of some modern amenities left gaps in the walls of this particular abode. A laborer tore open old plaster, laid eyes on what looked like handwritten text.

The owners, local historians, and Professor Karl Bardosh marveled at the magnitude of the find. Papers were carefully removed, examined and studied by various domestic and international scholars and organization.

The quality of the documents, ink remained readable after all these decades, was attributed to the heavy smoking of the apartment's prior owner. The papers were rendered waxy, calcified with a sick yellow patina. The extremely detailed outline of how Budapest had intended to rid its city of its 200,000 Jews in Nazi death camps was public knowledge; the irrefutable proof was present and in the form of the official Nazi census.

"All the names, all the families?" Zoli's voice cracked.

"We can talk more about it after we get your story on tape."

College-aged-kids rolled tape on the professor's mark, the sound guy yelled: "Speed!"

"Professor Karl Bardosh interviewing Zoltan Gluck..."

The two men sat face to face for close to two hours, full videotape swapped for fresh ones. Lungs parched by speech and emotion moved on, Zoli captivated the small crews with his firsthand-history lesson. He hosted them through time, colorful language led to powerful imagery painted by words and inflections. Stealing food from rabbits, drinking milk from the manure, the Germans who risked their own lives to help Jewish children in need, the farm widow and her daughter in particular: Zoli shared it all.

His storytelling left eyes welled, tears prompted when he detailed the last days of his brother's life, and the kids who suffered through the ordeal along with them.

"I vould never see him again," Zoli trailed off at the end of his testimonial. "I never knew what happened to Jenő after that day."

They sat under the weight of moments relived, silent. Cut tape.

"Maybe we can find something in our databanks..." was the only hope Bardosh could give to the unalterable history shared.

"From ze papers you found?" Zoli sparked at the possibilities.

"Yes, it was an astounding find. Most all the papers we have from the war are faded or rotten, the quality of the paper was poor, by '44 German supplies were running thin. Once we get it into the computer..." Bardosh explained as they stood over a focused young man digitizing archives, uploading Zoli's video to their blossoming website.

"Văt then? After it is all in ze computer."

"It will be available to visitors who can explore the database for names, relatives, histories, testimonials..." He led Zoli to another group of students working their way through lists of Jews counted in May 1944. "The Nazis established holding locations for Jews before relocating them to the ghettos in Pest's seventh district, by the *Dohány Utcai Zsinagóg*, before they were deported to the gas chambers of Auschwitz."

"And, you have all ze names? All the Hungarian Jews are on ze list?"

"Yes. The Nazis kept impeccable records. If they came through Budapest there's a good chance we know their whole history," Bardosh lit up, shared Zoli's amazement, "Jews filled their census forms out honestly, they had no idea what was in store. After they were counted, 200,000 Jews were moved into 2,000 tenements called Yellow Star Houses. All of this is on record."

Bardosh's continued narrative provoked imagery; memories from childhood urged Zoli's heart to skip a beat, then another. The moment Zoli watched his family dead and adrift, face down in the currents of the Danube were drawn out in the professor's speech.

"They were left to die crammed in ghettos. Many late arrivals were murdered by the river. There's a memorial of that atrocity..." the professor said.

"Another memorial?" Zoli questioned.

"Yes. Iron shoes."

"Iron shoes?"

"That's how they memorialized the location of the

massacre," Bardosh allowed himself into the scope of Zoli's reflection. "Around 600,000 Hungarian Jews perished in the Shoah, most of them at Auschwitz, but many of them were lost on the banks of the Danube. Their shoes were left behind..."

"I remember..." Words weighted down by consequences, forced histories indented impressions. Past and present fell indistinguishable in Zoli's amygdala; grief was close enough to breathe; smells and sounds rang through his senses, perpetually pressed against his innards. He was eternally trapped in a moment, then another, and another. "I văs there," he added.

The professor held his side, tried to ease a spasm induced by the horrid reality. He had developed sympathy pains in the course of collecting testimonials, it was impossible not share the discomfort with all those who had opened up about their past, some for the first time.

Danny had entered the room and took a seat behind them as his father saw information gather in a final configuration. An easily accessible matrix full of names and dates left Zoli in awe of the modern age.

"Here you can look up names, dates, locations, concentration camps."

Zoli placed his glasses on the tip of his nose, tilted his head back to accommodate a line of corrected sight.

Bardosh made way, slid the keyboard Zoli's way. The old man tilted his head, searched every key individually for the letters needed, an excruciating process; Zoli stabbed, spelled: J...E...N...O.

The computer whirled to life, the churn of gathering

data presented in an ordered manner. A list of names, Zoli's family, reflected in the blue eyes of a man who has seen the world and remained a little farm-boy concurrently.

"Just click the hyperlink," Danny broke in. "Roll the mouse until your cursor, that blinking arrow is over the blue link, yes that one, okay, click it, yes, click..."

"Click? Vat iz dis click?" Zoli followed directions as best he could, eventually opened a page dedicated to his brother.

The information provided was sparse, much of the form page was empty. Zoli remained glued to spaces left blank, in a voided family history; current city, marital status, time of death.

"Vat does this mean?"

"Looks like there isn't much on Jenő Glück," Bardosh hovered, looked from Zoli back to the pale glow of the computer screen. "Thanks to your testimonial we know he was liberated at Mauthausen sub-camp Gunskirchen..."

"I vas with him. He was in the hospital there. Vat happened to him next?"

"We don't know. We will add information as soon as we get any. The more we get the more we can cross-reference, build a fuller picture. We just started and there is already so much we have yet to put into the system." Tough news was never easy to deliver, Bardosh continued, "Take as much time as you like with the computer." He floated on a thought, the professor remembered, "We do have a list of survivors living in Budapest." He turned, left Zoli entranced in a new world.

Zoli was lost in the hypnotic buzz of the information

super highway. The well-filtered version of which displayed family history in each passing click. He toggled through each member on record, spent time on each page. An act that willfully sent him deep into each of their tragic ends.

He saw his mother's last moments in the darkness of his clenched eyes. Tears decades overdue kept them closed tight, fluttering in horror.

Danny had scooted in, helped his dad navigate cyberspace. Stories shared in concert with photos found branched out like chapters of his own biography: The Shoah, The Exodus, The Liberation of Israel illustrated online and in chronological order. Hours at the helm, piloting the rough seas of his struggle, finding long-lost friends and family among the ones and zeroes kept them glued to the screen. Zoli's story capped by his trip to America on the doomed Andrea Doria; the whole thing was right there, etched in light. Name after name, victims and survivors all recipients of the same well-documented brutality.

Danny watched his father lose all the color in his face. Zoli's usually rosy cheeks were as white as freshly washed sheets.

"Oh my God." Disbelief festered in a life reduced to archives. Zoli nearly fell out of his chair at the sight of a name he didn't know he had to find. "Click. Click there. Here," he exclaimed.

Danny led the cursor to a hover over a name that pulsed in the clarity of binary code and jumped into the information age.

Zoli's was reduced to a reflection, melded into a timeline, into his own history, into the name: Chaim Kemény.

They left the Shoah Foundation. Zoli walked under a new burden, it bunched up in his neck, shot down through his innards, infected his soul. They continued quietly towards the hotel. The adjacent Danube drowned brown in pollution, inundated by garbage and grief.

"Hey, check it out," Danny said. "It's that memorial the professor mentioned."

They turned to it, took a second to add the sight to the history they carried. Tourists walked by the unassuming Iron Shoes, only a few stopped for the photo op, its relevance left mostly unnoticed.

Zoli took a folded piece of paper out of his breast pocket, unfurled it to reveal the name of a hospital where Chaim was in hospice.

"Do you mind I go alone?" Zoli asked.

"You sure?"

Their gaze remained intact, made assurances.

"Yes, I'm sure... You don't need to return..." Zoli insisted. "I do..."

Halls crumbling from neglect, floors left in need of mopping, asbestos bubbled off the ceilings of an institution decades behind Western medical standards. The path led Zoli toward truths he didn't know if he wanted to know. His progress from the elevator was plagued by reluctance. He stopped, questioned himself. "Vhat am I doing?" One false start after another, as he considered, reconsidered: "Vhat is there left to know?"

The sounds of low toned beeps that tracked beats and drips from bags both inside and out chorused through a room half full of the bedridden. Zoli peeked in, turned to the closest patient, and proceeded inside. He worked his way from one bed to another, found an old man lying in his own decrepitude. A cloud of death visible over his dying days. Zoli tackled memory, attempted to place the face, questioned instinct, but continued all the same.

"Chaim?" he asked as he inched closer to the man who was once his minor. All manner of tubes and wires did him a disservice, kept him alive against his will. Zoli got close enough to recognize him, "Chaim?"

"Who is it?" Eyes cracked through yellowed crust, neglected health on full display, emaciated and diseased. Chaim Kemény's sight struggled to focus. "What do you want?"

"Chaim? Is that you?"

"Go away." The old man rustled out of restless slumber and into his unforgiving reality, shifted his weight from one side to the other, eluded ease. Sheets soiled by all manner of bodily fluid pronounced Chaim's discomfort with a stench, and a command: "Leave me alone."

"Chaim..." Zoli acclimated, leaned in. Hungarian dripped in pathos, he proclaimed, "It's me...."

Chaim locked on. A rush of adrenaline gifted him the strength to sit up and gawk in amazement. A slow realization hit him like a force of nature, a tsunami that leveled the past into the present.

"Zoli?"

"Yes, it's me." Zoli's proceeded carefully, tilted into what he knew would forever shatter his well-constructed truth. "How are you?

Pleasantries missed their mark, opened up a silence that drowned in the ocean of their shared past. There was nothing left to say, small talk insulted the gravity of their proximity.

"I know..."

The old man squared up, prepared to expend more energy than he had been asked to for a long time. Deep breaths and a cleared throat led the way for: "I have to get it off my chest, Zoli..." He struggled to continue, "Before it is too late."

"It's okay." Zoli grew tense with anticipation. "You don't have to..."

"I wasn't myself ..." Chaim interrupted. He fought with grief, talked through tears, battled death for the moments needed. "They changed me..."

"Chaim..." Zoli shook his head. "Please..."

The old man wouldn't let the subject change, kept explaining, "He cared for me when no one else would, he fed me, clothed me, gave me a bed to sleep in..."

A heavy silence fell over them, was accompanied by the erratic sound of Chaim's heart, as monitored. Grown men regressed, sat face to face with children battered by the fogs of war.

"It's not your fault," Zoli added. "You were just a child."

Chaim's beats turned frantic, a force of self-loathing charged by guilt and sorrow draped the large room in darkness. Still calm before the storm; blinders fell over Zoli's eyes as he focused in on his struggling friend.

"Everything... he made me do everything..." Chaim said, tilting away from Zoli. He closed his eyes in an attempt to deny himself the pain of a truth, and uttered, "And, and... I wanted to..."

Young Chaim Kemény was brought out of the cold rain

and into the warmth of Commandant Franz Ziereis's home. The crack of the fire and table full of food that the Nazi command enjoyed, and was dangled in front of their new recruits. Dr. Heim initiated Pavlovian instruction, offered Chaim sweets and praise. Dr. Dirlewanger joined in, allowed the boys in their service to gorge on Bavarian delicacies while their peers died starving on their feet less than a kilometer away.

"Please let me know if you would prefer it back at the camps," Dr. Heim would say while inspected nails and teeth, down the line of boys frigid with obedience. "Or, I can arrange for a job in the quarries. Say the word. It will be good for the Reich to have such well-fed workers."

Ziereis favored Chaim, set him apart from the other boys in their collection. For nights that turned to days, through baths and bedtimes, Ziereis kept his favorite curly haired Jew close and away from the doctor's wicked experimentations. His nine-year-old pet eased to the comforts provided.

"It wasn't your fault..." Zoli leaned in, put a hand on his battered friend's shoulder; bones and cancer to the touch, a shell of a human eaten by the onus of the Holocaust. He locked onto the regret in the dying man's eyes. "You were just a child."

"I was never a child, Zoli, they tore it out of me."

"I know."

"They made me into a... I am responsible..." Struggled breaths were wrecked by panic, forced gasps agitated by the long-overdue; anger boiled over, accented Chaim's final words with a gurgle of personal salvation. "I told them about the farmhouse, Zoli, they found you because of me..."

Zoli's concerns faded, acceptance struggled to make way; he stood in puddles of worry turned real, drowned in a long malignant moment, then uttered: "I know."

Chaim's percussive EKG dominated his shallow admission; tears ran down his face as he lunged for breaths, jutted for air like a fish out of water. He forced his secrets to the surface for the first time. "I remember begging to stay with him. I cried when, when the Soviets..." He struggled to draw oxygen, lungs failed between syllables uttered, "I remember everything. You don't know what I did. Me. A Jew..."

"It wasn't you."

"I brought them to the farm..." The tempo on his monitors chimed critical, a confluence of disjointed beats contorted his confession. "I saw them shoot Jenő, I saw him fall..." He reached for Zoli. Unable to make contact, Zoli instinctively met him halfway.

"They missed," Zoli interjected.

"Did he make it? Was he freed?" Chaim charged.

"I don't know what happened to him," Zoli uttered. A knot tied tight, stressed to near-tear, slowed fissures that promptly gave way to sudden lacerations; a pool of mixed emotions, actualized lives, and the situation at large poured from his pores.

"I am sorry. I am so sorry..." This was the moment Chaim had been saving his strength for, a lucidity long unseen emerged from the withered man. "Not a day goes by that I don't relive..."

"You don't have to..." Zoli's soft interruption relieved

Chaim of his effort. Zoli exhaled, in the moment, "I forgive you."

Chaim let go, fell back into his bed; inner peace introduced in a final exhale. The ease that ushered him into the great beyond wouldn't be disturbed by the doctors and nurses charged to resuscitate him from it.

25

———

Packed and ready to go, Lizzy and Danny extended their final farewells to the family, hugs and kisses were dealt and held. The entirety of the trip was encapsulated in the unsaid, and articulated in the obvious.

"I vish you vere coming vith us, kiddos," Zoli exuded.

"Yeah, why didn't we do the cruise too?" Lizzy teased her husband.

"You need more vacation?" Danny barbed.

Zoli watched their banter. A fulfilled grin grew across his face; his whole life invested in their union. The thought of grandchildren twinkled in his eyes, the sound of being called *nǎgypapa* rang through his mind.

"I know you don't," Lizzy joked as she set Danny's corduroy blazer aside, palmed his protruding gut. A collection of Eastern Europe's fattiest delicacies jiggled in place, sat to clog arteries, shortened his breath.

"Ok, goulash for breakfast, lunch, and dinner," Danny retorted.

"Not breakfast..."

"You for real?" Danny booty bumped her; lovely levity lived through their yin and yang. "I have eyes you know."

"Okay, one time." Her smile was infectious, spread through the morning huddle. "They were leftovers. It's not like I ordered it for breakfast."

"So good," Julika added.

"I like Hungarian food..." Lizzy and Danny put on their best old Hungarian lady affect to state the obvious, in unison, shoulder to shoulder, "It's taaasty."

Their ease was icing on Zoli's cake. He got to eat it too. A life of hardships washed away in the moment. He stood with his wife and watched their kids hop into a cab and disappear into an old city illuminated by the new dawn.

Friends congregated at the boat basin that extended out from the city and into the Danube, faces from Zoli and Julika's visit waited to see them off. Gabor, Marta, Cousin Szandor, old friend and artist Eszter Gyory all intermingled with the ghosts of their respective regressive pasts: parents left behind, siblings—Jenő—forgotten friends, and long lost relations, distant relatives whose names were never learned were all present at river's edge. The assemblage filled the couple with the totality of their lives lived, the weight of the bad, the relief of the good; festive with gifts of food made fresh and flowers homegrown fanned Zoli and Julika's departure.

"That was a nice trip with the kiddos." Zoli looked over the riverboat's railing. The winds of the moving watercraft blew through his thin grey hair, so habitually combed into place that it lifted off his head in a long flat quaff more suitable for a jazz bar than a luxury cruise. His eyes locked on the twists and turns they faced up river. Its current washed clean in their progress; the foul tint travelled through the bad and the worse before it cracked blue.

The 400-foot Explorer Class cruise ship, complete with limited and luxurious sleeping quarters and upscale amenities, set forth on its twelve-day journey. The public announcement system kept the passengers informed: "There will be day trips in Bratislava, Linz, and Nuremberg with overnights in both Vienna, Cologne, and Amsterdam," was repeated in the languages represented on the tour.

Within hours of their push upstream, in the smooth calm of the starry nocturne, they maneuvered past embankments, beyond ports that have bloomed from ruin and flourished through the ages. Modern cities rebuilt and brilliant against the pitch-black-backdrop of their collective history, under the peaks of the Little Carpathian Mountains, the ship pushed across the Hungarian border.

Zoli and Julika watched the country neither called home disappear in their wake with drinks in hand.

By morning, passengers were allowed to disembark, visit the 17th century old capital city of Bratislava in Slovakia. Julika's family had come to Hungary from Slovakia, some returned after the war, others stayed where they were. Borders changed around them. They immigrated at home.

"Julika!" the old man with an eternally waxed handlebar mustache yelled enthusiastically; the felted hat shifted on his head in his enthusiasm. Fritz continued with his hand on his head, "Zoli!"

They met with hugs and reintroductions. Uncle Fritzi,

as Julika had called him throughout her childhood, was the only recognizable relative among the extended family who waited for them. The gathering shuffled through introductions, Czech spoken and not understood.

Fritz raised his arms and yelled, "Family meet your family," in Hungarian, Czech, Yiddish, and English for good measure, and concluded in the language they preferred: "Let's eat."

The entire brood walked their American cousins through the 18th century town, under architecture that stood through tumult. Original hues were respected in restoration, a continuity of the brownish-orange rooftops distinguished the old parts of town from the new. Baroque palaces and ornate concert halls lined cobblestoned streets as they made their way toward a local vineyard.

Julika's relations felt that this rare reunion deserved a celebratory feast; the traditional meal featured a whole goose liver fried fresh in a pool of its own congealed fat, blood, liver, and pork sausages cut into bite-sized pieces, onion sautéed slabs of cured bacon, cold cuts, cheese, bread, fruit, sweets and pastries were all laid out; the whole thing washed down with an abundance of wine and *pálinka*.

Even after two heart attacks, Zoli successfully convinced Julika, with the help of the extended family, "It would be rude not to accept at least one plate full of the hospitality."

They ate and drank, stories of the past were never far from audible, perspectives draped out for all to consider. Zoli continued to contemplate a life in Eastern Europe, the way his family had intended, as was now splayed out in front of him. Their family was allowed to branch out, thrive in the old country. Life in Slovakia was good. Zoli watched babies rocked to sleep in new grandmothers' arms, young couples starting their lives together.

Zoli and Julika were cornered by a bunch of their youngest relatives; most of them wore Danny's hand-me-down. One wore the suit he was bar mitzvahed in; the blue and white New York Yankees pin-striped three-piece suit complete with vest was only taken out on careful occasions.

"Tell us about New York?"

"Where is your son?"

"Do you have grandchildren?"

They were bombarded in translation. Their answers couldn't keep up with the curiosity.

"Guys, give them a chance to eat," Uncle Fritzi interjected, tired of interpreting.

The walk back to the docks was long and deliberate, their drawn out farewell held up the cruise ship's departure. Crew waited on the Glucks as they went down the line with hugs and handshakes for the entire family.

Back onboard, veiled in the depths of night, the sound of the river's rush; a fork redirected the large craft towards the lights of the oldest European metropolis. Sparkles off the horizon rippled in the current. Vienna basked in innovation, cultural and scientific accomplishments lined its rich history. The moment the Iron Curtain shattered, Vienna reclaimed its place as the shining light of the lower Danube.

The three days and two nights they took in the city was filled with tours, where Mozart and Beethoven lived and now lay, Freud's offices, and the art school where Austrian-born Hitler was refused admittance. They spent nights out; the opera and concert halls were Julika's favorite. They were a reminder of a childhood filled with music that was forever lost.

Viennese liberties were held in high regard by Eastern Europeans who went without. Zoli remembered hearing of the ideal in dreams shared by old ladies who peeled potatoes or worked the gardens, tales of lives that eluded him in the country or at the camp. Residing in an American style four-star hotel had never once crossed into those childhood allowances.

They spent a day in Grinzing; a quant village established in the 14th century by winemakers was made up of a cluster of brightly painted homes and cellars; vineyards, restaurants, and cafés offered the freshest and the finest the area could afford. The Eastern European-born couple were elevated to tourists worth catering to. The fact that it was the antithesis of how Zoli was received his fist time up the Danube, by train, on foot, by force, was not overlooked by Zoli.

They walked aimlessly through time; Vienna's lights washed the old city in tungsten warmth, the old capital of the Habsburg Kingdom lived up to the honor, its Schön-brunn Palace stood as testament to Austria's opulence.

Zoli sat on a couch in a museum room full of works by old masters. He drowned in the depth of color, strong brush strokes, subtleties in the eyes of portraiture that bore down on the viewer. Imperial Jewels on display capped their day in the *Museumsquartier*. By design, after an early dinner, and by appointment only, they took the early evening to visit Otto Fine Art.

Still located at *Grünangergasse* 6, 1010 Wien, little had changed in the salon style gallery. They entered.

Glimpses into the bygone eras of European grandeur remained, antiques that reflected a refinement persevered in the midst of its declining relevance. Rudolf Otto's son, Heinz, took his father place behind a desk inside.

"Mr. Otto?" Zoli approached him, face to face for the first time.

"Yes?" English extended, as hands were clasped.

"Zoltan... Zoltan Gluck."

"Oh, Mr. Gluck." Required English drifted into habitual German, "What a pleasure to meet you."

Pleasantries shared led to aperitifs served in hand blown long stemmed glasses, "hand painted by local artisans," as explained by the proprietor as they made their way through the display.

"Your father was a very fair man..." Zoli stopped on a magnificent landscape, the great Hungarian Plain of his youth captured between four corners. "If it weren't for him, I may have never built my business from where Stern-*bacsi* left it," *bacsi* being the suffix used in respect for a male elder, *neni* for the feminine. Zoli had earned the honor of the suffix in recent years.

"I am honored to extend ze tradition, Zoli-*bacsi*..." the young Mr. Otto said. He stood straight with a well-groomed posture; his English broken into a thousand German digraphs, dripped in its inescapable cadence. "I vill consign za vay he did. Vhatever you vant."

"Thank you, Mr. Otto, but, I retired..."

"*Ach*, a salesman never retires, not vone like you..."

"Yes, but I sold my gallery."

"I think you enjoy it too much. You will continue with your customers on 'ze road,' no?" Heinz nodded, convinced himself. "Ya, I think so."

Zoli knew he was right as he investigated the quality of the large oils in ornate hand carved frames that occupied all the available space of the modest Viennese storefront. Standing before glimpses of European life, canvases of the way things were, Zoli stumbled over truths, up paths taken and down all the possibilities that existed along the way.

The thought of alternate lives penetrated Zoli's considerations; he was lost in one such indulgence where he was allowed to follow in his father's footsteps in Felsővadász, and so on. It was a thought that haunted him through the rest of the evening.

Pastries and strong coffee ended their overnight, few words were left to share. They were both exhausted, burdened by a proximal introspection.

Julika was forever tormented by abandonment issues, was left forever miserable; fatherlessness darkened her childhood more than the Holocaust, and lingered in her subconscious. Her anxiety was well-hidden but ever-present, revealed in tantrums of tears and raised voices that lasted through her life in behaviors unbecoming an older woman.

Zoli was open to the emotions that accompanied his many realizations. The truths that had eluded him filled memories, occupied thought. The knowledge was his. It comforted him.

On deck, the next morning, and the morning after, Zoli looked out onto the lush terrain floating by; a bounty grown from a mayhem laid upon the land, obliterated life and landscape bloomed in reclamation under the new sun.

The two spent nights in the casino onboard. They lost chips, drank Absolut martinis, up with two olives, then another. Dining was served fine behind expansive windows that panned the countryside's ever changing view.

Julika joined her husband on a nighttime topside walk. With champagne in hand, the cool wind in their hair, Zoli raise his glass, "to life," was the beginning of a toast unexpectedly interrupted.

Around the bend, and in an instant, all the transcendence of the luxury cruise was obliterated by a gruesome sight. A sore that oozed off the Bavarian banks of the Danube to infect the waterway, and seared Zoli to the core. He had no way out from under the tsunami of memories and emotions. He suffocated on the barrage, gasped for air.

"The notorious concentration camp Mauthausen can be seen off the starboard side," the P.A. system chimed, turned Zoli in its direction. "Please consult with our concierge to arrange a tour during your daytrip in Linz."

It was a stop more in service of the cruise-liner than the passengers, Linz's central location made it a perfect transportation hub. After the first half of the tour, the ship needed to refuel and restock food and services, accommodate new arrivals and connections for those traveling on excursions beyond.

The boat docked. Passengers congregated on deck, clouds rolled in in prelude. Darkness fell over the landscape. Summer storms dropped lightning, exploded thunder, like bombs over the waterfront's war torn history.

They retreated inside for the creature comforts that

awaited them: a cocktail reception in the best room the ship had to offer, then a mix of traditional and contemporary dances were all a part of that night's entertainment. They drank and gambled against the inevitability of the new dawn.

Weather cleared, sunlight burned the overcast, streaked in the new day. Julika made sure to sign up for the tour. "Two for Mauthausen," uttered Julika without an inkling of incongruity. The irony escaped her.

They ate their continental breakfast while waiting to board the bus.

The smell of communism presented itself in the cold war era vehicle, more like a converted truck than a tour bus, here to take tourists on a half-hour drive full of prepared remarks in struggled English.

"Linz vas Hitler's childhood home, the location of the camp so close is... uncanny," their young tour guide shared.

The van pulled up to the Mauthausen Memorial. The group disembarked and gathered around a large statue that stands outside the concentration camp; it depicted a prisoner of the camp, in ragged clothes, uncomfortably thin, with his hands up to the futility of those years. "*Lidebdete menschen seid wachsam*," was etched in its base, begged for awareness from all who had come to visit.

Tourists continued into the fortress-like structure, clean and presentable, the once overcrowded and uninhabitable barracks were kept museum pristine; "Mauthausen was established as a quarry, and assured profitability by keeping slave labor..."

Zoli shuffled along, fell behind, weighed down by his return. Familiarity made it difficult to keep up, sounds turned static, melted in Zoli's being. He curled and regressed to being back in his old home, shook like the child he was back then.

"Who the Nazis worked to death," the tour-guide continued.

Zoli caught up as the group entered the newly built visitors' center; a polished presentation of the horrors in the camps, rooms full of 81,007 names, victims, Glucks included, with 10,000 spaces still left blank for "victims unknown." Nazi tools of terror on display; whips used by guards, empty Zyklon-B gas canisters used in genocide, as well as identity bracelets retrieved from mass graves all sat behind an inch of protective Plexiglas.

Zoli stayed back, snagged on the past as it laid over the present, the two turned indistinguishable. The flavors of his time there remained fresh on his tongue, the taste of human ash in the air was forever stuck in his nostrils.

"We're going to miss the tour..." Julika chimed in, left ignored.

Zoli's non-answer was his only answer. He stood on defiled ground. Formative brutality permeated through him, where they were, where he was.

"This vas home," he turned into the discomfort, stared out toward the adjacent fields. His finger extended on familiar terrain, explained, "That's where we worked, just over the hill, ze displaced person camp vasn't that far away either." He stepped on his old path to work. "Oh my God," the sight of a long forgotten monastery snatched his breath.

The 13th century chapel, left within the 15th century compound the Catholic Church built around it, towered over the remnants of the displaced persons' camp. Zoli craned his neck to catch sight of a modest steeple within the Gothic angles and intricate details; flamboyant arches and flying buttresses built through recorded history.

He set off in its direction, strained uphill, and stood intimidated upon arrival. He looked up to catch sight of the immense cross that balanced on the cathedral's peak. It seemed so small, memory had deceived him.

Julika followed him directly toward the house of worship.

The sound of their entrance echoed off walls, reverberated through the space, made their presence felt.

"I can'ts believe it," Zoli slowed to a sensation, the familiarity of an unchanged church. "Just like I remember."

A nun in her early eighties shimmied out of a room adjacent to the gothic entrance. The heavy wood door creaked closed behind her.

"Hello, my name es Sister Mary Kessler." English thick with a German timbre, aged in the shadow of death, bounced through the nave. Slow and careful, she was sure to annunciate. "Can I help you?"

Zoli's solemn expression deepened; blue eyes that belonged to the teenager transported affections through time. "Do you keep records?"

"Records?" Sister Mary Kessler tilted her head, intrigued. Her tone adjusted to the subject matter. "We kept records after the war, before the allies took over."

"I remember coming in here looking for my brother... here... in '46..." Haunted by the utterance, he continued, "His name was Jenő, Jenő Glück, born 1926."

Zoli regressed, fought tears. His eyes welled regardless,

red and sore, nerves tingled top to toes, popped through his central nervous system like electricity on fire. Jitters developed in a manmade cool by success in America. He was replaced by the child who stood in that exact same spot as he had so long ago.

Sister Mary Kessler watched Zoli squirm, body movements and affects of a child facing the worst truths. A damp silence fell over the space, saturated the walls; lingered discomfort infected every word shared.

"You came in after ze var?" Her accent deepened the further her recollections were drawn.

"Yes..." Zoli looked to his wife, found his bearings, turned back to the nun, and continued, "To look for my brother."

Long churning quiets that lived solemnly in this church screamed out at once, joined in an avalanche of inaudible grief. Silence imposed by those there in spirit, the unsaid accessible in every inch of surrounding earth.

"I was here... then..." Sister Mary Kessler broke the silence with a gentle caring, a soothing empathy.

"You were?" Zoli questioned, amazed.

"I have been here all this time." She led them into a side office, "Did you say Jenő..."

"Gluck, Jenő Gluck, born 1926." Zoli followed close behind. A new enthusiasm welled from within, was urged on by Julika. They kept quiet, careful not to rattle the new reality around them.

Sister Mary Kessler moved toward old shelves loaded full of cobwebs and accumulation. Long unmoved ledgers filed away in their permanent homes. She urged her old tired bones through appropriated Nazi records, hospital admissions forms. Determined, her fingers ran through one alphabetical list after another, eventually landed on Gluck, Jenő, 1926 within a book of the then recently departed.

The sight stopped her cold. Memory-induced understanding ran cold through her veins with the sting of repressed truths.

"I remember you..." Sister Mary Kessler whispered in confession, a reconciliation, in German and solely for her own benefit. "You had been through too much... I didn't have the heart. You were so young."

"Ya? Did you say something?" was Zoli's immediate reaction. He leaned in to further inquire, "Did you find something?"

"Yes." The elderly nun struggled to reach audibility, faced her past in Zoli's eyes. She focused in on his brutalized soul, "It is all here..."

Zoli quivered inward, molecules long dormant shook conflicted, panicked. Julika remained beside him in a pool of anxiety.

"Just like it was when you came in so long ago..." The nun continued to look through the detailed records of refugees registered, opened long stationary bound volumes filled with the names of prisoners, survivors, and the deceased. The sorrow in her eyes was a constant as she perused through the fate of the countless affected. "I will never forget that day."

"What?"

They locked eyes.

"The day you came in," Sister Mary Kessler dropped her head, and confessed, "The day I lied to you." She continued, shamed and repentant, "The truth was too painful."

"That was you?"

She nodded, flipped a large leather bound book around to face Zoli. He moved in for a closer look. "It says right here," the nun pointed as needed. "He was liberated with you, 1945. That is marked here by the Americans."

Zoli ran through it all, over and over, maddening ruminations, infuriating sorrow. He wiped a tear that held all the loss in its slow roll down his cheek.

"But he didn't make it to the hospital..." Sister Mary Kessler stammered, took pause, checked her emotions. "It says here that he is buried in a mass grave on the southwest side of the cemetery."

Zoli cleared his throat, croaked, "This cemetery?"

A long deep silence affirmed his question, and lingered.

"We already missed the boat," Julika chimed, then encouraged, "Let's go."

They entered a cemetery steeped in generations of Deutschland's heaviest humidity, the thrash of perpetual storms, and dropping pressure. Through large black wrought iron gates that weren't there in '45, the two continued past rows and groupings, Christian tombstones modest and prewar left cracked by the ages, no new graves erected after the unholy desecration of the land.

Displaced dirt scarred the earth; what lay beneath the mound prevented the grass from growing, matched the landscape, incongruity incarnate. The absence marked an unholy spot.

They sat on a nearby bench in silence for hours that folded like minutes through the seconds that remained.

under his breath, for his brother, for his whole family, Zoli prayed:

Yit-ga-dal v'yit-ka-dash sh'mei ra-ba, b'al-ma di-v'ra chi-ru-tei, v'yam-lich mal-chu-tei b'chai-yei-chon uv'yo-mei-chon uv'chai-yei d'chol-beit Yis-ra-eil, ba-a-ga-la u-viz-man ka-riv, v'im'ru: A-mein.

Words barely audible under excruciating grief, Zoli allowed himself tears for the first time. Julika comforted him. Her attempt to stay strong proved futile. They cried together.

The sun fell under the horizon. Clouds filthy with history hawked dusk's peaceful commencement into night. The void had come too soon.

"We could have gone to Bratislava, like your family." Zoli's attempt to fill the absence was frenetic, out of his control, perpetually fought the hurt. "We were right there, on the border... Or America, he could have been Eugene, or Johnny, or Jimmy, Jim." Dreams of what could have been, what could have been done, charged into his head; possibilities fired from all available synapses. "Maybe we can rebury him closer to us, by our plots in New Jersey?"

Julika put her hand on his shoulder as they considered the impossible. They remained in place till the temperature dropped and nocturnal life stirred awake around them. A hollow chill tore through the Bavarian woods, urged them to their feet.

They walked away from the mass grave, past aisles of deteriorating headstones. The howl of the wind accompanied screams from the past that built the closer they got to the large wrought iron gate that surrounded the cemetery.

"I don't believes it." Zoli uttered as he caught sight of the closed exit-way.

They stepped to the imposing barrier that loomed meters over the senior citizens. Zoli attempted to open its door for a good half hour. They didn't know whether to laugh or cry, feelings determined by the company they kept. Panic began to fester.

Julika was at a loss. She called into the blinding fog, "HELP!"

They waited behind bars. The gates of Mauthausen once again kept Zoli in place. He rested his head in his hands as the culmination of past, present, and future intermingled in his marrow.

Time failed.

"Hello? You need some help?" German rang through the mist, out of the darkness. A bark of a German Shepherd led two armed guards their way.

"Ya, we need help," Zoli said, his best German was good enough.

The soldiers approached, examined the situation. "How did you get locked in there?"

"I have no idea," Zoli answered. "They locked us in."

The young men jumped to action, helped one another up and over the fence. One stayed atop the gate to help the other hoist the old timers over; Zoli first so as to be able to help bring his wife comfortably to her feet. The hour long exercise left them all on the freedom side with cheers and laughter.

"Danke," Zoli extended his hand to their young saviors. *"Danke schoen."*

They stood face to face with the guards. Zoli caught their Aryan eyes; a long silence replaced the initial thrill of their escape.

Irony flooded in, drowned them all in place.

The young men considered their location, the age of the visitors, and their act of helping them escape. They fell solemn. The truth swelled, regurgitated history, infected both sides of the same coin.

Zoli's eyes twinkled their signature blue. The limits of his youth turned expansive in his thoughtful glance, worked to soothe, to understand, to forgive and ascend.

The Earth continued to spin under their feet, remained on its eternal journey through time and space, the past ever-present.